Janice Horton writes contemporary romantic fiction with a dash of humour and a sense of adventure. In 2014, after her children had left home, Janice and her husband set off to explore the Caribbean. In 2015, they returned to the UK only to sell their material possessions in favour of travelling around the world. They are currently housesitting in France after travelling around South East Asia.

@JaniceHorton
www.facebook.com/JaniceHortonAuthor/
janicehortonwriter

The Backpacking Housewife

The Next Adventure

JANICE HORTON

OneMoreChapter
A division of HarperCollins*Publishers*
www.harpercollins.co.uk

One More Chapter an imprint of
HarperCollins*Publishers*
The News Building
1 London Bridge Street
London SE1 9GF

www.harpercollins.co.uk

This paperback edition 2019

First published in Great Britain in ebook format by
HarperCollins*Publishers* 2019

A catalogue record for this book
is available from the British Library

ISBN: 9780008340636

Typeset in Birka by Palimpsest Book Production Ltd,
Falkirk, Stirlingshire

Printed and bound in Great Britain by
CPI Group (UK) Ltd, Croydon CR0 4YY

To my family … with love. xx

Chapter 1

Tortola, British Virgin Islands

This morning, in bright sunshine and on calm waters, we're heading back to Road Town, Tortola, the capital of the British Virgin Islands: the starting point of our round the world adventure eight months ago and today our final port of call. I gaze out from my viewpoint on the forward deck at the shimmering vista ahead of me and at what must certainly be one of the most beautiful sights in the world; a chain of tropical islands laid out like an emerald necklace.

I know I should be feeling elated, excited, or even triumphant about our return, but I'm feeling rather overwhelmed about it instead. That's because I woke up this morning to realise that its's exactly one year ago today that I grabbed my passport and got on a plane at Gatwick, leaving my whole life and my old life, behind me. A whole year.

And today, it feels quite literally and figuratively, like my life has come full circle.

So, while everyone else is busy and getting ready to disembark and celebrate our homecoming, I can't help but to look back, rather than forward. I can't help but to wonder what happens next for this backpacking housewife.

If this is the end of my journey? Or just another new beginning?

I'm torn in two by my conscience and my heart.

I have a big decision to make and it's not going to be an easy one.

Do I continue to travel the world with Ethan? Or do I head back home to the UK?

I know that Ethan wants me to be with him. I know he loves me. And I love him.

But how do you tell someone who is something of a real-life Indiana Jones and who thrives on a life filled with endless adventure that you've started to think it might not be the life for you after all? That a life spent in perpetual sunshine while saving the planet has become too difficult for you? That the weeks and months and the thousands of miles of distance between you and those you've left behind is all too much?

I have two grown up kids and an aged mother who I haven't seen in a very long time.

My heart aches as I realise it's almost the end of November and Christmas is coming.

I missed Christmas with my family last year. I spent last Christmas on a tiny island in the middle of the South China Sea. If you looked it up on a map, you'd see it really is as far away from anywhere else as you can possibly get. I imagine, as far as my family were concerned, I might as well have been on the moon. On Christmas Day, I remember sitting crying on the beach, under a scorching sun, thinking of the place I used to call home and imagining them all opening presents without me, which brought on another kind of guilt. The kind that tells you how spoiled and ungrateful you are for not appreciating what you have and where you are now.

I've missed a whole year of birthdays and anniversaries and other special family days too.

When I last checked in with my family, via a wi-fi signal in a port of call just several days ago, I discovered that my eldest son, Josh, and his girlfriend, Zoey, had just got engaged. That was unexpected. I mean, he didn't even have a girlfriend on the scene when I'd left.

He sent me a lovely photo of the two of them taken at their engagement party.

A party that I missed.

I'd called the happy couple as soon as I could to offer my heartfelt congratulations. But then our conversation had quickly resorted back to the question of when I might be coming home.

And that was awkward, as I really didn't have an answer.

When I speak with my younger son, Lucas, he often sounds surly and uncommunicative and he makes our long-distance conversations hard work. I ask him about his day and what he's been doing over the weekend and how his work is going and he's dismissive. Call it mother's intuition, but I worry if there is something going on that perhaps he's not telling me?

I also worry if I even *have* any mother's intuition left these days.

I could of course be worrying for nothing. But getting any information from Lucas about his life is impossible when he immediately switches the topic of conversation from him back to me. And I'm told once again, how most people's middle-aged mothers (and I'm only forty-eight for goodness sakes) take daytrips to The Lake District and join Book Clubs, rather than go backpacking around the world and then join the crew of an ocean-going ship.

I listen and I agree. I know both my sons are missing me and they also worry about me.

I worry about them too. I worry about missing them. I constantly stress over whether I've done a good enough job as a mother to leave them to it now that they are both in their twenties?

What if they do need me? Even though they are grown up successful young men.

And, because I'm not there, who do they turn to if they need advice or emotional support?

Their father? What kind of example is he when he's proved to be an untrustworthy liar?

And how do they really feel about their parents being divorced now?

Perhaps it's because I haven't exactly been able to talk to

them about their anxieties or concerns in any depth over the past twelve months? Not since that time just before Christmas last year, when they both flew out to Kuala Lumpur to see if I'd lost my mind as well as my homing beacon. In speaking face to face, I'd been able to reassure them. Whereas now, I find it frustrating how feelings are a difficult subject to tackle by text message.

Somehow, words seem to get scrambled and become devoid of sensitivity.

That they don't reflect what's really in the heart.

Not to mention autocorrect issues and textspeak which often make matters so much worse.

Only this week did Josh question my overt use of: *WTF.*

I thought it meant: *Well That's Fantastic*.

And so, of course, I've been using it rather a lot.

For the last couple of months, I've been tossing and turning more than this ship.

I've been losing sleep, while trying to work out how I can continue to live a nomadic lifestyle with Ethan, while also maintaining a tangible and meaningful connection with my family. But having it all seems impossible.

I don't feel Ethan is the kind of man to step back from the helm and retire.

And I simply can't be in two places or on both sides of the world at one time.

I've had to confide in him over feeling permanently at sea these days. Although, I was using that as a metaphor for our nomadic lifestyle, rather than our ocean-going situation. He'd listened to me and he'd said he understood. He said that he understands all my angst and guilt.

But, I'm not sure that he does fully understand, because he has no family of his own.

I tried to explain about my mum to him. 'She's not getting any younger.' I said.

Which, in hindsight, didn't best explain how I really feel about her needs, her age, her fragility, and not being there for her.

Ethan had simply replied. 'Well, Lori, my darling. None of us are getting any younger.'

And, of course, he's quite right. Yet another reason for us all to grab life and really live it.

Ethan's parents died a long time ago and, from what I can gather, he was still in his teens at the time. I don't know exactly what or how it happened. But they do seem to have passed away at around the same time as each other. I wonder if they were in some kind of accident.

Only, he doesn't talk about them very much. Maybe it's too painful for him?

It's also entirely understandable that he is perhaps unable to truly empathise with me and all my worries over my two sons or an aging parent. Although, with his roots in Scotland, I find it hard to accept there isn't at least someone somewhere in the world who is related to him.

An uncle twice removed or even perhaps a distant cousin?

When we had briefly talked about it once, I'd suggested

doing a bit of genealogy research to check for anyone who might be a relative, or even a black sheep in his clan. But then I'd noticed a vein in his temple starting to visibly pulsate and how quickly he changed the subject.

A shout disrupts my thoughts and I turn around to see Ethan on deck.

'Lori! I have news. I have great news!'

A smile spreads across my face. I watch him in amusement as he struts his stuff, wiggling his hips and dancing through the early morning sunbeams and across the main deck towards me, wearing an unbuttoned shirt and baggy khaki shorts, while waving his satellite phone in the air. I laugh. I do love his boundless energy and passion.

Ethan has the heart of a lion, but he extrudes all the enthusiasm of a child.

I mean, just yesterday, as we sailed past the island of St Martin, he was positively whooping about a pilot whale and her calf swimming off our bow. Last week, he sounded the muster alarm when he spotted a record number of dolphins following in our wake. And, last month, when our research vessel *Freedom of the Ocean* rallied on a conservational issue off the coast of Costa Rica to stop illegal shark finning, he stood out on deck beating his chest like Tarzan.

But I have perhaps not seen him quite as exuberant as he is today.

Several of the crew whoop loudly in response, as I wait to hear what crazy escapade he might have conjured up for us next. Life with Ethan is always an adventure and to my certain knowledge every one of those adventures has been the result of a phone call.

'My darling, I believe I've found us a piece of dry land that we can finally call home.'

I catch my breath and my heart skips a beat. His words wash over me through the warm and salty air between us. Did I hear him correctly? Did Ethan Goldman, nomadic eco-warrior and king of the seven seas, just say *dry land* and *home* in the very same sentence?

Had he really been listening to my worldly woes?

To my worries about my family and how much I miss them?

Had he really understood and been putting together a plan for when we got back here?

'Really? Oh Ethan, that's fantastic! Where is it?' I gasp.

'Here. In the BVI's. Although I'll have to head over to Grand Cayman to sign the lease.'

'Here, in the British Virgin Islands? A lease? Are we renting a house?'

My brain clicked into overdrive. Is this plan of his both the answer and the compromise?

The resolution to the conflict in my double life?

A base for us to work from and for us to call home?

Only moments earlier, I'd been imagining a heart-breaking and distressing scenario, where I was sobbing into Ethan's pineapple patterned shirt and saying goodbye to him this afternoon.

I had imagined that the very next phone call he took would be the catalyst to him taking off on some new and fabulous adventure and that he'd have to go saving something somewhere in the world without me. But now, instead, I'm suddenly and happily conjuring up in my imagination a traditional clapperboard Caribbean style house, surrounded by palm trees, either here on Tortola or Virgin Gorda. I'm imagining myself holding out my arms in welcome to my family as they arrive to spend Christmas with us this year. And, next year, planning with them a visit over the summer holidays and lots of other special family times too. I imagined my mum sitting on a comfortable chair under our shaded porch, looking out at a beautiful tropical garden, rather than sitting in an old armchair in front of the fire and looking outside at her small winter ravaged patio. I imagined Ethan teaching Josh and Lucas to scuba dive in the warm sea and them all having an amazing time together.

That's my dream – a big happy family – all spending quality time together.

And, when my mum and my two boys step off a plane into my new world – and they see for themselves what kind of life I'm living and what kind of man I'm living with now – then they can be happy for me at last. Then they wouldn't worry about me so much. Or continue to question my state of mind. And demand, in every long-distance conversation, that it's time I came home. What a perfect way that would be for me to introduce them to Ethan too.

Part of my angst and guilt is because I haven't yet told them I have a new man in my life.

I've only explained about going off with a new friend to do some conservation work.

I certainly hadn't told them how I'd met a gorgeous man in Thailand, fallen head over heels in love with him, and that we were now travelling all over the world together.

I don't feel it's the kind of news that's best shared in an email or a message.

Although, I'm sure, if they ever did manage to get over the shock of me having a new man friend, then they would be impressed that he's a renowned environmentalist and the founder and CEO of The Goldman Global Foundation. And, when my mum eventually picked herself up off the floor at the thought of me having another man in my life, she might be thrilled to hear that Sir Ethan had been knighted for his services to global ecology and endangered animal conservation.

Right now, I'm excited. I find Ethan's idea of a renting somewhere entirely acceptable.

Although, it is certainly a little unusual – simply because as a rule Ethan doesn't rent – Ethan buys. Probably because he can afford to buy anything he wants. Like this ship, for example.

While many fifty-year old men might choose to buy a classic motorbike or a flashy car, this middle-aged philanthropist prefers to spend his small change on a state-of-the-art fully equipped ocean liner, with the world's most advanced gadgetry and marine research facilities on board. But renting a house will be far quicker than buying one.

We might even be able to move in today!

'It's not a house,' Ethan tells me with great gusto. 'It's an island no one has lived on in a hundred years!'

And, suddenly, I can feel my elated heart sinking ever so slowly down into my deck shoes.

The image of an idyllic Caribbean colonial style house with my mum on the porch immediately crumbles away to be replaced by something far less decant and far more decayed looking. I sigh and take a deep breath. I do love that he cares so passionately about preserving ecosystems and saving the endangered creatures of the world. But after eight months spent mostly at sea, and while working on the most pressing conservational issues in the world today - that of plastic pollution in our seas and the study of global warming on our oceans – what I really meant when I'd tentatively hinted to him that we might settle down and find a home together, was somewhere with an actual address.

I'd thought we might live in a place that can be found without satellite imaging or having to use longitude and latitude coordinates. Somewhere civilised with a population and civil amenities and a transportation system that includes an international airport and not just a precarious landing strip. Somewhere with shops. A supermarket where I can buy milk that doesn't necessarily have to come from a coconut. A house with a proper kitchen rather than a galley with a floating stove. A bathroom with a tub instead of a tiny shower and with a proper toilet rather than one in a tiny claustrophobic cubicle like the kind you find on an airplane.

Was I expecting too much? I guess so. This was Ethan *Indiana Jones* after all.

Because now I fear he has another adventurous project in mind rather than an actual home.

On an island that no one has lived on in a hundred years no less!

But was that even possible these days in the BVIs?

Jeff, one of our marine biologists, laughed. 'You've gotta admit it, Lori. This is so Ethan!'

So Ethan had become a popular adage with all the scientists onboard for when anyone had a crazy idea. Never crazy to Ethan, of course, who was still enthusiastically strutting his stuff on deck. I roll my eyes as I consider yet another desert island where we can live like castaways.

I know how cynical and ungrateful that sounds, but I'm kind of fed up with shifting sand.

I'm missing solid ground. I'm missing being in one place for a while.

But more than all of that I'm really missing my family.

Chapter 2

At Road Town, Tortola, *The Freedom of the Ocean* is now safely docked in the harbour and no one has wasted any time getting onto dry land. Ethan has wasted no time either in securing a small boat to take us – just the two of us – on what he describes as a romantic voyage of discovery. So, I'm now standing on a wooden jetty in a very busy part of the marina, with my cell phone firmly clamped to my ear, while I'm trying to reach my family back home.

Ethan is chatting to a very distinguished looking man who is wearing a linen suit and a panama hat. I'm casting my eyes over some incredibly impressive yachts and catamarans in what is known as the boating capital of the Caribbean, and as I can already feel my long wavy hair becoming even crazier in this ridiculous humidity, I'm regretting not bringing along a hat myself. I'm already perspiring profusely in my white cotton shirt and shorts that I'm wearing over my swimsuit. The tops of my flip-flopped feet are being scorched by the hot morning sunshine.

I watch the two men gesticulate over a very sleek looking motor boat. It's expensive looking with white padded seats and two powerful outboard engines and I can't help but to wonder why, when I have a full signal on my phone for the first time in absolutely ages, is no one answering my calls? I then realise 10am here is 2pm in London. My boys will be at work and my mum will no doubt still be at her afternoon pensioner's bingo session.

Then I see Ethan and the distinguished looking man shaking hands and there is a set of keys being handed over. Suddenly he is waving at me with great enthusiasm. 'Okay, Lori. Let's go!'

I dash over to untie the mooring rope from the cleat and jump into the boat that Ethan has procured. We set off into the sparkling sunshine and soon made good progress through the stretch of water between the islands that is known as the Sir Frances Drake Channel. As we leave the harbour and the bay, I can clearly see the verdant shapes of the larger islands across the straights from us. In the far distance there is Norman Island, said to be the inspiration for Robert Louis Stevenson's book *Treasure Island*, and Peter Island, with its broad curve of white sand beaches and exclusive high-class hotel resort.

I do know a little about the Virgin Islands from my own days as a travel agent. Many moons ago, while I was also a housewife and mother bringing up two little boys, my ex-husband and I had our own very successful travel business. Only, in those days, I used to plan other people's adventurous itineraries and could have only dreamed of the life I have now.

The Virgin Islands are split into American and British territories. The largest of the British owned islands is Tortola. The second largest is Anegada - also called Drowned Island - as it's flat and low lying and often flooded by high tides. Although, I know next to nothing about the smaller islands except that there are lots of them – over fifty – and that's just in the British Virgin Islands or BVIs as everyone calls them for short.

I point a finger across the straights towards a small islet. 'I know those are Salt and Cooper and Ginger Island, but do you know what that little round one with no trees on it is called?'

'Aye. That's Dead Chest Island.' Ethan answered. 'There's nothing growing on it because there's no freshwater. It's where Blackbeard the pirate once abandoned fifteen of his crewmen with one keg of rum and a pistol with one shot between them. I suppose he'd assumed they'd all get drunk and then fight over the pistol to commit suicide.'

'Couldn't they have just all swam over to Peter Island instead?' I asked, thinking it didn't look too far away.

'It looks close enough but there are dangerous currents between the islands. The story is that they did all try to swim for it but only one of them made it. That's why there's a Dead Man's Bay on Peter Island.' He remarked.

I stared over at Dead Chest Island and tried to imagine the horror of being stuck in a place where nowhere actually looked too far away and yet everywhere was impossible to reach.

Ethan then boldly opened the engines and began to heartily sing at the top of his voice.

'Fifteen men on the Dead Man's Chest, yo-ho-ho and a bottle of rum!'

I sat back and enjoyed the warm wind blowing through my hair and took in the dramatic shape of Virgin Gorda, the third largest island in the BVIs off our starboard or right side, looking like a giant woman reclining in the shimmering Caribbean heat.

We are heading towards the outer islands now. I know that some are still uninhabited, but others are now the exclusive hideaways of the rich and famous; rock stars, movie moguls and rich entrepreneurs. I decide to look out for Tom Cruise because I'm sure someone mentioned that he'd recently bought one of these outlying atolls.

Ethan saw me peering ahead with eagerness.

'We're heading northwest towards The Dogs,' he informed me.

'What kind of dogs are they?' I asked cautiously, wondering if we'd needed rabies jabs.

Ethan laughed. 'There are no dogs. It's a group of islands named so because sailors once thought the barking they could hear came from dogs on the islands.'

'And, if it wasn't dogs, what was it?'

'Caribbean Monk Seals,' he clarified. 'Sadly, they're now extinct.'

He looked gloomy for a little while as he considered this awful loss.

We soon approached a group of five small rocky islets that made up The Dog Islands.

They looked wild and rugged against the calm deep blue of the surrounding sea.

'Now we're truly in virgin territory!' Ethan proclaimed.

He sounded excited as he stood proudly at the helm, inhaling deeply, as if the air around here was purer too. 'Many years ago, the sailors who came here thought this was the very end of the world, and they imagined the horizon line that you see now was the drop off point. All these islands around here are privately owned. But some are also protected wildlife sanctuaries for creatures that can be found nowhere else in the world. See that island up ahead?'

I peer through my sunshades at the shape of an irregular mound in the distance.

'That's Mosquito Island. It's where I first learned to scuba dive. My instructor, Booty Bill, was known as the last pirate in the Caribbean. He was a real character. There's so many rumours about him finding shipwrecks and treasure around here. No one ever really knew fact from fiction. When I first came here, at eighteen years old, Booty was like a father to me.'

Ethan sighed happily as he remembered those times.

'He sounds like an amazing man. Is he still here? I'd love to meet him.'

'No. He retired to Florida. But now, of course, Richard owns the island.'

'Are you talking about Richard Branson?' I gasped.

'Aye, in 2007, he swiped Mosquito from under my nose for just twenty million.'

Ethan shook his head as if 2007 was just yesterday and twenty million was small change.

'But I thought Richard Branson owned Necker Island?'

'Aye, he does. He bought Necker way back in '79. Although, interestingly, on one very old map of the BVIs it's shown as 'Knicker Island'. As you might imagine, Richard, with his sense of humour, thought that was downright hilarious!'

I laughed. 'Yes, I expect you'd have to be British to appreciate that joke.'

I'm guessing he and Richard Branson have an interesting alliance.

'So, is that why you know this area so well? Because you lived here as a young man?'

'Aye. I spent a whole summer down here before I started university. I love these islands. I know these waters like I know the back of my own hand. It's long been an ambition of mine to buy a boat and an island here and make my home in the BVIs. A dream, actually'

'But I thought Scotland was your home?' I said in some surprise.

'Nah. Not really. I've gone soft in my old age. Scotland's too damn cold. I'd rather follow in the footsteps of my fellow Scot, Robert Louis Stephenson, and live in warmer climes.'

And, I suddenly realised, that although I do know certain things about this man – his recent history, his passion for conservation, his determination to save the planet, and how much I love him – there is still so much that I don't know about him. His childhood in Scotland. His earlier life. How he single-handedly built up the Goldman Global Foundation. And this dream of his.

I suspect Ethan is as deep as these waters all around us and as equally intriguing.

'And, this island we're going to see today,' I said. 'Do you think this might be your dream?'

He turned from the helm to grin at me. He had such a handsome face in any regard, but when he smiled, Ethan looked movie star handsome and my heart did a little flip.

'Lori, my love, believe me when I tell you this is a once in a lifetime opportunity. Unfortunately, this island's not for sale or I'd be snapping it up. It's held in an ancient trust. One hundred years ago, it was leased to someone who died with a hold over on the lease agreement, so the island was left to inheritors for the remainder of the lease despite them having no plans nor interest in the island. My guess is they forgot all about it until the lease finally expired this year. I got my lawyers straight onto securing it for the next hundred years.'

'And that's why no one has lived on it in all that time?'

'Aye. It's a rare find. The last private island with an

untouched eco-system in the Virgin Islands. That's just like finding a virgin in a brothel!' He chuckled at his own joke.

'So, what you're actually talking about is another research facility!' I remarked a little sourly. I couldn't help it. I loved his enthusiasm. But how could an abandoned island possibly be our permeant home? How could we possibly thrive, never mind survive, out here on a small rock? I imagined the two of us sitting on a deserted island beach together, sun scorched and dehydrated, with nothing more than one bottle of rum between us – like those poor abandoned pirates – and fighting over one gun with one bullet in it with which to end our awful misery.

As we made our approach, to what I could easily understand being thought the very edge of the old world, Ethan's untouched virgin island rose dreamily from the sea and it was breath-taking to behold. At first glimpse, I see white crested waves crashing into rocky inlets and small sandy coves. But then I spotted a small heart-shaped cove with a tiny curved beach and with swaying palm trees and a labyrinth of boulders forming natural pools and seawater-flooded grottoes. I hear the call of seabirds, egrets, herons, pelicans, frigates, and drag my eyes upward over sheer rugged cliffs to see undulating hills covered in misty jungle, as Ethan steered us straight into the heart-shaped cove, where the shallow waters were teeming with colourful fish.

He puts down the anchor onto a sandy bed. 'The boat will be safe here. This is the only safe way to approach the island because the lagoon on the other side is protected by a coral reef.'

Then carefully he pulls out an old battered map from a folder he's brought along, and we stand together on the gently swaying deck to study it carefully. It's deeply creased and faded with age. It looks exactly like a treasure map with its star shaped compass drawing and little illustrations showing landmarks. In excitement, I spot an outcrop marked 'Treasure Point' at the most northerly aspect.

Treasure Point: so called by ye freebooters from the gold and silver supposed to be bury'd thereabouts after the Wreck of a Spanish Galleon.

'Oh, it's a real treasure map!' I gasp. 'But who are the freebooters?'

Ethan looked amused as he passed me a bottle of cold drinking water from the cooler.

'I'm guessing any treasure buried here would have been lifted a long time ago by my mate, Booty Bill. Freebooters, hence booty, was a name for pirates in the old days.'

My eyes flitted across the rest of the map. I see the island is long and shaped like a figure eight, or a symbol of infinity, with two distinct volcanic ranges and a narrow middle area.

'Oh, look, there's a house here!' I shake my finger in excitement at an illustration of a dwelling. I immediately imagine us living there overlooking the beach and the lagoon.

'I wouldn't get your hopes up too much. I doubt it's still here. Not after all this time.'

Ethan tapped a finger at the top of the document where it said: *Map of Waterfall Cay by Thomas Jeffreys, Surveyor and Geographer to The King. The Virgin Islands, 1775.*

'This island is called Waterfall Cay? How beautiful. But surely it will still have a waterfall?'

My imagination conjured up a romantic scene in which Ethan and I were swimming naked below a tropical waterfall with rainbow coloured mists all around us. Ethan, who might have been imagining the same thing, slung an arm around me and pulled me closer to kiss me slowly on the lips. As we touched, our skin was hot and damp through the light cotton of our shirts.

His lips tasted of sea spray but in a nice way. More mythical merman than dirty pirate.

When he spoke, his voice was low and sexy. 'Shall we go exploring to find out?'

We left the boat in the little bay and we slipped into thigh-high warm clear waters with soft sand underfoot and waded ashore. Once ashore, we made our way east through the steamy interior and then began a climb through steep and rugged jungle terrain. We stepped carefully along what appeared to be remnants of an ancient trail of flat rocks that must have been laid down and trodden smooth by many feet so many years before us. Pirates, castaways, sailors, explorers, wanderlusters—who knew?

We leapt across narrow rushing streams that cut through our path and in all the places where the path had collapsed. Ethan, being a gentleman, held my hand and guided me as we traipsed along muddy banks and through the deep forest foliage.

We quickened our pace once we heard the thundering sound of a waterfall ahead.

Then we fought our way through a curtain of hanging vines, to emerge breathless and dirty and sweaty, and to find that we were standing inside an open-air grotto filled with cool misty air in which countless shiny reflective green butterflies fluttered in streams of filtered sunshine.

It was breath-takingly beautiful.

Inside this grotto, there was also a large round emerald green pool of water, surrounded by many other smaller round emerald pools, separated and interspersed at differing levels by giant granite boulders. Some of these giant boulders were shiny volcanic black. They were round and flat and smooth from centuries of rising and declining water levels washing over them. Others were white, limestone or marble, and also flat and smooth.

Ethan took my hand again as we leapt from one to another, like we were playing a game of giant checkers, to reach the deep main emerald pool beneath the tall and writhing and thundering white-water stream that fed it from high above.

In the smaller pools, the water was as still and smooth and reflective as a mirror. I peered down at my reflection.

I'd like to say that what I saw was the face of a gypsy wanderer. Someone with the heart of an adventurer and the spirit of a mermaid. But what I actually saw was a middle-aged woman with a happy face, sparkling bright eyes, and long and messy and dirty wild hair. I decided I liked what I saw. This was Lori, the world explorer.

Not Lorraine, the ex-housewife from London.

Lori was a happier and more fun person than the anxious always unsure version of herself.

And then suddenly the mirror became a window into what lay beneath. Large translucent fish suddenly appeared as if by magic. They'd been completely invisible until the sharp rays of filtered sunlight revealed them. 'Look—' I called out to Ethan.

He was suddenly beside me and when our eyes met, my thoughts of love were clearly reflected in his eyes too. Our lips crashed together. Our breath quickened between our hasty kisses as we tugged and pulled at each other's clothing. Not that there was much in the way of our bare skin. I dipped my fingers into the waistband of his shorts, flipping open the button fastening with one hand and boldly pulling down his zipper with the other and soon they were discarded, flicked away onto a nearby rock. In response, with a practiced dexterity, he lifted my vest top over my head and pulled down my shorts in one swift move. My bikini soon went the same way. Then we were together as one, turning and twirling, in the cool emerald pool.

At one with nature and with each other in what appeared to be a paradise.

Happily, after making love, we lay back in the wonderfully cool rippling water, listening to the rhythmic background of the cascading falls and gazing up at the small patch of blue sky that could be seen high above the walls of tall verdant vines that reflected in the pools of water.

It looked unreal. It was like being wrapped up in swirling northern lights. Like in a dream.

'This place is magical. This island is incredible. Look at all these butterflies!' I gasped.

I lifted a hand out of the water, sending tiny droplets of rainbow glazed water into the air.

I splayed my fingers wide apart under the wings of a hovering and shimmering and glimmering green butterfly. To my astonishment it settled itself down onto the tip of my thumb.

'Oh look. It's tame. I've never seen anything quite like this!'

'Many years ago, this island was a butterfly sanctuary.' Ethan told me, as he also lay back relaxing in the water. 'One of my heroes, Alfred Russel Wallace, who was a 19th Century Scottish biologist and explorer and a direct descendent of William Wallace, discovered a unique species of giant butterfly right here on this little island.'

'Do you mean William Wallace of Braveheart fame?'

'Yes, that's right. Alfred reported that the butterflies here were as large as dinner plates. At that time, the Victorians were keen collectors of tropical butterflies and so The Green Morpho butterfly of Waterfall Cay soon became highly sought after and so incredibly valuable that it was prized above all others. Eventually, Wallace came back to this island to find that his special discovery, one of the largest butterflies in the known world, had been almost wiped out. That's when he established the sanctuary. To try and protect and save them. But, over the years, the island continued to attract butterfly poachers and so The Green Morpho is now sadly extinct.'

'And that's what led to its extinction? People collecting them?'

I couldn't take my eyes of this tiny butterfly as it settled onto my hand, undulating slowly, showing off how it could magically change its wings from green to gold in an instant.

'And these little fellows, although very pretty, aren't so rare.' Ethan told me knowledgably.

'But maybe this island could be a protected sanctuary for butterflies again?' I suggested.

'Perhaps. Only, to apply for the protected status from the government, we'd need to find an indigenous species here or at the very least an endangered one.'

'Indigenous? That means a native species?'

'That's right. Like the Green Morpho.' Ethan leaned forward to kiss my bare shoulder.

As if offended at not being deemed special enough, the little butterfly fluttered away.

'There's only one problem. 'I adore butterflies, but I really can't abide caterpillars.'

Ethan laughed in surprise. 'Why ever not? I mean, it's not like they can hurt you.'

'Because I think I had a traumatic experience involving caterpillars when I was a little girl,' I confessed. If I closed my eyes, I could recall a misty memory of myself as a child, standing at a big leafy shrub in the garden. 'I was picking caterpillars off a plant and collecting them into a plastic bucket. I have no idea why.'

Back then, like today, there's hot sunshine on the top of my head and the earthy scent of damp soil and vegetation all around me. I remember the simple childish pleasure I felt at collecting dozens – if not hundreds – of tiny new creepy crawly friends.

'I suppose it was some kind of a childhood game.' I continued. 'Except, I'm still not entirely sure if it was something that really happened to me, or if it was just a horrible nightmare. When I heard my mother calling me, I left my bucket of caterpillars on a workbench inside our garden shed for safekeeping.' I paused and shuddered at the thought of retelling it.

'So how is that traumatic?' Ethan scoffed, not seeing anything offensive in my story at all.

'Because, when I returned to the shed to play with my caterpillar friends, I remember the wooden door slamming behind me and finding my bucket almost empty, except for just a few green caterpillars and some leaves.

I can remember looking around to see only one or two caterpillars crawling along the bucket rim and wondering where they'd all gone?'

'That doesn't sound anywhere near as bad as the time I found my ant farm unexpectedly empty.' Ethan interrupted me to say. 'Except it wasn't kept in a shed. It was in my bedroom!'

He laughed at the memory. I ignored him to continue with my own story of icky trauma.

'I then suddenly realised that there were hundreds of caterpillars covering the walls and the glass windows. They were also crawling on the wooden beams and ceiling. When they started to drop onto me, I began to scream. They didn't look cute to me anymore. They didn't look like tiny friendly toys that wriggled. They looked like tiny bloated chomping hairy monsters and I screamed and screamed. I remember feeling the pitter patter of them falling onto my head and getting caught up in my hair and sticking to my dress and my bare arms. I remember trying to flee. Only to find the door handle and my escape route covered in caterpillars. I was trapped. They all looked like tiny wriggly scary snakes. Yuck!'

I shuddered again and pulled a face to show my revulsion to both snakes and caterpillars.

Ethan laughed and discreetly pinched my bottom 'Oh, look, there's a snake in the water!'

But I wasn't falling for it and so we had a splash fight until we were suddenly aware of the time and how the whole morning had somehow escaped us. We reluctantly left the waterfall grotto and made our way back through the rainforest towards our boat, where Ethan said that included in our charter was a cooler with fresh drinking water and a packed picnic lunch of sandwiches and fruit. He was always so thoughtful and thorough about everything.

Although, being Ethan, of course, he would call it being prepared.

Once back on board, after our packed lunch, to get our bearings, we cast our eyes over the ancient map once again. I traced my finger along the line that formed this side of the island.

'Okay, so this is the bay where we're at anchor just now. And here is headland and the lagoon and the long stretch of beach that's protected by this coral reef.'

'Yes. That's right. And that's where I want to build our house.' Ethan declared.

I dragged my eyes up from the map to look at his handsome face and wondered how I'd ever thought to doubt him over these past few weeks. He had been listening and sympathising with all my concerns. He had understood me when I'd tried to explain how I loved my life with him but couldn't help but to feel anxiety over being separated from my family. He'd said then that he'd find us somewhere for us to call home and he'd been true to his word. All this, despite my reservations that Ethan Goldman could no more settle down somewhere, than a butterfly could choose to land on my hand. Happily, I'd been proved wrong on both counts.

'I want to build us a big beautiful traditional style Caribbean house. Using only natural materials and with features that will provide us with a zero-carbon footprint.' His eyes sparkled as he told me his plans. 'We'll use solar panels to generate our own electricity. We'll dig a well and tap into the fresh water source here for our drinking water. We'll finally have somewhere to call home. A perfect place to take time out and a base to return to between our travels. Where we can invite your family over to spend their holidays and where we can both grow old together. How does that sound to you, Lori?'

'I think it sounds perfect,' I told him with tears of happiness blurring my vision.

We gathered up our things to find the beach where he wanted to build our house.

Then Ethan opened the cooler again, to haul out a bottle of chilled champagne.

He waved it at me momentarily before stuffing it into his small backpack.

'When we find exactly the spot to build our house, Lori, then we'll open this to celebrate!'

I laughed and clapped my hands in excitement and approval at this wonderful idea.

We waded from the boat and back onto the little sandy beach in the heart-shaped bay from where we made our way into the steamy jungle once more. This time, we ventured in a westerly direction, into what looked like a beautiful and exotic tropical garden with giant vegetation and flowers everywhere and with butterflies and hummingbirds and other colourful birds in the trees. We stepped carefully over twisted roots and through feather-like grasses and wound our way through wild sugar cane and tall bamboo and trees with long hanging tendrils. We craned our necks to look up at the tallest of palm trees, laden with coconuts, and with their fronds waving back and to in the warm humid breeze. I saw bananas growing in great clumps, hanging down on storks, weighted down by the hefty purple cones of the banana flower.

There were breadfruits the size of footballs. Mangos and starfruits ripe and tantalisingly ready to eat. The tropical flowers that I recognised looked like those grown in heated botanical gardens back home. Others looked so vibrantly colourful and oversized and waxy that they looked completely unreal. With every step, I started to realise this island had an awful lot going for it. Ethan kept stopping along the route to take photos on his phone of the flora and fauna.

'This island might look like a total escape from the outside world but as far as locations go it's in the middle of the tropical suburbs,' he told me. 'It has protected waters. Consistent trade winds. Line of sight neighbours and it's just a short boat ride from Tortola and its regional airport and the international airports on St. Thomas, Antigua, and San Juan.'

I started to get it. I began to understand.

Excitement fizzed up inside me like the effervescent

bubbles in our soon to be popped champagne bottle. I could now see how this island was a middle ground for us between remote and accessible, public and private, and a perfect place for us to call home. It ticked all the boxes. It really was that perfect compromise that I'd been looking for and longing to find.

Suddenly, we reached a place where lush vegetation stopped and beach began, and we stepped out of the shaded surrounding jungle with its cool dampness underfoot into hot sunshine and hot powder fine white sand. I laughed and pointed out a discarded beer bottle in the sand. 'I'm starting to doubt your claim no one has been on this island for a hundred years!'

'Maybe there's a message in it?' Ethan suggested, with a mischievous twinkle in his eye.

I checked, just be sure, but only found a small hermit crab. Then an iguana crossed our path – a big one – looking like a fearsome prehistoric creature and I jumped back in surprise. Ethan reassuringly grabbed my hand, and then we both ran with our bare feet burning across the hot sand towards the water's edge, where he pulled me into the clear and shallow waters of the calm blue lagoon and into his arms once more.

He kissed me long and hard until I was breathless and dizzy with desire for him. His big hands gently held my face then moved down my neck and my body and then holding me closely, he said to me in what was almost a whisper. 'Lori, my darling, I know I've been acting a bit crazy lately.

But, to be honest, I've been ridiculously nervous about coming out here with you today.'

'Nervous? No way. The Ethan I know doesn't do nervous!' I protested, laughing.

I've seen Ethan keep his cool in the scariest of situations. Like the time he'd managed to keep his sensibilities about him when, in the middle of a vast ocean, everyone else was freaking out at the ships generator failing on us while we were engulfed in three hundred and sixty degrees of thick soupy sea fog, and all the noise and vibrations we'd all become used to had become an eerie and deafening silence. He'd proved unshakable.

'Well, okay. Then I've been ridiculously excited,' he relinquished with a grin.

'Well, now I understand. This place is beautiful. And, like you said, it's a rare find.'

He gazed deeply into my eyes, making my heart melt and butterflies flutter in my stomach.

'It's not just the island that's got me excited. It's because I knew that today it would be just you and me here. I knew it would be the perfect place. The perfect moment.'

And then he did something totally unexpected.

He got down on one knee, reached into a pocket in his shorts, and produced an exquisite solitaire diamond ring. 'My darling, Lori, will you marry me?'

And, I fell down in front of him onto my own knees, in absolute astonishment.

My legs were shaking. My whole body quivering. I

couldn't breathe. My mouth was dry. I couldn't swallow. I was dizzy. My heart was suddenly pounding so hard in my chest and so loudly in my ears that I couldn't think properly. My mind and my thoughts, so clear just a mere moment ago, were now as fractured and streaming as the sunlight being refracted by the beautiful diamond being presented to me. What do I do? What do I say? What do I think?

The man I love is asking me to marry him.

This island, our new home, is an absolute paradise.

It's perfect and he's perfect.

So why do the obvious words escape me?

What's not to love about him and this idyllic proposal?

Why am I hesitating and not immediately saying yes?

A searing silence hung in the air between us.

It was like the whole world and time itself had all stopped still.

There was not a breath of wind nor a ripple of movement in the lagoon.

And, instead of thinking with my heart, and saying yes because I love him, my head is once again filled with confusion. All I can think about is how my family who are back home will react? What will they say if I tell them I'm getting married again?

Then my own reservations surfaced too to present their side of the argument.

I'd been married before. So had Ethan. So why do it over again?

Tears welled up in my eyes. I tried desperately to blink them away.

Ethan's handsome face was becoming oddly distorted.

I fought my panic and conflicting emotions and prepared to explain myself to him.

Perhaps I needed a little more time? Time to think.

Surely there was no urgency or reason for us to rush into anything?

Wasn't us just being together and loving each other enough?

But when my vision cleared, I could see that his expression had indeed changed from romantically anxious to something that resembled downright furious. His eyes, just a moment ago were soft and loving and kind, were now wide and blazing and murderous.

Had I offended him so badly, with my hesitation, my reluctance?

And then I realised that he wasn't looking at me at all.

He was looking right past me and over my left shoulder.

So, I turned to follow his distracted gaze and my mouth dropped open in astonishment.

At the far end of the beach, at the headland, where there where some giant boulders, there was also a giant construction crane. There was also a man-made jetty type structure jutting out into the sea with its concrete piles buried into the coral reef.

What the Hell was happening here!?

What about the pristine virgin eco-system? What about the untouched reef?

And what had happened to Ethan's lawyers securing the hundred-year lease?

Suddenly, Ethan was no longer down on one knee. He was on his feet and running along the beach. I ran after him. My heart racing. My breath dry and rasping in the salt laden air. Sweat pumped and rolled from every pore on my body in the heat and humidity and under the ferocity of the midday sun. When I caught up with him, for a moment we stood side by side, panting in disbelief, at the offending machinery and chaos of construction that had already destroyed a whole section of coral reef. 'I just don't understand. It's supposed to be ours!' Ethan hissed.

Then, in a glimmering shimmering mirage, I saw a group of people.

Before I could even say a word, Ethan had spotted them too, and he was already scrambling in their direction. Again, I followed him in hot pursuit and saw that there were in fact four people standing in a huddle, perusing a document that looked like it might be a building plan.

There were three men and a woman. Two of the men, wearing hi-vis vests and construction helmets, were obviously the labour workforce here because they appeared to be listening to instructions from the other man. The one doing the talking was tall and well built, deeply tanned, silver haired, and smartly dressed in tailored shorts and a white linen short-sleeved shirt. This man had the air about him of someone incredibly important and affluent.

The woman standing beside him was willowy slim. She

was wearing a pale-yellow sundress and large brimmed white straw hat. Beneath the hat, I could see she had a small heart-shaped face and that she had long bright red hair that she wore in a heavy braid over one shoulder. All four wore sunglasses, but still managed to look surprised to see us as we approached them.

I stopped a short distance from them and wrung my hands anxiously. This was awful.

I'd never seen Ethan so angry. Not even that time when we'd come across a gang of rogue fishermen using sticks of dynamite to fish on a coral reef in the Sulu Sea.

'What the fuck are you doing here?' He exploded, as soon as he'd got close enough.

The woman whipped off her sunglasses to reveal wide steely grey eyes. She fixed her gaze on Ethan, with what appeared to be familiarity. Then she suddenly started to laugh through her shimmering red lip-gloss. Her laughter sounding like the playful tinkle of sleigh bells. I couldn't decide if she was brave or incredibly foolish to mock Ethan in such a way. The last time someone had dared to laugh in his face, he'd performed a citizen's arrest and locked the offender in the hold, until he could be handed over to the authorities at our next port of call.

'Well, what a surprise. If it isn't the famous Ethan Goldman!'

Had she recognised him because he was quite famous? Or did she actually know him?

Oh Lord, please tell me this isn't another ex-wife!

'I could ask you the very same question, brother!' Snapped the smartly dressed man.

Brother? Was that a term of endearment or was this man Ethan's actual brother?!

I narrowed my eyes and recognised the line of this man's hair, the broadness of his brow, the strength of his jawline, the shape of his eyebrows, the contour of his profile and the clincher that was his aquiline nose. This man *was* Ethan but perhaps in ten years' time.

Otherwise they were clones. Time twins. Doppelgangers.

What did this mean exactly?

Did it mean that this man – whom I trust implicitly with my life and whom I love with all my heart and who has caused me so much angst over whether or not to return to my own family and who had just proposed to me with a diamond ring on a perfect beach on bended knee – has blatantly *lied* to me all this time about his so-called lack of family?

Chapter 3

George Town, Grand Cayman

When Ethan is upset, he's a man of very few words. I know this from experience because after a particularly traumatic incident at sea, involving a fully grown female whale and a Japanese whaling ship off the coast of the Philippines, when our ship *The Freedom of the Ocean* had arrived a little too late to save the whale but just in time to witness the terrible distress caused to her young calf, Ethan had hardly spoken a word for days afterwards.

When I'm upset, however, I need to talk it through. I need to micro-thrash the details.

So as we hurtled back towards Tortola at breakneck speed in our speedboat, I wanted to know how and why these people were drilling holes in Waterfall Cay – when it was supposed to be our island and our new home – and why, out of nowhere, it turns out that Ethan has a brother called Damion and a sister in law called Gloria.

But, when I voice my concerns and my confusion to him, I get the silent treatment.

Once we are back on Tortola, however, it appears we are on speaking terms again.

He tells me he's taking a flight over to Grand Cayman to talk with his lawyers.

I point out that it's already late in the afternoon. He assures me it can't wait.

I say I'm going with him. The next thing I know we're in a car heading to the airport.

I broach the subject again. It's killing me that he's lied to me. I need to know why.

My heart is so heavy right now that it hurts and I'm drowning in my own disappointment.

I've been the victim of lies once before and I'd promised myself never again.

My ex-husband lied to me and so did my best friend. It was cruel and soul destroying.

But Ethan? My strong, unshakable, dependable, rock? Well, that is truly heartbreaking.

Now, I look at him and I can't help but to wonder what else I don't know about him?

How many other secrets he might be hiding and keeping from me?

What other aspects about himself he might currently deny but eventually admit?

Ethan is slumped in his seat, his hand rubbing his forehead, as if he's easing a pain.

'I didn't lie to you, Lori. He's just no longer my brother. Hasn't been for a long time.'

'But he's your sibling.' I argued. 'Just because you disowned each other doesn't mean you're no longer related. It's not like divorcing Marielle. Your brother is family. He's blood!'

'Lori, forgive me, but this is not the time. I have to find out what happened with the lease.'

I bite my tongue and steel myself to stay silent. Not easy when I have so many questions.

And then, of course, there's the elephant between us.

His marriage proposal is still hanging in the air.

At the airport, Ethan quickly charters a private jet. It takes us two hours to fly over to George Town on Grand Cayman. On the plane, in my big comfortable seat opposite Ethan, I sip a glass of champagne that was spontaneously offered to us after take-off. Only, it tastes sour in my mouth. Ethan didn't even touch his. He just stared out of the small oval window, frowning.

At the lawyer's office, I prefer to sit in the reception area listening to the heated exchange going on at the other side of a closed door. I check my phone. It's 6pm here and so that means 11pm in the UK. It's now too late to call my mum or my boys.

I decided to call Josh anyway and to leave another message.

When Ethan comes out of the lawyer's office his face is red with rage.

'Come on, Lori. Let's get out of here. I need a drink.'

We walked two blocks and into a bar. I order a glass of wine.

Ethan orders straight bourbon. A double.

'Are you going to tell me what's going on now?' I asked him tentatively.

He threw back his bourbon and swallowed it. 'We lost it.'

I'm starting to feel sorry for him now. My heart softens. My anger dissipates.

I actually consider wrapping my arms around him to offer him some comfort because if Ethan's drinking doubles then he's having the worst day ever. And I've seen Ethan having bad days. Like the time we just happen to lose an underwater (thankfully unmanned) research drone that was apparently worth over a million US dollars. I consider his words for a moment.

'How? I don't understand. How did you lose an island?'

'He got to the lease before us. His plan is to build a luxury hotel resort on the island.'

I shrug. 'This isn't like you, Ethan. If he got there first, then why all the resentment?'

Ethan was usually so philosophical about everything. I've never seen him harbour any hard feelings towards anyone. The need for justice, yes, absolutely. But, when faced with an unfairness, he's normally the first person to say, 'whit's fur ye'll no go by ye' which in Scottish, is the same as 'what is meant for you by fate won't pass you by.'

Obviously, he felt very differently regarding this particular situation.

'Because he played dirty. I can't believe he actually pretended to be me to get hold of that lease and then he took it for himself. He cheated us out of that island. Now do you understand?'

I nod my head slowly and I feel badly. I remember my ex-husband Charles doing something like that to me. He'd taken out a loan in my name because he'd been refused the credit. I only found out about it when he'd defaulted on the payments. 'Yes. I think I do.'

'Do you want to go back to Geluk Island for a while, Lori?'

I nod and offer a little smile and place my hand on his and give it a little squeeze.

Last January, we'd spent a blissful six weeks together on the island paradise called Geluk.

The name, pronounced *Gluck,* means 'place of happiness' and indeed we were very happy there. Ethan, or rather his foundation, the GGF, has an oceanic research centre on the Caribbean island. We'd spent our mornings working and diving on the coral reef and our afternoons upstairs in our private quarters making love. In the early evenings, we'd meet up with locals and friends at a beach bar at sundown, to enjoy rum cocktails and grilled seafood and spectacular sunsets. Then, hand in hand and under a sky full of stars, we'd stroll lazily back up the beach to our simple loft room under the swaying palm trees with its bamboo furniture and wooden shuttered windows. It was a perfect way of life. Idyllic, in fact.

The island, like Ethan, had quickly claimed my heart.

It was easy for me to imagine that we might have stayed on Geluk Island forever. Ethan had said that he'd once felt the same way about it. The island is situated in a sheltered bay between the Cayman Islands and the coast of Honduras. It's often described by those who know of it as a well-kept secret – and they'd liken it to a Key West of the 1930's era; a laid back and sleepy little gem of an island in the eastern Caribbean Sea.

Until of course that secret got out and the tiny tropical paradise became invaded by tourists.

On most days, it looked exactly how you might imagine a Caribbean island before any commercial tourism arrived. With just one main street and locally owned shops and businesses and quiet bars and restaurants. A commercial boat came in twice a week with imported supplies and the islanders principally trade in fish and shellfish and are self-sufficient in tropical fruits and coconuts. There are no cars there and there's no pollution. People get about on bicycles or they simply walked everywhere as nowhere is too far away from anything else on Geluk.

There's a real and very special sense of community amongst the population.

But, being so conveniently close to the Cayman Islands and now part of the new and popular cruise routes, means that half the time there are hordes of people on the island spoiling the ideal and the idyllic. Plus, Ethan is a kind of celebrity. Lots of people know of him and his work. Especially those in the diving community. He's often recognised in the street and approached by strangers in bars and while simply trying to have a quiet drink and minding his own business.

He hates all the fuss. Especially if he's being asked for his autograph.

So, I guess we'll just have to move on and find our paradise home somewhere else now.

Or not. I mean, now that his dream of living on a private island in the BVIs has been taken away from him, I must once again wonder if he will ever want to settle down anywhere else?

And, is it even in Ethan's nature to live in one place?

He's an activist. A man of the world. And what about me?

I must question whether or not I am truly a woman of the world?

I can't help but to doubt myself. Yes, I want to travel. Yes, I want to be with Ethan.

I'm still being torn in two by my wanderlust and my desire for stability.

But all those 'wants' feel so selfish when to claim them for myself means I have to treat my family like they no longer exist. I met a Buddhist monk in a golden temple in Thailand once, and he told me that Buddha says that you should remove the 'I' from 'I want something' because it is your ego, and you should remove the 'want' also because it is your greed. Then you'll be left with your 'something.'

And, as much as I try to reason with myself and apply all that I've learned over this past year into my decision making, that angel and devil of good and bad and positive and negative, sit on my shoulders to this very day to constantly whisper into my ears and taunt me.

And, of the two, I'm never sure which one of them is being entirely truthful.

I can't help but to agonise over what it is that I must compromise on?

Today, with Waterfall Cay, it really seemed like I'd found the answer.

It seemed, in a moment of hope and glory, that I'd found my compromise.

But now that option has disappeared as fast as it came and I'm back to the same question.

How can I possibly choose to love a man over my own family?

How can I ever allow myself to really trust anyone ever again?

How can I trust another person when I can't seem to trust my own instincts anymore?

When having it all is impossible and so means having to choose?

Ethan dragged his eyes away from staring at the bottom of his empty bourbon glass to look at me. I really don't think I've ever seen him so dismayed. Not even when together we'd nursed a turtle, who'd been hit by the rudder of a longtail boat in Thailand, and its carapace was cracked open and its right flipper gone and a chunk missing from the edge of its shell.

'Oh Lori, I lost something else today too —' he confessed miserably. 'I lost your ring.'

I didn't know what to say. It was a beautiful ring. I just hoped it was insured.

'I must have dropped it in the sand. I expect the chances of finding it again will be remote.'

I looked deeply into his soulful eyes. Those very beautiful but now incredibly sad pools of light and love and emotion. I couldn't help myself. A great surge of love came crashing over my own fiery feelings and doused them out in a wave of both passion and compassion for him.

'Ethan, losing a ring doesn't mean you've lost my love. I love you. I want to be with you. But, despite what you call the cruise ship invasion, I still think that Geluk Island would be our next best choice as a perfect place for us to build a home together. Then we can have something that resembles a home life between our work projects. I need that stability. I want a door to close when I need to shut out the problems of the world. I want somewhere to rest when I'm feeling tired. I want walls on which to hang my favourite photographs. I'm afraid, I just can't carry on like this —as a homeless nomad.'

Ethan shrugged and sighed and sulked and he didn't look either convinced or happy.

'I suppose I've always thought that one day, I'd settle down in the BVIs.' He confessed. 'I really wanted that island to be our home, Lori. I really felt we belonged there. Strangely, I've never felt that way about anywhere, not even Scotland. But, you're right. I'll just have to accept it's not going to happen and move on. Just give me some time and I promise I'll find us somewhere else to call home.' He looked so incredibly sad and disappointed.

For someone who always seemed ready and prepared and who knew exactly how and when it was time to move on, I've never known Ethan to drag his heels, or to be so reluctant before.

'Look —' I tried to reason with him. 'If this island is really that important to you, why don't we go and talk to your brother about it? If he only knew how you feel – how very special this island is to you – then he might be prepared to back off and give it back to us?'

Ethan vehemently shook his head. 'No way. Lori, you simply don't understand who you are dealing with here. Damion will not give up the island. Especially, if he knew how special it was to me. There's nothing that you or I can do about it. It's gone.'

'I simply can't believe that to be true. You are brothers. Surely this can be worked out?'

Ethan shrugged again but it was more like an acknowledgement of defeat than of acquiesce.

'If it was anyone else but him then I'd be inclined to agree with you,' he said to me while signalling the bartender for another drink. 'But Damion and I don't get on and we never have.'

'Never? Not even when you were small boys together?' I queried.

'No. Especially when we were kids. We were born ten years apart and it's like we were born to be complete opposites in every way. We could never agree on anything. Damion would make everything into a competition that he would win no matter the cost or the consequence. If he wants something, then believe me, he will not stop until he has it and he will never give up or ever back down. It won't work. So why don't we just forget all about Waterfall Cay?'

'Forget? But you said it was a rare find. You said it was your dream? There has to be another way. There must be something we can do. He is your brother and he must have some redeeming qualities. Surely, it's time you two agreed on something and made amends?'

I pondered on my own childhood. I'd been an only child, but I'd always longed for a sister.

I'd imagined a sister to be a constant and reliable forever friend who would never let you down. I'd brought up my own two boys to be good friends and allies and to support each other.

'Not while he is as stubborn as he is ruthless.' Ethan noted sourly.

And just at that moment my phone rang. 'Oh, I'll need to take this. It's Josh.'

A feeling of something that I can only describe as pure

unadulterated dread washed over me in the moment when I saw that it was Josh calling. My stomach turned over because I knew it was well after midnight in the UK. It was the middle of the night. It was so unlike him to call at this time. Unless something was wrong?

And that's when I heard the news about my mum and my mind and my body and my whole world went into a freefall of absolute and total panic.

'What? Josh, slow down! What did you just say?'

I looked to Ethan. 'My mum has had a heart attack. I need to go home right now!'

And Ethan did what he always does best. He immediately sprang into action.

He hailed us a taxi and we headed straight to the airport.

At the British Airways desk, he wanted to buy two first-class tickets to London, and we argued about it for a while, but I insisted that I needed to go home alone.

'I need time to deal with this myself. My boys don't know anything about us yet, Ethan. This is absolutely not the right time to tell them. I'll call you. I'll speak to them. I promise.'

Then in my rush to get to my gate and onto the plane that was already boarding, I turned to say goodbye to him, only to realise that I'd already gone through the point of no return.

And, suddenly, Ethan was nowhere to be seen.

Chapter 4

London UK

It's early morning in London when I step off my overnight flight and it's very dark outside. The temperature is reported to be well below zero degrees and everyone else has deplaned wrapped up in coats and scarfs and boots. To my embarrassment, I'm wearing a flimsy summer dress and flip-flops. I have a small backpack with me and no checked luggage because I've left the mainstay of my sparse belongings back in the Caribbean.

I emerge from the green zone of customs into the brightly lit bustle of the arrivals area at Gatwick airport and I'm feeling like an exile after being away for a whole year. I know I look different. I feel different. I'm also shivering violently from an assault of icy cold air that's being sucked inside the terminal from the doors leading to the outside world. I'm chilled to the bone.

Goosebumps are doing a Mexican Wave across my entire body and it feels as if my skin, that just yesterday was warm and brown and supple in the humid tropical air, has suddenly become grey and shrunken and icy in response to the dry air on the plane and now the cold damp atmosphere in the UK. My eyes feel sore and heavy as I look around me in confusion at the faceless crowd. Then, to my relief, I hear a shout from a familiar voice.

'Mum!' And my heart leaps as if it's been shocked back to life by a defibrillator.

Then I'm standing in front of Josh, my darling eldest son, who looks even taller and more handsome than I can ever recall. I throw myself into his arms before noticing he's with someone; a pretty young woman with big dark eyes and long brown hair.

'Mum, this is Zoey, my fiancée.'

I embrace Zoey and kiss her cheek and say how pleased I am to meet her.

'Hello, Mrs Anderson. Wow—you are so suntanned!' said Zoey, who was staring at me as if I'd just arrived from another planet and she'd never seen anyone quite like me before.

'Oh, please, call me Lori.'

'We've brought you a warm coat, Mum. We guessed you'd be getting off the plane in summer clothes!' Josh was now helping me take off my small backpack, so that he could wrap a padded jacket around my shoulders, to save me from freezing to death.

'Oh thank you! I feel so ridiculously underdressed. Oh, that feels lovely and warm!'

It smelled of a young person's scent: light and fruity and fresh.

'And thank you, Zoey. I assume this is your coat?'

'Yes, but I have others, so you can keep it for as long as you need.'

Then I saw her looking down in sympathy at my stone-cold blue-tinged toes.

And I could tell she was wishing that she'd also brought me some socks and boots.

I turned to Josh for an update on my mother's condition.

'How is your Gran? Can we go straight to the hospital to see her?'

When I saw Josh and Zoey exchange uncomfortable glances my heart dropped like a stone.

Tears filled my eyes and I was now shaking so much I could hear my teeth rattling.

Clearly, I'd arrived too late and she was gone. I'll never see her or speak to her or hug her ever again. There would be no joyful reunions here or in the Caribbean. I'd never be able to tell her about all my adventures and the people I'd met over the past year.

There is no time left in which to celebrate or to tell her how much I've missed her.

None of that was ever going to happen now. I was too damned late.

I let out a sob of grief and felt a great stab of sorrow and guilt rip through my breaking heart.

I've been so heartless and selfish in abandoning my family when they'd needed me here.

What had I been thinking? Taking off without a care or a thought for my loved ones?

I'd behaved appallingly. I'd thought of only myself, when one year ago I'd grabbed my handbag and my passport and ran from the house to get as far away as possible, thinking of nothing but leaving behind my adulterous husband and treacherous best friend. When, what I'd really done, is to selfishly abandon my whole family. I'd ran away and left my kids and my mother to deal with the aftermath of what happened that day and then to face the mess of divorce without me here. What must my kids think of me now?

Selfish? Indulgent? Weak?

For a whole year I've been travelling all over the world looking for purpose and happiness when that purpose and happiness was right here all the time – with my family. I hadn't really needed to travel great distances or pray in golden temples or take guidance from monks in saffron robes or find ways to make a difference in the world. I'd already made a difference. I might not be a wife anymore, or a housewife, but I was still a daughter and a mother.

The full impact of this realisation and the consequences – that I'd never see my lovely mum ever again – was more than I thought I could take. I just stood there with tears streaming down my face. 'Oh, Josh! I'm s-s-s-so very sorry!'

'Mum. No. It's not what you think!' Josh responded rapidly to my deathly reaction. 'Gran's fine. In fact, she's just been discharged from hospital. We feel badly now, for telling you over the phone that she'd had a heart attack, when actually it just turned out to be bad indigestion.'

I stood speechless and in shock with my mouth open for what seemed like an age.

I'm relieved, of course, that my poor mother isn't dead or on death's door, but part of me is now also somewhat annoyed. I've just flown half way around the world in a terrible state of panic. I'd left Ethan in a very bad situation and I'd practically given myself a coronary in my rush to get to the airport and onto a flight immediately after getting Josh's phone call.

I hadn't stopped to think. I'd just reacted.

And I suppose that's exactly what I did this time last year too.

My instinct to run has by fate and circumstance brought me right back here.

And now the gruelling flight is over, and the awful panic dispersed and the weight lifted from my shoulders, I feel like I've just woken up from a nightmare and with a terrible hangover.

Maybe I'm suffering some kind of post-traumatic stress?

'Come on, let's get you out of here before you freeze to death,' said Josh, rattling car keys.

We walked briskly outside of the terminal and crossed a dark wet and busy road filled with the noise of screeching taxis and the roar of busses and the clatter of people dragging enormous suitcases or pushing precarious piles of luggage on stiff wheeled trollies. Josh fed a parking ticket machine with notes and coins. When I saw how much it had cost him to park the car, I searched for my purse, before realising I didn't have any money in Sterling to offer him.

'Oh, can we stop at an ATM? I had meant to go and swap my dollars for pounds.'

'No problem. I've got it. We can sort that out later, mum.'

I slid into the back seat of the car and soon we were driving away from the airport. It was the morning rush-hour and I peered out of the window at the foreboding sight of shiny slate grey streets and a background of darkness. It's as if I've been transported from a world of technicolour into a one of monochrome. It was raining hard. I watched Josh's head move from side to side in sync with the wind-screen wipers as he negotiated the heavy traffic, checked the rear-view mirror, changed lanes and twiddled with the air con all at the same time.

'We'll soon have you warm, Mum,' he said, setting the dial to red and the blower to full.

I took a deep breath and tried to calm myself by staring down at the goose bumps standing to attention on my bare knees and wondered if I'd ever feel warm again.

It had been thirty-six degrees C when I'd left Grand Cayman.

It was, of course, the middle of winter in the UK, so what could I expect?

But had it always been this awfully dark and dreary looking?

'We'll go straight over to Gran's.' Josh said. 'She's got the spare bedroom ready for you. She's looking forward to having you stay with her until you get yourself sorted.'

I bit down on my lower lip and realised I was a homeless burden until I 'get myself sorted'.

Sorted with what? My own place? I suppose that all depended on how long I stay.

And then I realise that I'm already contemplating leaving when I've only just arrived.

In the same front room of the small terraced house where I'd been born forty-eight years ago, my mum was sitting in her armchair with a cup of tea and a shortbread biscuit when we arrived. The house was warm, the TV was blaring, and she was watching *Good Morning*.

Her face broke into an immediate expression of joy when she saw me, and she leapt to her slipper-shod feet without any hesitation. 'Lorraine! You've come home!'

'How are you, Mum? You gave us all quite a scare.' I said, hugging her tightly.

She ignored my comment and insisted on pouring me a cup of tea to warm me up.

Then she fussed over us and force fed us cakes and biscuits. When I asked how she was feeling, she replied that she was 'feeling much better now' but wouldn't look me in the eye.

Then my younger son, Lucas, arrived and it felt so wonderful to be in the same room as both my sons again. I'd missed them so much that I didn't want to stop hugging them. I found myself stroking their shirt sleeves and touching their faces and ruffling their hair. Checking they were real. And of course, it was lovely to meet and chat to Zoey, and admire the engagement ring she was wearing. Even though it made me emotional and tearful on two counts. I was full of joy for them both, but I couldn't help but to be reminded of Ethan and the ring he'd offered me.

I wiped my tears and blew my nose and pulled myself together.

Zoey is a lovely girl and, although we've only just met, I immediately approved of her.

I see the way Josh looks at her and it's clear that he loves her and that she loves him.

That's good enough for me.

Oh goodness—my boy has become a grown man in my absence.

After an hour or so, Lucas and Josh and Zoey, said they had to get on as they had previously made plans for the day. It was a Saturday, so Mum insisted that they all come back again tomorrow, for Sunday lunch. Just knowing that I'd be seeing them the next day to catch up more on their lives made seeing them all leave a little easier. Then, once they'd gone, Mum insisted that she and I go upstairs to sort through her wardrobe to find me something warm to wear. I was incredibly tired. I just wanted to take a bath and have a good long sleep. But I knew that if I gave in to the jet-lag now, then I was likely to be wide awake in the middle of the night.

I followed my mum up her narrow and carpeted staircase, thinking that despite the generous gesture, I really didn't want to wear any of her clothes. But I was hardly in a position to refuse.

She emptied the content of her entire wardrobe onto her bed and made me try things on.

Her trousers were all two inches too short on me. Her dresses were too wide. At least we were the same size in shoes. In the end, I chose a matching brown wool sweater and skirt ensemble and some one hundred denier tights and a pair of sturdy tan brogues. Teamed with Zoey's jacket, I felt like a twenty-years-older version of myself, trying too hard to look trendy.

Once suitably clothed, Mum said we needed to 'pop out to the shops' to buy some more teabags and enough food for tomorrow's family lunch. I stifled another yawn and checked my phone, wondering if I had any messages, only to find the battery was totally flat.

I put it on charge while we went out to the shops in mum's old car.

Mum drove us and it was a terrifying experience. I'd felt safer in a tuk-tuk on the streets of Bangkok or hacking my way through the jungles of Borneo or fleeing pirates in the South China Sea than being in the passenger seat of my mother's little car. Had she always been this bad a driver or had this only happened over the past year? She seemed to have lost all her road sense and also her sense of direction. The route to town was incredibly busy and the traffic was stopping and starting at every roundabout and set of traffic lights. It was now early-afternoon, but it was quite dark – twilight at best – and it was still raining heavily. The roads were so wet that they reflected every passing car's headlights and my tired eyes felt dazzled. Mum chatted non-stop the whole time that it took us to get to the shopping mall, animating her laughter and conversation by waving her arms around her head, instead of holding onto the steering wheel and focussing on the road.

I sat rigid with fear in the passenger seat as we ran a set of red traffic lights and narrowly missed being hit by a lorry. The irate lorry driver had the nerve to stick his fingers up at me, while mum seemed oblivious to any other traffic on the road and drove around the roundabout twice because she'd missed the turn off onto the by-pass.

Eventually, after battling with an automatic ticket machine and a barrier at the entrance to the underground car park, we arrived at the shopping mall and found a space to park. I wearily followed mum's hurried steps inside, where thanks to a blast of hot air from a blower over the entrance door, it was warmer and more comfortable.

There were already Christmas garlands decking the shopping aisles and a huge Christmas tree, fully decorated with lots of twinkly lights, stood in the main square. It looked quite wonderous. I stood staring at the tree for a moment, feeling surprisingly emotional and suddenly extremely grateful for being back here. It was all such a wonderful relief.

I turned to my mum and hugged her warmly and wiped a tear from my eye.

She hugged me too, laughing at my unexpected show of affection. Then she suggested that while she went into the supermarket, I should go off and buy myself some new winter clothes.

I agreed it was a good idea and we said we'd meet up with each other again in the square.

I know this mall very well. I know its lanes and avenues like Ethan must know the waters of the Caribbean. I must have walked through here many hundreds, if not thousands of times, as a housewife. I used to come here several times a week to do all my shopping.

Yet today, it doesn't feel at all familiar to me in the same way it once did.

I really don't understand it because all the shops that were here before are all still here.

Yet, it's like I'm having a déjà vu experience and attributing it to another lifetime.

It feels surreal to me. I'm noticing things that I've never noticed before. I see how incredibly pale and pallid and stressed people look as they rush around and pass me, pushing loaded shopping trolleys, prams and pushchairs, dragging screaming toddlers, all while chatting incessantly into their mobile phones or to each other. There are so many droning voices being punctuated by piercing high pitched shrieks and background music and other sounds that it has all become a buzzing white noise to my ears. It's bouncing off the steel and glass and cold white tiles that clad the walls and floor of the shopping mall.

It feels quite suffocating and all consuming.

After spending so much time in the third world, where people have so little by comparison, everything here suddenly seems so abundant and glossy and extravagant. Shop windows are full of unpractical stuff that no one really needs but will buy because its Christmas. People proudly carry a clutch of bags showing off that they've been and bought the big brands.

Clothing. Shoes. Cosmetics. It's all so excessive.

But I've never noticed it before. Not that I used to be any different. I used to do it too.

I once felt it was important to have the designer handbag, the new coat, the right shoes for every occasion, and a new dress because I couldn't possibly be seen out in the same one twice.

Not to maintain modesty or to keep warm but to impress and keep up appearances.

A child, of maybe ten years of age, ran into me without an apology. He'd almost knocked me off my feet but without a care he yelled and swore at me as if it had been my fault we'd collided. I noticed how well dressed he was in an expensive premier league football shirt and training shoes. The same branded trainers that I know my son Lucas loves to wear.

For some reason, I was reminded of something that happened to me not too long ago when I'd been shopping for fresh fruit on a street on one of the lesser known of the Caribbean islands.

The shops on the street were just wooden tables, some made from old doors, piled high with a selection of locally grown fruits or they were simply a battered looking wheelbarrow that was filled with ripe bananas fresh from a nearby tree. A young boy, again around ten years old, had spotted me doing my shopping that day and was soon running alongside me to beg to be allowed to carry my shopping bag. I guess that with my western looks and my blonde hair, I'd been an easy target for his attentions.

'Let me help you, lady. Let me carry your heavy bags today?' he pleaded so politely.

I'd been immediately charmed by his smile and his entrepreneurial spirit and so I let him carry my bag containing a few mangos, a couple of pineapples, a hand of bananas, knowing that I'd be soon asked for a dollar in return. The day was scorching. Blisteringly hot. And, as we walked along side by side, with the sun beating down on our heads and heating up the hot hard dry sand base that formed the street, I could feel the heat burning through the rubber soles of my flip-flops. Yet, I noticed this boy wore no shoes. I asked him 'where are your shoes?'

And he simply smiled at me and shrugged and then shook his head.

And that too had made me stop and reflect on how in the western world we have so much.

A thought that I suppose simply wouldn't have ever crossed my mind before I'd travelled.

Of course, we confuse the price of material things with the price of happiness, don't we?

It's only by stepping out of the material mindset that we can appreciate that confusion.

But I do need some new clothes today. I need some practical clothes to keep me warm.

So I head across the mall to a shop where I know I'm likely to be able to pick up what I need for a reasonable price. It's a charity shop where I used to work several mornings a week as a volunteer. Where, for many years, I'd worked with the same group of women who I called my closest friends. One of them, Sally, had been my very best friend in the world.

I used to confide in her. We'd had a laugh together. And a cry, sometimes, too.

But I didn't want to see Sally today. Not yet. Not now.

Not dressed in my mum's clothes and looking red-eyed and exhausted.

I know that's incredibly vain of me, but I'll freely admit to being a proud woman.

In Buddhism, pride and vanity are considered poisons, as they are part of a selfish ego.

No doubt, here in this small suburban town, where everyone knows everyone and everyone else's business, I will bump into Sally soon enough. But, by then, I hoped I'd be more up for the challenge. More prepared. Because, if I was being honest, the thought of seeing Sally again filled me with anxiety and dread and a great dollop of despair.

What would we say to each other after what had happened and after all this time?

It's not as if the past year has changed what I saw or diminished what she was doing with my husband in our marital bed on the day I came home unexpectedly early. If anything, it has amplified it. It's like that horrific moment has being preserved – frozen in time – until it can be properly addressed and Sally and I face both the consequences and each other in real time.

Yet seeing Sally used to fill me with joy. She was my best friend.

More than that, she was like the sister that I'd never had and always wished for.

I suppose that's what made this whole thing worse. Even more heartbreaking.

Why couldn't Charles have had an affair with his secretary instead?

Why did it have to be the woman whom I'd allowed to become my soul sister?

I suppose it was for all the same reasons that I'd once loved her too. Sally was an attractive and sophisticated woman. She was great company and she was always upbeat and fun. She never seemed to run out of interesting things to say or exciting things for us to do together.

When Sally decided to lose weight and get fit, we joined the gym together. When she needed new clothes and makeup, we went shopping together. When she decided to learn French, we signed up for evening classes. We confided in each other completely and talked for hours over a cup of coffee or a glass of wine in each other's kitchens. We confessed our most intimate secrets. I now cringed at the thought of telling her that Charles and I rarely had sex.

When I reached the charity shop, I see another co-worker and friend at the counter and so I go inside. I walk along the sale rail and pick out a couple of sweaters, a pair of jeans and a warm coat, a thick wool scarf and then head over to the till. When Taryn sees me, her eyes light up and she gasps in surprise. 'Lorraine! You're back! And, oh my gosh, you look fantastic!'

'Yeah, I just got back today. I need a few things to wear. How are you?'

'I'm fine. Just the same as ever. You know how it is. Nothing ever changes here.'

I nod my agreement as she rings up my purchases and I hand over my bank card.

'We're still short staffed, if you want your old job back, it's yours!' she said, while bagging my new-to-me things and putting me right on the spot with her immediate job offer.

I panicked a little and shrugged. 'Oh, erm—I don't think that's such a good idea.'

'Sally doesn't work here anymore. Just in case you were

wondering. None of us liked what she did to you. Taking your husband. Moving into your house. If that helps?'

'Maybe—' I said, feeling a little flustered and trying to think of what to say in response and failing miserably. My jet lag was suddenly making me dizzy and giving me a headache. 'Let me think about it and I'll call you. Thanks, Taryn.'

I walked away not feeling as pleased as I might but feeling slightly horrified.

How easy it might be to slip straight back into my old life here?

Not all of it. Not back to being a housewife or a best friend. But the rest of it.

In many ways, being back here so abruptly, it feels like the past year has only been a dream.

That heading straight for the airport and arriving in Bangkok, then exploring Thailand, island hopping down the Andaman Sea all the way down to Malaysia; then having to convince Josh and Lucas – after they'd flown all the way out to Kuala Lumpur to bring me back – that I was still relatively sane and wanted to continue to travel, had only happened in my imagination.

But it did happen and because of it I knew I wasn't the same person anymore.

I wasn't Lorraine Anderson, housewife. I'd become someone else entirely.

I was now Lori Anderson, a world explorer.

I'd crossed continents and sailed the oceans and seen the most amazing things.

Yet nothing here in this town seemed to have changed at all.

And there was undoubtably something strange and disconcerting about that fact.

I thought back to yesterday, when I'd been on a beautiful Caribbean tropical island, swimming naked in an emerald green lagoon fed by a waterfall, with a tiny butterfly sitting on my hand. The symbolism hadn't escaped me. In the same way that a caterpillar becomes a butterfly, I felt that I too, in travelling, had emerged from a cocoon and found my wings.

And then, of course, I'd met and fallen in love with Ethan.

At a time when I never thought I'd ever find love again.

Whom I'd left reeling and alone in Grand Cayman.

Who still deserved an answer to the question he'd asked me on the beach yesterday.

Had it really only been yesterday?

Chapter 5

I woke the next morning with an anxious jolt and in surprise at finding myself back in my old bedroom at my mother's house in London. I'd been dreaming about being onboard *The Freedom of the Ocean* and so that's exactly where I'd expected to wake up – in our cabin and in our small bed – with Ethan beside me. The creaking sound I'd heard in my sleep wasn't caused by the ropes and the sway of the boat as I'd thought but by a tree in my mum's garden.

I'd woken expecting Ethan's big warm body to be stretched out next to mine, his long and tanned legs in a tangle with the sheet that had covered us in the chill of night. The sheet that would always end up discarded as soon as the sun had risen over the line of the horizon, sending pale pink shimmers of light through the small porthole above our heads followed by an intense yellow blinding light that quickly heated up our little cabin, until we lay splayed out and soaked with perspiration in our nakedness.

Then in our drowsy state, we would reach out to each other without opening our heavy-eyes and we would rouse each other with a tender touch, a sweeping finger, a tentative kiss from drowsy lips on hot sensitive skin. Then our breathing would quicken, and our tender touches would become something more urgent, and without a word uttered we would welcome this brand new day and greet each other, with a celebration of our lovemaking.

Realising I was quite alone and that the room was chilly and dark, I quickly grasped the reality of my new situation. My mind flitted over all that had happened over the last forty-eight hours. The island. Ethan's brother. The news. The panic. The flight. Being back home.

I snuggled back under the duvet and sank into the warm comfortable mattress and let my head lay heavy on the soft pillow. A feeling of peace and relaxation and acceptance washed over me. I heaved a great sigh of relief that my mother's heart attack had been a false alarm.

I found myself smiling until my smile became a ridiculously happy grin in knowing that my mum was perfectly all right and it was just a few weeks until Christmas and I was back here with my family. Just like I'd wanted. After all the pining and moping, and all the missing and the wishing that I'd done over the past few months, I really should be making the most of every precious minute with my family. I really should be making up for all the time I'd been away.

So, with a lightness of heart, I grabbed my phone from

its charger on the bedside table to find that because I'd turned the sound down to sleep blissfully uninterrupted, I'd missed four calls from Ethan. On the last attempt, he'd left me a voice message, saying how relieved he was to hear that my mum was okay. He'd also said that he was missing me and that he still regretted not travelling back with me to the UK. I played the message twice over to listen to his deep and smooth and oh so sexy voice with his gorgeous Scottish lilt. I knew I could listen to him talk forever because his voice melted my heart and soothed my soul.

And I was missing him too. I was missing him so much that it hurt.

So much that my heart was heavy again and my thoughts conflicted and confused.

Arrrgghhhh! Was it even possible for me to ever feel completely contented with life?

What did Buddha say about contentment? That it is the 'greatest wealth'.

I tried to call Ethan back but to my disappointment I got his automated answer again.

And that was the problem in having an entire ocean between us and being on two different time zones. I left him another message saying I'd just slept off my jet lag. That I was fine and I was looking forward to spending the day with my family. That I would try to call him again later if he didn't call me first. And that I loved him.

Then I realised I could smell cooked bacon wafting upstairs from the kitchen.

Oh my goodness – I smell British bacon! Big fat rashers of lean and meaty goodness.

For a while now, I've been a vegetarian. It's a personal choice but it's one that fits in with my new beliefs and my life as a conservationist. I do feel passionately about animal welfare and greenhouse gas emissions and global warming and so not eating meat seems ethical to me.

In joining *The Freedom of the Ocean*, I had been correct in assuming that everyone else onboard would also be vegetarian. What I hadn't expected, however, was that marine biologists generally don't eat fish either and so are mostly vegan. I had happily and perhaps naively considered that living on ship, surrounded by water and therefore a bounty of seafood, would have meant me having to find a zillion different ways to serve fish for dinner.

It makes perfect sense to me now of course that people who protect and study fish don't actually eat them. But I must admit (although certainly not publicly) that I love eating seafood.

So, I was quite gutted – pun intended – by the dietary restrictions and also in having to find a zillion different ways to serve tofu. Ethan, who like most men will happily eat anything he's given on a plate, would if pressed always describe himself as a 'flexitarian.' In that he takes a more environmentally sustainable approach to the source of his food in occasionally eating meat and fish and other animal products. I'd always thought this was cheating and like having your beef cake and eating it. So, I did now feel terribly guilty, as I leapt out of bed and into the slippers and dressing gown that mum had kindly loaned me and padded down the stairs following the scent of cooked bacon into the kitchen.

My mum was at the stove waving a spatula at me. 'Good morning, Lorraine!'

I was so overjoyed to see her, alive and well and real, that I rushed across the kitchen to put my arms around her and squeeze her tightly. 'Good morning. I love you, mum!'

She laughed and kissed my forehead and ruffled my bed head hair, saying I should pour us both a cup of tea. Then we sat at the kitchen table eating good old British bacon sandwiches with HP sauce squidging out of them and drinking our strong tea and putting the world to rights.

We talked about all the things I'd missed as well as my family – TV soaps, British magazines, proper tea, fish and chips with mushy peas, Yorkshire pudding, proper gravy, Victoria sponge cakes and steamed pudding with thick creamy custard. Until we realised that we'd chatted half way through the morning and, as Lucas and Josh and Zoey where coming over for lunch, it was now time to start preparing the main meal. I was so excited.

This was going to be the kind of family day that I'd dreamed about for so long.

One that I'd dreamed of while standing onboard ship, looking across an endless ocean.

While sitting on hot sand with my toes in the tideline, gazing at an unbroken horizon.

Walking through a tropical forest, staring up through palm fronds into a cloudless blue sky.

Thinking about my precious and beautiful family so many thousands of miles away.

So, while I was helping mum and peeling vegetables and setting the table with a pristine white cloth and her best china, I happily continued to listen to her chatting away and telling me all about her social clubs and the pensioner trips she'd taken over the summer, all about her friends and what they were doing, and how busy she's been with her church activities all year.

She told me how she'd recently started helping out at a homeless charity. That she still volunteered at the hospice and the local hospital and the food bank. This was all on top of the reams of stuff she did through her church. My mum is a kind and generous woman. She seems to have boundless energy and keeps her days incredibly full and active. I've noticed that some of the people she helps and refers to as the 'older ones' or 'the elders' are actually a lot younger than she is and I find myself wondering how she even has the time to sit here chatting with me.

'Oh, don't worry!' she assures me when I ask if she's going to miss church today. 'Joan's handing out the bibles today. As I've just come out of the hospital, John, that's our Minister, has insisted I take this Sunday off. But maybe you and I can do it together next week, Lorraine?'

'I'd really love that—' I said, deciding that rather like my vegetarianism, I might be best to keep my new belief in Buddhism to myself.

Mum asked about my travels again. She wanted to hear more about places I'd seen.

So I regaled her with my adventures in Thailand at the turtle sanctuary and in Borneo learning about the Orangutans. How I'd learned to be a scuba diver and how amazing it was to be underwater and helping to restore coral reefs that had been damaged by either man or nature and about the lovely people I'd met and the incredible experiences I'd had along the way.

But I also continued to stress how I'd really missed her and the boys the whole time.

How I was really and truly happy to be home.

In turn, she confessed how worried she'd been about me.

'I want you to know that every Sunday in church, I prayed to The Lord to protect you.'

Then she put down her teacloth and I saw she was trembling and had become a little tearful.

'Mum, are you okay? What is it? What's the matter?'

'Lorraine, I do understand about you going off to Thailand. I understand why you felt the need to run away from that bloody no-good husband of yours after what he did with that no-good woman who'd called herself your friend. But all this time you've been away, a whole year, I've been hardly able to bear the thought of you out there all alone and so far away from us. And, for the life of me,

I just don't understand how you ended up running away to sea on that damned ship and going all the way around the whole world on it!'

I took a deep breath and decided this was exactly the right time to tell her about Ethan.

'Look, mum, if we are being honest with each other then I have something to tell you too. I wasn't all alone out there. I have someone. I've met someone quite wonderful and that's why I went on the ship. I wanted to be with him and it was the only way for us to be together.'

'He's a sailor?' she gasped in horror, as if sailors were the absolute depths.

'No. He's not a sailor. His name is Sir Ethan Goldman and he's a famous explorer.'

Mum's eyes practically popped right out of her head and into her tea cup.

'He's a philanthropist, which means he does amazing things all over the world to help people and animals and to save the planet, and that's why he was knighted by Her Majesty the Queen.'

Mum, who was a big fan of The Queen, was immediately smitten.

'Oh, go on, Lorraine. Tell me some more about Sir Ethan and your trip around the world?'

As she took a seat and dunked another shortbread into yet another cup of tea, I obliged.

I explained how after first meeting Ethan in Asia, and

after a month or so of us living in the Caribbean together, he had been called to an important meeting in Grand Cayman. 'It was to discuss a high-profile project to do with climate change with the world organisations. Naturally, they all wanted Ethan heading up the team. I knew at once when he returned to me that he'd already agreed to go. And, why wouldn't he?'

'So, Sir Ethan asked you to go along with him?'

I nodded. I couldn't help but to wobble a bit at this point. Recalling this special moment in my life brought a great lump of emotion to my throat and caused tears to well up in my own eyes. 'Ethan said to me; 'Lori, there's always a place for you in my heart and by my side.'

Mum's shortbread hung in mid-air for a moment before falling into her cup with a splosh.

'The thing is, Mum. I knew that I didn't want to lose him. I'd fallen in love with him.'

She passed me a tissue when she saw the tears spilling down my face. I blew my nose.

'But the whole assignment was to last eight months and the entire mission was at sea!'

'Oh heavens!' Mum sympathised. 'And with your tendency for sea sickness too.'

'Exactly. It turns out that the ship, called the *Freedom of the Ocean,* is the best equipped ocean research vessel in the world. It has a specially equipped laboratory designed for climate studies and high-tech computer gear and equipment for ocean floor mapping and an underwater drone that collects plankton and microscopic plastic particles for analysis.'

'But you aren't even a scientist, Lorraine. I remember you barely got a CSE in science.'

I shrugged. 'I know. But Ethan insisted that my previous skills as a housewife more than qualified me for Head of Housekeeping, which on a ship, is a senior crew position.'

I laughed at the irony, but mum's expression was still deadly serious.

'But, Loraine, didn't you think it would be dangerous?'

I shrugged. 'No. My concern was how to tell you and the boys what I was doing.'

'Well, you certainly had us worried, Lorraine. But now, this morning, listening to you talk so passionately about all the places you've been and all the people you have met, I realise that I was perhaps being terribly selfish in wanting you to come home. I do love hearing about all these amazing experiences you've had and how you've travelled to all these places that most can only dream about. So, now I feel terrible about you having to rush back here unnecessarily and on a completely false alarm. I'm so sorry, Lorraine.'

'Oh, Mum. Please. I'm happy to be here. I've told you how much I was missing you all!'

'Well, from what I've heard this morning, you might have preferred to stay where you were.'

'Mum, I'm just so relieved you're okay. Honestly, I was ready to come home.'

My mother studied me for a moment as if she was trying to decide on how to respond.

She patted my hand. 'But what about Ethan? Don't you still want to be with him?'

'It's complicated, Mum. I don't know. I'm still thinking about it.'

'You mean that you don't really know if you do love him after all?'

'No. It's not that. It's just that—well, he's asked me to marry him.'

'Oh. I see. And, you're not sure if you want to marry him?'

I bit my lower lip to stop it trembling. 'I'm not sure if I ever want to be married again.'

Conscious of the morning getting away from us, we quickly cleared up the kitchen and set the table for lunch and then went our separate ways to get dressed and ready for the boys and Zoey arriving. I was so looking forward to us all spending the whole afternoon together catching up.

When they arrived, we had lunch and then remained sitting around the table, drinking tea.

I wanted to know more about Zoey and how she and Josh had met and fallen in love.

'Zoey is a reporter with the local paper.' Josh told me proudly.

'Actually, I'm a junior journalist with the Shamfold Herald.' Zoey corrected him.

'Zoey's brother, Zack, is one of my friends from university.' Josh told me.

'My brother set us up on a blind date!' Zoey explained, blushing.

I wanted to know if they'd set a date for a wedding yet and where they were going to live when they got married. I know Josh is currently sharing an apartment with another male friend.

But, no matter how many more questions I asked them or how hard I tried to steer the conversation to them and their exciting future plans, they keep giving me short sharp answers and then drawing me off course and onto the proverbial rocks, with yet more questions about my voyage. They did all seem to be overly fascinated by my time spent travelling the world.

Or, rather, Zoey did. Maybe it's in her journalistic training to ask lots of in-depth questions.

She explained how she was really interested in marine conservation and so she wanted to know all about the mission and about the day to day life on an ocean-going conservation ship.

The boys wanted to know if I'd ever been caught up in storms and how I'd coped being in the middle of the ocean and so far away from land. My mum wanted to know what the ships kitchen was like and what my job actually entailed. I tried to answer all their questions honestly.

I explained that a ship's kitchen is called a galley and that the rooms are called cabins. I tried to make light of all that I'd experienced. When in truth, they were asking me to describe to them in mere words what had certainly been the most incredible and the most intense experience of my whole life, perhaps aside from having given birth twice.

'But how did you prepare for it, mum? Was there some kind of special training?' asked Josh.

'Of course.' I assured him. 'Every crew member gets survival training. We were always doing drills. For example, we had to practice how to fight a fire onboard. We also did man overboard drills and learned how to safely abandon ship if we were ever in danger of sinking.'

'Wow. It all sounds amazing and incredible. The ultimate adventure!' Zoey enthused.

'It certainly was.' I agreed. 'Although, looking back, I think I might have been a bit naïve in thinking that life on a ship would be something like living on a small island.' I laughed.

I remember Ethan using that line on me when I'd admitted my inexperience as a sailor.

'There are in fact only two similarities; lack of privacy and lack of space. And, as you wake up every morning in a totally different time zone and a different part of the world, it can be a little disorientating!'

'Especially as you've always suffered with motion sickness.' Mum reminded me stoically.

'But you sailed around the whole world!' Zoey cheered, looking at me in wide-eyed wonder.

'Yes, after our sail away from the Virgin Islands, we

crossed the Atlantic to head down the coast of Africa and onto Asia before crossing the Pacific to sail through the Panama Canal and right back to where we started.'

'How many others were with you on the ship? Were there other women too?' Lucas asked.

'Yes, there were always lots of other women. We had eight crew members plus around twenty scientists, all top marine researchers and biologists, who came aboard or departed at various ports of call. Some stayed with us for just a few weeks and others for a few months depending on their studies. During our months at sea, mapping and collecting data, we all saw first-hand evidence of man's destruction and pollution of the seas and oceans – we sailed through oil spills and vast areas of floating plastic debris, we stopped to help dolphins trapped in discarded fishing nets, and we've freed turtles caught up in old ropes. All the people I met on the ship were really lovely and amazingly capable. We were all part of a wonderful team working hard to make a real difference in the world. And, on the tough days, when we faced real trauma or trouble, everyone pulled together seamlessly to help and support each other.'

'What kind of traumas and troubles?' Josh asked me in sudden concern.

'Like the times we battled high-seas and gale-force winds or when we tried to avoid storms or to outrun hurricanes. Trauma, like the time Ethan cracked his head open and we all thought he had a dangerous concussion. Or trouble, when we came across illegal trawling vessels. Except, of course, Ethan doesn't call it trouble. He calls it dispute.'

'What kind of dispute?' Lucas's eyes were now wide in alarm.

'Well, we had the good fortune to be spared any run-ins with high-seas pirates, but we did have the misfortune of coming across illegal fishing vessels at various times. Our protocol in these situations was always to call for back up from the nearest coastguard or from one of the *Sea Marshal* conservation fleet who often patrolled the same waters.'

'I'm a supporter of *Sea Marshal* and *Sea Shepherd* myself.' Zoey told me stoically.

'But sometimes, when we came across illegal fishing, it wasn't always possible to maintain our impartiality.' I continued. 'And of course, it certainly wasn't in anyone's nature onboard *The Freedom of the Ocean* to allow the killing of whales for their oils or the slaughter of sharks for their fins. So, sometimes, we had no choice but to get involved to try to stop it.'

'Really? Whales? And sharks are killed just for their fins?' Josh gasped in horror.

'For shark's fin soup.' Zoey informed him. 'It's still a delicacy in some places.'

Everybody went quiet for a moment as they contemplated the atrocities I must have seen.

'Mrs Anderson, if there was just one thing – one experience that you will never be able to forget from that amazing voyage –what would it be? Can you tell us?' Zoey investigated.

'One thing?' I considered, wondering if it was really wise to speak of it.

They all sat back waiting quietly in encouragement and eager anticipation. Even my mum.

'Well ... it was without doubt the time we sighted an illegal whaling ship in the South China Sea. As our ship approached, we discovered a great slick of dark red steaming whale blood and a dying fully-grown female whale on the surface, with a young calf next to her who was still alive. It was a terrible sight. One I'll never forget.'

'Oh, my gosh! So what happened? What did you do, Mrs Anderson?'

'Oh Zoey, please, call me Lori or Lorraine. I remember watching in horror as the whaling ship's crew reloaded their harpoons. Our captain was bringing us about, changing our direction, so to position our much smaller vessel between the whaling ship and the whale and her calf. I suppose we were gambling on the hope that the whalers wouldn't harpoon us. Ethan was hailing the captain of the whaling ship over the radio and ordering him to cease and desist. Our crew were all up on deck yelling at the other ship's crew. Our scientists had appeared from below decks to offer their voices and to record the video evidence on their phones; something we did in the hope that being identified and outed on social media might send them away, but it just seemed to aggravate them instead.'

'And what were you thinking while all this was happening around you?' Zoey breathed.

'I remember thinking that the sun was hot and the sea was incredibly calm and the winds were light on what should have been a beautiful morning. But instead, all around us, the air was thick with the smell of blood and the reek of oil and vibrations from the ship's engines and the low moan of the dying whale. I remember thinking that the whaling ship was huge and rusty and scary looking. I could see its deck was a dirty cluttered mess of coiled lines and hoists, winches, and it had two huge harpoon canons. Not only was their ship much bigger than ours, we were outmanned too, as I saw around thirty or more, filthy looking, ugly, very mean men, who were all yelling at us in a language I didn't understand. Once we were close enough to smell their sweat and the overwhelming stench of dead fish coming from the bowels of their ship, they were shaking their fists at us for gate-crashing their killing party. Then there was a bang and a crack, that sounded like a firework going off, and I saw a harpoon with a train of long rope arc through the air and then I heard a dull thud as it hit its target. I heard her scream, and in response, I remember that I screamed too. It was terrifying.'

'And what happened to the young whale?' Josh pleaded, his face pale with anxiety.

'I did something entirely instinctive because I'm a mother myself.' I told them, my voice betraying the boiling indignation that I'd felt in my heart at that time. 'I jumped from our ship into the sea and I swam as fast as I could towards the whale and her calf. When I was in the water, I could hear people yelling and suddenly the man overboard siren was sounding, but I didn't stop swimming. When I reached the mother whale, I could see the pain and the look of despair in her huge eye, just before it became a blank stare.'

'Oh my God!' Zoey cried out; her own eyes wide in anguish.

'At this point, I'm crying with rage and trying to tread water rather than swallow it, when I saw the young one disappear beneath the surface only to resurface right next to me. With a blast of his hot breath, I'm now covered in a gory pink foam mix of blood and sea spray. I turn my head to look for the position of the whaling ship and then back to where I can see Ethan leaning over the deck rails waving his arms at me in warning. I'm in a total panic. My only thought is how to stop the next harpoon hitting this calf.'

'What did you do, mum? What happened next?' Lucas begged.

'I reached out to grab the mother's lifeless fin and I haul myself out of the water and onto her enormous body. Then, for a moment, I have to stop to catch my breath and get my balance before I crawl up her slippery wet skin and up and onto my knees and onto my feet. Then I'm standing on top of the mother whale and waving my arms and shouting at the evil whale killers in the hope that they won't fire their harpoon. And then, with a great belch of black smoke, I see the whaling vessel turning to leave and I started cheering. And then I see that Ethan is shaking his head at me but he's also cheering and waving too.'

When I stopped telling my story there was a poignant and stunned silence in the room.

Eventually, Lucas asked me if I thought the calf had been old enough to live on its own.

I nodded. 'Yes, it would grieve for its mother, but it was old enough to survive.'

'We all think you're a real hero and incredibly brave.' Zoey added compassionately.

'Oh, no. Please. I didn't feel brave. I'd been quite terrified!' I heartily admitted.

'Well it was all incredibly daring.' Josh insisted.

'And dangerous.' Lucas spluttered. 'Not exactly the kind of thing mums normally do, is it?'

'Oh Lucas, come here and give me a hug!' I said, seeing how much I'd worried him.

I grappled him in my arms and hugged him like I used to do when he was a toddler.

'It was the adventure of a lifetime.' I insisted. 'And, for the rest of my life, I'll never forget the day I stood on top of a dead whale in the middle of the South China Sea, waving my arms at its murderers and yelling like a crazy woman. I don't regret what I did for a minute.'

'I'm proud of you, mum. We all are.' Lucas told me earnestly.

'Thank you. But you should also know that for all

the lows and anxieties there were just as many, if not more, highs and moments of pure joy. I'll never forget the long days of peace and tranquillity at sea. The incredible unbroken horizons. The shimmering shades of blue.

And in that moment, I was transported back to a very special time in my life. It was a beautifully warm and clear starry night and the sea was as calm as a mill pond. Ethan and I lay up on the top deck, gazing up at millions of stars and ageless constellations. Who knew that star gazing was so much better in the southern hemisphere? And, that south of the equator, the northern hemisphere constellations all appear upside down?

Ethan had pointed out the Southern Cross to me. 'Look, it's right in the centre of the Milky Way. In the constellation Crux. The bright yellow star you can see at the far left is Alpha Centauri.' And, as we were gazing up in wonder, a shooting star had streaked across the sky.

I remember that I caught my breath and took Ethan's hand in mine and squeezed it in a tight grip. Neither of us wanted to say anything until the star had fully dissipated.

'What did you wish for?' he asked me out of curiosity.

'For us to always remember this moment together and how special it is.' I replied.

And Ethan said in a whisper that sounded to me like a lover's sigh of errant longing.

'Oh ... I love you, Lori.'

'And I expect that all these experiences have changed you?' Zoey suggested to me.

I gave myself a mental shake back to the present and I looked at her and smiled.

Something tells me I might have just inspired Zoey to go off and live a life of adventure on the high seas. I smile because I think she understands me in a way that perhaps my sons don't.

I feel I have found a new ally in my future daughter-in-law.

'I expect so, Zoey. I think travelling and meeting new people and having experiences, especially those that take us out of our comfort zone, can make us rethink our own place in the world. It's too easy to sit back and let life happen. We should all be taking a positive and interactive stance. Ever since I've met Ethan, I feel much more inclined to take a stand against wrongdoing and take positive action against injustice. One person really can make a difference. I'm very grateful to him for teaching me that.'

'And who *is* this Ethan you keep mentioning?' Lucas demanded.

Chapter 6

'So, tell us, Mum. Are you home for good or just for Christmas?' Josh asked me boldly, after I'd been back a whole week and he and Zoey and Lucas had popped over to their gran's house for a quick weekend visit. Today just happens to be 1st December, so naturally, our conversation had turned to our plans for the Christmas holidays.

'Oh, I'm definitely home for Christmas!' I enthused. 'I want this Christmas to be really special. I want us all to have a wonderful family Christmas together this year. I'll cook. We'll have a traditional turkey and bacon rolls and roasted potatoes and all the trimmings. It'll be a three-day festive extravaganza from Christmas Eve through to Boxing Day, with fun and games and gifts under the tree!' I was quite breathless with excitement just telling them about it.

My mind wandered back to last year, when I'd been on a small tropical island in the Sulu Sea, just off the coast of Northern Malaysia with Ethan. We'd roasted a Christmas lobster on an open fire on the beach. It had been wonderful. But I'd really missed my family.

I'd missed them so much that I'd sobbed my heart out on the beach.

And my Christmas gift last year from Ethan had been a satellite video link call home.

It must have cost him an absolute fortune.

Mum piped up to interrupt my thoughts. 'Well, just so you know, Lorraine, I'm serving Christmas lunch to the homeless on Christmas Day. I could try and get back here at around 4p.m. but I can't promise.' I stared at her blankly for a moment while I processed her words.

I could hardly believe it. She'd wanted me home. She'd told me how she'd prayed every Sunday in church for me and in particular she'd wanted me to come home for Christmas.

Yet she wasn't actually going to be home for Christmas herself.

I really wanted to point this out to her in no uncertain terms. But instead, I reminded myself that I must admire my mother for her charitable considerations and for giving up her own time, so that she can serve turkey to the homeless and those who might otherwise go hungry. It's such a kind and worthy thing to do. Even if it did put a big prickly holly leaf right in the middle of my very special family Christmas Day plans. With an uncharitable sigh, I revised my schedule. I moved serving Christmas dinner to later in the day.

'Okay. I suggest dinner at 6p.m. Would that work for everyone?'

I looked at both my sons and Zoey who were sitting on the sofa with long faces.

I was reminded of the three wise monkey statues I'd seen in Thailand.

Bapu, Ketan, and Bandar. *See No evil. Hear no evil. Speak no evil.*

Surely the promise of a fabulous festive feast and a bit of fun over pulling crackers and wearing paper hats and an exciting game of charades in front of the fire would soon get the smiles back on their faces. 'But you three can come over earlier, if you like. I'll be cooking all day, so there'll be plenty of nibbles. We can open some champagne while we wait for Gran to come home. Then we can all open our presents together from under the tree. It'll be wonderful. What do you think?'

I was already imagining the scene: snow falling gently outside, logs on the fire, the twinkling lights of the Christmas tree in the corner, the scent of fresh pine needles in the air, a stack of presents in Christmas wrap and ribbons, the table decorated and beautifully set with candles and flowers, the smell of lovely food coming from the kitchen, the crooning sounds of The Rat Pack or Michael Bublé in the background and our laughter filling the room as my mum arrived home. A perfect family Christmas.

I forced myself not to think of Ethan right at that moment, whom I'd briefly spoken with on the phone several times this week, who was still asking about whether he could jump on a plane and join us here for Christmas.

But I'd been adamant that until I could broach the subject (of him) and properly explain (to my kids) how I was in a relationship (with him) then he would had to wait patiently in the wings for my signal that that it was safe for him to arrive.

Then I spotted Zoey and Josh elbowing each other in the ribs.

Until Zoey spoke up in a small and apologetic voice.

'Erm—actually, Lori. I'm really sorry, but Josh and I have already agreed that we'll be spending Christmas this year with my family. It's all been arranged.'

I forced myself to adopt an expression of understanding.

Even though I actually felt like I'd just been slapped hard across the face by the Grinch.

'Oh, please, don't apologise!' I fussed. 'I mean, I've just arrived back and so I wouldn't dream of asking you to change your plans and disappoint your family. But, I'm sure that you and Josh can still come over at some point during the day, can't you? To open presents and have a mince pie?' I paused expectantly and maintained my upside-down sulk.

'Not really. You see, Zoey's parents live in Cornwall.' Josh explained. 'And we said we'd drive down there on Christmas Eve. But we could try and get back here for New Year?'

'Oh. Well, that does kind of make it difficult, doesn't it?' I remarked, trying not to weep.

It never occurred to me that Josh and Zoey might have prior arrangements for Christmas.

'And what about you, Lucas?' I said, turning to my younger son and now my only hope, whose face was now as pale and waning as a moon on a misty winter's night.

'Well, that's a difficult one for me too. I've already promised Dad that I'd spend the day with him. He's booked a table at the pub. If I don't go, then he'll be all alone at Christmas.'

I wanted to shout out: 'But then I'll be all alone for Christmas!'

Of course, I didn't. Instead, I sat quietly with my hands clasped tightly together on my lap.

'You can come to the pub too, if you like, Mum? In fact, I know Dad would like that!'

I smiled and gritted my teeth while thinking that I'd rather stick pins in my own eyes than spend Christmas Day with my cheating no good ex-husband. And how, rather sadly, it seemed that I'd been expecting rather too much and been entirely mistaken in assuming my family would be available to spend time with me this Christmas. I was destined to be all alone.

Unless, of course, I covertly invited Ethan over to spend Christmas with me here?

Except that he wouldn't want to be a secret or go along with any platonic games.

He'll want to hold my hand. He'll want to kiss me under the mistletoe.

He'll want to flirt with me and share my bed. He'll want to sleep with me.

But how does a mother tell her kids that she has a boyfriend?

When even to me that sounds completely ridiculous at my age?

Oh, how excruciatingly embarrassing.

How do I explain about Ethan to my kids?

They do already know of him because I've mentioned his name on several occasions.

I've guessed they have their suspicions that he might be 'someone' and they do know that we work together, and I've known him for quite some time. So really, it should be relatively easy for me to gently introduce the mere idea of him and me being an item into our conversation. And, if I choose the right moment, and if I'm careful to slip in a mention of his credentials first – his knighthood – they'll know straight away he is a man of great social standing and reputation. My mum already knows, of course, but that is another matter of concern. I'm worried that if I don't say something soon—then she undoubtably will.

I'm already fending off questions as fast as my mother can instigate them.

'What about Ethan?' My mum suddenly pipes up as if she's reading my mind.

'Yeah, Ethan. Who is he? You've mentioned him a couple of times.' Lucas noted once more.

I took a deep breath and gathered my thoughts and in that moment my mum did the unthinkable. She snatched away my moment and told them everything in no uncertain terms.

'Sir Ethan has asked your mum to marry him!' She announced proudly on my behalf.

'Oh Mum!' I groaned, thinking I could have quite cheerfully strangled her at that moment.

'What? So, you're saying, that all this time, you've had a boyfriend?' Lucas demanded.

'Not a boyfriend by the sound of things – but a fiancé!' Josh clarified, sounding horrified.

Then came the onslaught of questions and demands for answers.

'Didn't we have a right to know that you're thinking of getting married again?'

'Where will you live if you marry this man?'

'If you do marry him, will we ever see you again?'

I held up my hands against their barrage of words and anxiety.

'Woah, boys, before you all get too carried away, you should know that I haven't decided if I will marry him. Right now, Ethan is looking for somewhere for us to live and settle down, so that we won't always be travelling all the time. That means that if I do marry him, or even just decide to be with him, you can all come and visit anytime, and we will all still be a family.'

The silence was palpable. Eyes were staring. Mouths were gaping.

Until my mother started laughing and cheering and clapping her hands.

Determined that the subject was now closed I turned to Zoey to help me out.

'Zoey, I want to hear all about yours and Josh's plans now that you're engaged!'

Josh was still shaking his head. 'It sounds to us like you will marry him.'

Lucas was sulking. 'Dad will be gutted when he hears about this.'

With yet another mention of my damned ex-husband from Lucas, anger flared up inside me and it took all my resolve to remain calm. The last thing I wanted was an argument with my sons about their father or to bring Charles into this already heated conversation. And, I'm sure Lucas didn't mean to offend me, but I do know that from what my mum was telling me during our catch-up conversation earlier this morning, that Sally and Charles had not lasted more than a few months together. That Sally had moved out and afterwards both Josh and Lucas had reconciled with their father. I'll admit, hearing about Charles and Sally splitting up soon after I'd left and how the scandal of their affair had been made public knowledge had pleased me.

Not that they hadn't deserved each other. Not because I'd wanted any kind of reconciliation or retribution. It was simply a feeling of satisfaction that Karma had prevailed.

'Anyway, Dad said he wants to see you. He wants to talk with you.' Lucas informed me.

'He says you have unfinished business to discuss.' Josh clarified.

'Ah, so your father already knows I'm back here?' I replied.

'Yeah. I told him.' Lucas admitted. 'He always calls me on a Sunday morning for a chat.'

I nodded in approval. 'Well, of course. That's very nice.'

'Good. You'll see him, then. You'll talk things over with him?'

'No. I don't mean it's nice that he wants to see me. I mean it's nice you both still see him.'

'Well, why wouldn't we? He's our dad. He's the one who's been around for the past year!'

I felt like I'd just been slapped. All my guilt over not being here for my kids rose up like a monster from somewhere in the middle of my chest and threatened to choke me. Despite this, I lifted my chin stoically and reminded myself that I must acknowledge that my sons have a right to voice their true feelings. It's only healthy and being connected to their father is good. It should be encouraged. That said, my sons are not children anymore, and I too have a right to stand up for myself. So, I rose to my feet and gave my sons the benefit of my own feelings.

'Well, I'm here now, and there's nothing that I want or need to say to your father!'

'But you don't understand. He's sorry. I know it. He's told me!' Lucas continued.

'Look. I don't care if he's sorry. Your father and his other woman, my best friend, betrayed me and it wasn't even a onetime fling. They'd both lied to me for a year. They cavorted and conspired together and they didn't give a jot about me and what was *my* marriage and *my* friendship. He might be sorry but I'm not.'

My voice was rising like a crescendo as I got more and more agitated.

Everyone had shrunken back into their seats as if I'd gone completely ranting crazy.

'And, do you know what? Now that's it's done, I'm really glad it happened. Do you want to know *why* I'm glad about it? Well, I'm going to tell you why. Because now I have found a decent man. Someone with morals and ethics and who truly loves me. Someone who, unlike your father, would never do anything to deliberately hurt or betray me!'

There was a stunned silence in the room.

The boys were horrified. Zoey looked embarrassed.

I too was shocked at my own vehement defence of both myself and my relationship with Ethan. Wow, did I really trust Ethan that much? With my heart? With my love? With my future? Did this mean that he had somehow restored my faith in love and marriage?

Did this mean I was now actually considering his proposal?

And I saw my mum was looking at me with a small smile playing on her lips.

It seems that I just can't win. When I'm away from my family and travelling I'm unhappy because I miss them all and when I'm away from Ethan I also feel lonely and incomplete.

I'm so frustrated. It seems the only way to get any peace in my life is to develop a thick skin and not care so much. But I *do* care. I can't *not* care. I also realise that I'm in a bit of a sulk because my family aren't including me in their plans for Christmas. I know they aren't doing it to be intentionally unkind. It's just the way things have turned out. I can't really expect them to make changes to accommodate me. Can I?

And, I'm not only missing Ethan, I'm also missing the feeling of action and adventure he evokes in me. For a whole year, my life had been an exciting journey. It's been a quest for something or a mission to accomplish important things. Now, suddenly, it's like time is standing still for me and I'll admit that I'm feeling incredibly bored.

It's like the novelty of me being home has worn off and now it's life as boring usual.

And it has me thinking and rethinking all that has happened between Ethan and I over the past year. I'm going over and over in my mind what happened on Tortola and Waterfall Cay.

I'm mulling over the words he spoke to me about his lifelong dream: 'I love these islands. I know these waters like I know the back of my hand. It's long been an ambition of mine to buy a boat and live on an island here in the BVIs. A dream, actually.'

And it's really grating on me that Ethan, a wealthy man who has properties all over the world, has absolutely nowhere to call home. A man who has unselfishly dedicated his life to helping others – man and beast – as well as trying to save the world for future generations. A man who travels the world like a crusader to protect and salvage and save. Who has never knowingly given up on anyone or anything – other than his despicable brother – and whose one and only dream for himself is of living on the last untouched private island in the BVIs.

A dream that has been so cruelly snatched away from him.

And, whether I marry him or not, with every fibre of my being I want him to have it back.

If Ethan won't do something, then I need to devise a plan to turn things around for him.

Surely there must be a way to get the island back?

This morning, it's quiet in the house. Mum is out playing bingo at the pensioner's centre.

So I fire up my tablet and do an internet search on Damion Goldman.

I discover straight away that Ethan's estranged brother is a high-profile businessman in the USA, where he lives in California with his ex-model wife, Gloria. He's a wealthy man too.

He owns hi-tech businesses in Silicon Valley and he also has commercial interests all over the world including in oil and banking. I read several recent news reports about Damion Goldman playing golf with one of the founders of Google and a CEO of Microsoft and then attending meetings with coal mining companies in China, despite calls for global carbon control. I note he also has interests in a controversial palm oil production company currently being implemented in the destruction of rainforest and the endangerment of Orangutans.

For that reason alone, I was starting to understand why Ethan despised him.

But hatred wasn't a healthy emotion to hold onto and family was family after all.

Although Ethan's opinion of Damion being ruthless must be deeply-rooted.

I couldn't help but to ponder over what might have caused such a rift between the two brothers and if it could be fixed? Despite Ethan's earlier objections, I once again mulled over the idea that if Damion knew exactly why his brother wanted Waterfall Cay – and how the island was uniquely special to Ethan – then perhaps a mutual understanding could be forged and a resolution could be found? I started to feel excited about this idea.

Many times, on small islands throughout Indonesia, where people's livelihoods and the welfare of their families depended wholly on the sea and in the industry of fishing, I'd witnessed Ethan acting as a mediator between government fisheries and fishermen who couldn't see the sense in establishing fishing quotas. They'd thought they could just carry on fishing, because that's what their ancestors had always done, with no consequence for the environment or thought of ever running out of fish to catch. But, once Ethan had managed to actually get them to sit down and to listen, they could see the mutual and the long-term benefits.

Surely, in the same way, Damion and Gloria could be persuaded to compromise and to find another island on which to build their grand hotel resort? A plan started to form in my mind. A plan that, if it worked, could bring these two estranged brothers back together again and result in Damion handing over Waterfall Cay to Ethan. All that was needed here was clear communication and thoughtful mediation.

When I spoke with Ethan on the phone later that evening, I broached the subject of the island by asking if he'd heard anything more from his lawyers. He replied that he had and that they'd completed their investigations on how the lease and the island had been hijacked by his brother.

'They confirmed how the trustees, having seen the Goldman name on the asset application and in the email address, had mistakenly emailed the draft to Damion's lawyers,' he explained to me. 'And no one had questioned the redrafted lease documentation even after he'd damned well signed it!'

'How can that happen?' I queried, thinking this was highly irregular and certainly unethical.

'Because they were tricked.' Ethan's tone was laced with loathing.

'There must be something that can be done about it?'

'They're full of apologies but it seems there's nothing that can be done.'

'Did you ask if they'd take another look over the small print? Maybe there's a clause about damage to the island that could get him evicted? I mean, he's drilling into a coral reef!'

'Lori, stop. There's no point. There's no way that Damion will have overlooked something as simple. He'll have greased some very powerful palms to get all his plans approved. I know that you are disappointed. I'm disappointed too. But we're going to have to let this one go and move on. We'll have to find another island somewhere else to call our own.'

'But you said that it was a rare find.' I protested. 'You said it was your dream!'

Ethan paused for a moment before changing his tone into one that sounded much softer.

'Look, Lori, you said you needed to spend Christmas with your family. I absolutely understand. Really, I do. But I miss you and so you must understand that I can't just sit around here moping for the next few weeks. I have to do something or I'll just go crazy.'

I smiled down the phone. It pulled at my heart strings to think of him missing me and moping and going crazy. 'Then you are going to be very happy to hear that I've told my family all about you and me and us. Although, I should warn you that Josh and Lucas might need a little winning over. My mum, on the other hand, can't wait to meet you but will insist on calling you Sir Ethan. So, why don't you get your gorgeous crazy self on the next flight over here, because now there's nothing stopping us from spending Christmas together in London?'

But, instead of a cheer at my good news, I heard him sigh despondently down the phone.

My heart was suddenly in my mouth. This wasn't exactly the response I was expecting.

Why the sigh? Had he changed his mind? Wasn't he really missing me after all?

'What? What is it? Ethan?'

'Oh Lori—you see, when you insisted that you didn't want me there, I made other plans.'

'Other plans? For Christmas? What on earth do you mean?'

'I've been offered an assignment. It's just for a few weeks. While you're over in the UK.'

'An assignment ...' I repeated, trying to hide my hurt and disappointment.

'Aye. In the South Atlantic. It's a National Geographic study on Elephant Seals.'

From the tone of his voice, I guessed he was already really looking forward to it.

'Oh, Elephant Seals—that sounds wonderful.' I breathed.

I suddenly hated the thought of him going on any assignment without me.

'Lori, you'd hate it. It'll be cold and windy with snow and sub-zero temperatures.'

'Which sounds exactly like the weather here.' I sulked. 'When do you leave?'

'Tomorrow. I'm going out to the Falklands to meet up with the rest of the team. I should warn you, that as I'm heading into Antarctica, I could be out of touch for some time.'

'So, it'll be a case of no news is good news?' I acknowledged.

'Aye. You got it. I should be back in time for Hogmanay. Can I come over then?'

'Sure. Hogmanay it is. Ethan, can you please do me a favour before you go?'

'Sure. Anything. You name it.'

'Can you please ask your lawyers to email me a copy of the lease for Waterfall Cay?'

His bated hesitation and the moment of silence between us spoke volumes.

I could tell he was reluctant to grant me my request.

'Okay, I'll ask them to email you a copy of the lease. But I want you to know that my dream isn't with a particular place anymore. It's with a certain person. I love you, Lori. Don't ever forget that. And I'm really glad that you've told your family about us at last. It means a lot to me. But when we do get together again, we need to talk about our future. I'll want to know if I need to buy you another ring?'

When our call was over, I sat quietly contemplating. Trying to make sense of my feelings.

I hated how unsure I was – not about him – and not of my love for him.

It was the whole marriage thing. Maybe it was a case of once bitten twice shy?

We'd both been married before and it hadn't worked out.

I wasn't sure if it made any sense for us to be together as man and wife.

Why did we even need to get married anyway?

I'm divorced from Charles. But is my relationship with him entirely over?

To me, it feels like there is still unfinished business here. Part of me never wants to see Charles ever again. But another part of me wants the satisfaction of saying to his face all the things that my mind has been screaming at him from the other side of the world.

It's been easy to be stay emotionally detached and to close myself off and ignore the consequences of his betrayal and our separation and divorce after twenty-five long years of marriage while there has been a distance between us. Like keeping my head buried in the sand.

But now that I'm back here, it's like my emotional scar tissue has once again become an open wound. I'm still angry. I still harbour resentment for all the years that I'd spent mindlessly dedicating myself to him and to our home. Cooking and cleaning for him. Ironing his shirts.

All while being overlooked, stifled, ignored, and treated with complete indifference.

Then, of course, there are our two children. Not that they are children anymore.

And Ethan? Well, he doesn't have children—as far as I know.

At this thought I stop myself and roll my eyes in exasperation and in new realisation.

It seems that since Ethan's surprise brother turned up, I might have developed a new trust issue. I can't help but to wonder if there's any other skeletons in his closet that I should know about before I can possibly consider marrying him? Then, there's his ex-wife, Marielle. She's French, attractive, but highly unstable. I met her last year at the same time that I'd met Ethan.

I didn't know they were married then, of course. I'd watched her slap his face before she left us and after she'd almost successfully warned me off him. She'd been angry too. Not at me I hasten to add. But all slighted women are angry in my experience.

That said, I do love Ethan. Of that fact I am totally sure. And, he's nothing like Charles.

But surely, co-habitation seemed a far safer and uncommitted option for people of our age?

When he proposed to me, I thought it seemed inappropriate somehow.

Although, it was also terribly romantic.

But what if my boys never came around to liking him when they met? What if they remained vehemently opposed to me being in another relationship never mind a marriage? I couldn't just ignore their feelings because they didn't know which parent to blame for their pain over our divorce. Oh dear, the angel and devil on each of my shoulders were busy arguing again.

I decided that I'd just let them get on with it because I now had something important to do.

I decided I would very much look forward to Hogmanay, as Ethan (being Scottish) liked to call New Year. But, in the meantime, I would focus my mind on what mattered in the present.

For as Buddha said: *Do not dwell on the past. Do not dream of the future. Concentrate the mind only on the present moment.*

Chapter 7

It's the first week in December and weather warnings have been issued for the whole of the UK. All bets are on for a white Christmas in London. The big high street shops are now playing Christmas tunes in store and streaming their festive commercials on TV. There's one advent advert that's really winding me up. It has a catchy tune. It's beautifully filmed. There's dancing elves and real reindeer. But it shows Santa coming out of a well-known supermarket pushing a shopping trolley that is overfilled with plastic carrier bags full of festive food.

The advert goes on to suggest what festive items are entirely necessary for yule time joy and the magic of Christmas but it's the trolley loaded with plastic bags that's really ruffling my say-no-to-plastic feathers. I mean ... what on earth are they (not) thinking?

Plastic carrier bags! Really?

We have plastic pollution all over the world and most of it ends up in our seas and oceans.

It's a sad fact that every single piece of plastic ever made still exists in one form or another to this very day. This plastic pollution must stop. There are now more ethical options. But of course, it costs more to provide shoppers with biodegradable bags or to promote reusable non-plastic carrier bags and this supermarket is clearly guarding their profit margins at the expense of the planet. I see that I'm not the only one to think this way about this particular advertisement as there is already a backlash storm brewing on social media against said supermarket.

Feeling motivated to do something about it, I made a quick banner from a roll of spare wallpaper that I found in the cupboard under the stairs and I wrote on it in thick marker pen and in very large letters. *SAVE THE PLANET! SAY NO TO ONE USE PLASTIC BAGS!*

Then I stood outside the well-known supermarket for an hour holding up my banner, until my feet where soaking wet and my toes were frozen, and the icy rain had made my homemade banner too soggy to hold up anymore and the two example supermarket plastic bags I'd stapled to it had filled up with water. Most people had ignored me, including the supermarket staff collecting discarded trollies from the carpark, but a handful of interested shoppers had stopped to ask me what I was doing with my say-no-to-plastic crusade and so I felt it had been worthwhile. I was just rolling up my soggy banner when a woman tapped me on the shoulder.

'I'd heard you were back, Lorraine. What on earth are you doing here?'

I looked up and my heart sank to see it was Sally. My ex-friend and husband stealer.

'Isn't it obvious?' I snapped. 'I'm educating people about plastic pollution.'

She looked at me from under the shelter of her umbrella with her eyes raised, as if I'd just said that I was telling people Santa was an alien and that Christmas was a commercial scam.

'It's something I feel very strongly about,' I clarified, trying to not to look horrified and hopelessly unprepared at seeing her so unexpectedly. I lifted my head in an attempt to look dignified while knowing I was soaking wet and slightly steamy in my mother's sodden woolly hat and heavy coat.

'Well you do look like you've just stepped out of a rainforest. Do you fancy a cup of tea?'

Sally gestured towards the supermarket café, which I'll admit looked warm and inviting.

I did fancy a cup of tea but not with the woman who had betrayed our friendship and slept with my husband. We weren't the best of friends anymore. We weren't friends at all.

But I nodded in resignation and we went into the bright lights of the warm café.

We took our cups of tea and sat down opposite each other on shiny plastic seats at a wipe-clean plastic table. Sally propped up her wet umbrella and slipped a silk scarf from around her neck, while I pulled off my coat and hat, knowing my hair would be a flat mess stuck to my head. I glanced up at her with reticence to notice how along with her perfectly made up eyes she was wearing a bright shade of red lipstick. But in the harsh bright lights, it all looked too much, and her skin looked pale and her face insipid and pinched-looking. Her silver-grey shoulder length hair that had always looked so natural and chic was now pulled back into a far too severe-looking chignon and looked oddly unreal. As she slipped her cashmere coat from her shoulders, I noticed how much thinner she was looking these days to the point of being bony.

'You've lost a lot of weight.' I told her in a way that might convey it wasn't a compliment.

'And so have you.' She answered with her red lips quivering. 'Only it suits you.'

We sipped our hot tea silently for a few minutes while I wrestled with every negative emotion that I've had to endure over the past year racing from my heart and ending up in a colossal collision in my brain. Carnage. Then the floodgates finally opened. Hers not mine.

I braced myself for the resulting tsunami as Sally disintegrated into shuddering sobs.

'Lorraine, I'm really s-s-sorry for what I did to you. I want you to know that I'm paying for it now. You might take some c-c-comfort from knowing, after you left, I l-l-lost everything.'

I could hardly believe her nerve. Was she expecting my forgiveness? My sympathy?

'You know, I really doubt that, Sally.' I cut in waspishly. 'You see, from where I'm sitting, it still looks to me like you took everything!'

She shook her head insistently while her shoulders shook and tears ran down her face.

'I lost my home, my husband, all my friends, and my job. I loved that job. I was s-s-sacked from a voluntary job for h-h-heaven's sakes. When you left, no one wanted anything t-t-to do with me. They all b-b-blamed me. Not C-C-Charles of course. Just me!'

I watched her rummage frantically through her designer handbag for a tissue to soak up her tears and her runny nose and I thought about the time when Sally and I had first met. I'd been so impressed with her. She'd seemed so glamorous and stylish at a time in my life when I was feeling drab and outdated. She'd always worn makeup and nice clothes. She'd looked so sophisticated. It was laughable now that Charles had called her 'my high-maintenance friend'.

Both mine and Sally's fathers were under palliative care in the same hospice and that's how we became friends. Over a few long weeks, during that summer, we'd got chatting in the visitor's kitchen and consoled each other over cups of tea as both our father's health deteriorated. I'd enjoyed and looked forward to her company. She told me she had two girls and I had my two boys. Sally was married to Craig, a bank manager, and they had a townhouse at the other side of town. I was married to Charles, who ran our travel agency, and we lived in a three-bedroomed home in suburbia. She had a top of the range BMW and I had a little old budget run-around car. She'd always donated her worn once designer clothes to a charity shop and I'd always bought all my clothes from a charity shop. Then, after both our fathers sadly passed away and our youngest children had happily started school, Sally and I met up again.

We'd both responded to a 'volunteers wanted' poster in the charity shop window in town.

I remember on that first day working together, while sorting through and pricing donations, she'd confided in me that she was terribly lonely living outside of town. I told her how, now both my boys were at school, I was feeling bored. Especially as I'd given up work to become a full-time housewife. Then we became really good friends. Better than that, we became like sisters. Until, of course, the day she'd crossed boundaries both literally and figuratively.

But now, sitting here and watching her face crumple and tears spurt from her eyes, I regretted being so generous to this woman. What a fool I was to trust her. To confide in her.

Her affair with Charles had been one thing; calculated and quite unforgivable.

But what was worse – far worse and more hurtful – was that she'd betrayed our friendship.

Sisters simply didn't do that to each other. There was supposed to be an unbreakable bond.

People sitting around us started to stare as Sally wiped away her tears with a flailing hand.

I noticed how the large collection of rings she always wore were now rattling against her knuckles and swinging loose on her long thin fingers. That her nails that were once famously long and always professionally manicured, were now nothing more than chewed stumps.

'We never meant to hurt you, Lorraine. It all sort of happened in the heat of the moment.'

I leaned forward across the table and whispered to keep my voice down.

'Hardly. You were shagging him for a whole year behind my back.'

When Sally looked up, she was an absolute mess with red watery eyes and with mascara streaking in black lines down her cheeks and her previously perfect makeup now smeared across her face, making her look something like a tragic clown. I stared at her for a moment.

I'm not used to feeling hard-hearted. Since I've been with Ethan, I'm quite the opposite.

Seeing Sally this way made me feel pity for her and incredibly sad for both of us.

'I don't expect you to f-f-forgive me. I just want you to know that I'm truly s-s-sorry.'

I stood up to leave. I'd let go of my anger towards her but certainly not my pride.

I reminded myself that Buddha had once said: 'If there is something you're not ready to forgive yet, then you can forgive yourself for that.'

'Happy Christmas, Sally.'

I walked away, not taking any comfort from her situation, as she suggested I might.

I headed straight through the shopping mall and over to the charity shop, where I saw Taryn stoically working alone again, while a backlog of people were queuing up to pay at the till. I could see she was frazzled. I picked up a couple of tops that I wanted from the sale rail and then I offered to help her out just for the hour that it took to disperse the queues.

Taryn was so appreciative and so I suggested that she might want to give Sally a call.

She looked surprised. 'Really? Sally? Are you sure?'

'Yes. I think she might really appreciate it. Especially at this time of the year.'

Taryn smiled and nodded. 'Okay, if you say so, Lorraine. I'll certainly give her a call.'

I've now been waiting for a week to receive a copy of the lease to Waterfall Cay from Ethan's lawyers by email. But it still hasn't arrived. I'm starting to wonder if he's forgotten to ask them for it or they have simply decided not to send it to me. I really wanted to check it over to see if there were any clauses that might clearly constitute an offence – something that would get Damion and Gloria Goldman evicted from Waterfall Cay – because surely drilling through coral reef and pouring concrete on a pristine habitat where turtles might nest must be a crime.

Plus, I'm now dithering over the plausibility of my Plan

A, which was to gently but persuasively talk Damion and Gloria into giving up Waterfall Cay voluntarily for the sake of family and common decency. I still happened to think, based on our short but eventful meeting on the island, that Gloria might be approachable, but I have my doubts and misgivings about her despicable husband. Ethan has certainly portrayed him as a formidable opponent.

Today, to curb my boredom, I've been up in the loft to retrieve the family decorations and tinsel, despite our low-key Christmas plans. I've found a box of Christmas themed candles and a nativity set and a set of outdoor twinkly lights that would look lovely on the small fir tree in mum's small front garden. I've pleaded with her to let me make a start on putting up the decorations, but she has refutably said 'no' because no one else in the cul-de-sac has started decorating yet, and so therefore neither should we.

It's true. In the street outside there's not one single light bulb or sprig of holly or Christmas tree on display yet. It seems people around here are not so keen on starting their Christmas celebrations too soon. Mum's in the same camp. She absolutely insists that Christmas decorations can't possibly go up until the third Sunday of Advent. That's in mid-December.

I do remember her being staunch about this when I was a child too.

No amount of pleading or persuasion then or now seems to be able to change her mind.

Instead, she's tried very hard to get me to join her in whatever it is she does all day.

I've politely resisted and insisted that I've plenty to do and she should carry on regardless.

Since then she's taken me at my word and I've hardly seen her during daylight hours.

She seems far busier and much more capable than I'd ever previously given her credit.

When I was married to Charles and we lived twenty miles away, I used to come into town and take mum to the cinema one afternoon a week. It was our special time together. I'd really thought I was being a dutiful daughter and doing her a huge favour in taking time out of my busy life to spend some time with her. Now, it seems quite clear that it was entirely the other way around, and she had been taking time out of her busy life to spend time with me.

Don't get me wrong, after being away for so long and after the shock of thinking I'd lost her, I'm delighted to see that my mum is fabulously busy and independent. But it seems achingly unreasonable for me to be so physically close to her and in such proximity to my darling boys and yet only see them for a short period of time on weekends.

Knowing that I won't see my boys much over Christmas either, I've been trying to make arrangements – appointment or so it seems – to see my sons for just an hour this week. Of course, I do know they are both busy men. Josh is a scientist and works in a laboratory on the outskirts of town. Lucas works in marketing for a big company in

London and he commutes every day and so keeps long hours. Their work sounds very interesting and important and I'm so very proud of them both. I've made it perfectly clear I don't want to be a nuisance. I've also told them that I'm entirely flexible. I'm willing to fit in with whatever time they happened to be free. I'm happy to meet up for lunch or in the evenings for dinner.

But, disappointingly, it turns out they rarely have time to spare and no time suits them.

'Sorry Mum. I never get a full hour for lunch. I really don't have the time.'

'Sorry Mum. I often have to take clients out at lunch-time.'

I phoned Zoey to suggest we might meet up for a girly lunch, but she said she wasn't feeling very well with 'winter flu' and so she was best avoided all this week in case she passed it on.

It just seems practically impossible for me to spend any time with my kids.

'What about after work? In the evenings?' I suggested, trying not to sound desperate.

Hello – I'm here now! I've been away for a whole year and I might go away again!

But Josh and Lucas say that after work they need to 'relax and chill' and they both apparently do this by staying home in their apartments playing Xbox Online with their cyber-friends.

To prevent complete boredom and total misery setting

in, I've cleaned and tidied the house and I've been shopping. I've made soup and cooked a meal and I've set the table nicely for when mum comes home at around 6p.m. But when she does get home (closer to 7p.m.) she tells me that she's already eaten. So, I eat my dinner alone while she takes a long soak in the bath.

After which, we sit by the fire and watch a couple of hours of TV together.

Mum loves all the soaps and the family quiz shows. She has the TV set up to record all her favourites. So, we don't have much in the way of conversation before she goes to bed at ten p.m. Not that there is much left to say now as we've talked nonstop for a couple of weeks.

We must have exhausted every subject on earth.

I open a bottle of wine and a packet of crisps and flick through channels on the TV.

It's all the same old stuff I've seen before on repeat.

I feel like I've somehow slipped back into something that could resemble my boring old life before I'd travelled. Only now, because I have lived a more adventurous life, it all rather feels like tedium and monotony. I settle on watching the National Geographic channel in the hope of catching a conservation programme that features Ethan. I know he's done lots of filming for programmes featuring on the likes of the NG and for Animal Planet. But disappointingly there's no sign of him.

Instead I watch a fascinating programme on the Galapagos Islands – a group of over a dozen islands in the Pacific Ocean some 1000km off the coast of South America – and very much somewhere I'd love to explore one day. These islands are so isolated that they have the most unusual animal life on them. Iguana and giant tortoises and unique birds. The narrator explains that it was on Galapagos that Charles Darwin had been inspired to come up with his theory of evolution by natural selection. At this point, I wanted to yell at the TV screen.

This was because Ethan had recently told me that it wasn't only Darwin who had discovered the theory of evolution. According to Ethan – and I'm sure he is absolutely correct – the theory of evolution was co-founded by one of his all-time heroes, Alfred Russel Wallace. This was the same nineteenth Century biologist and explorer and direct descendent of William Wallace who had discovered the giant butterflies of Waterfall Cay and had tried to save them from extinction.

And it was Wallace who, while he was in Galapagos, also according to Ethan, had discovered that insects and birds and small mammals can successfully migrate between islands – usually during storms and clinging to chunks of driftwood – and establish themselves elsewhere. A perfect example of the survival of the fittest and the theory of evolution.

I knew that if Ethan was here with me right now, we'd have had a lengthy and interesting discussion about this subject. I sigh and can't help but to wonder what he's doing right at this moment. I picture him in Antarctica leading a dog sled over glaciers on a mission to save penguins and seals. And I wonder if he might be missing me as much as I'm missing him.

It's Friday again and I've hardly seen my mum. I've been housebound most of the week as the weather is cold and miserable outside and I'm a bit cross because I haven't seen my kids since last weekend. Even though we've all still been here in the same small town as each other. In the very same country. On the same side of the world. That's not to say we haven't been in contact – I've chatted with them several times over our group chats as usual using Facebook, Messenger, Snapchat and WhatsApp – in exactly the same way I would have done if I'd been away. So I could in fact be anywhere and I'd be missing them in exactly the same way!

On Saturday morning, I get a call from Josh. He says that he and Lucas want to meet me for lunch. I'm beyond excited. I know the pub. It's one of those lovely old traditional pubs a few miles out of town with real ales behind the bar and low beams in the ceiling and a menu that is traditional with meals like steak and ale pie and fish and chips.

It's freezing cold and pouring with rain outside, so I start to look up the bus time tables.

Mum kindly offers me her car. All she asks in return is that I drop her off at the food bank this morning and pick her up again afterwards. I accept and I'm grateful.

But then I realise that I haven't driven a car in a whole year.

I do hope I haven't forgotten how to drive or lost my confidence.

Now, what to wear for a lunch with my sons? Not that I have many options.

In the bathroom mirror, I sigh and curse the layers of woolly clothing in which my body looks to be mummified. And what about my hair? On a beach or onboard ship, my long heavy tresses would be left to dry naturally in the warm and humid air and might look a bit salty or windswept until I'd tamed it with a bit of coconut oil. But here, in the UK, I have the look of an unkempt wild woman. I give it a brush and decide I look quite mad.

I pick out a plain black long-sleeved high-neck jumper and decide I'll wear it with the same pair of jeans I've been wearing all week, albeit alternatively with my chavvie-looking fleecy jogging pants. I spray a bit of deodorant under my arms and around and about and resign myself to the fact that I haven't knowingly perspired even once since arriving back in the UK.

After dropping off mum at the food bank, I drive slowly and cautiously along the bypass as the roads are slushy with wet snow. When I arrive at the pub, I spot Josh's car in the car park and go dashing inside with a happy spring in my step. It might be cold and miserable outside but it's busy and warm and cosy and welcoming inside. The contrast between the two environments doubles my pleasure. I pause to admire a lovely big Christmas tree at the entrance decorated with oversized gold bauble decorations and there's a festive menu on a chalk board on the wall offering turkey or baked ham. I realise how much I've really missed a British pub.

Of course, there's a lot to be said for sipping beer while sitting on a beach, but in my experience, in reality, there's always those pesky sand-flies to spoil the ideal. Whereas here, there's a real fire flickering in the fireplace and Bing Crosby is crooning *White Christmas* in the background. I'm asked by a rushing waitress if I have a table reservation just as I see Josh at the bar. I wave to him and dash over to kiss and say hello.

He buys me an orange juice when he hears that I'm driving and then I dutifully trot behind him and follow him back to the table where I can now see Lucas. He's sitting next to someone; an older man who is tall and slim and balding and whom I now recognise as my philandering ex-husband. Bowled over by shock and with legs suddenly like jelly, I take a step back into my own tracks. Charles stands up when he sees me. 'Hello, Lorraine, you're looking well.'

For a moment we stare at each other without blinking. I can't help but to think back to the last time I saw him: in our bed, butt naked, and on top of Sally. It's not the most attractive vision to hold onto for a whole year and certainly not a welcome memory right at this very moment. I consider how the time between then and now hasn't been very kind to him.

He looks so much thinner and leaner, which makes him look somehow taller and bent, in the same way that an old knurled tree might look bent after spending a year braced against a consistently cold wind. I turn to my sons. 'I can't believe you've done this. This is entrapment.'

'Yeah, well, we thought it's about time you two talked to each other.' Lucas declared.

'About that unfinished business.' Josh reminded me.

I hissed between my gritted teeth. 'You could have told me you'd invited your father.'

Not knowing what else to do, I tentatively took a seat opposite Charles. Then in that very same moment, to my horror, our boys got up and disappeared together into the pub's snug room to claim the pool table. Leaving Charles and I alone. Even though the pub was crowded and noisy, it still felt like there were just the two of us in this face-off and in this room.

Just me and the man with whom I'd had two children. Me and the man I'd once been married to for twenty-five years. The man who'd betrayed me. The man whom I'd once loved. This was not how I expected to confront Charles for the first time since he'd become my ex-husband: in a pub, without a stiff drink in my hand, wearing unflattering clothes and a very red face. I realised I was now perspiring profusely and all the words I'd specially crafted in my mind over the past year for his benefit – the scathing come backs and the witty responses – all escaped me now.

'I meant it when I said you looked well, Lorraine.'

Charles continued to say. 'Forgive me for staring, but I'd swear you look ten years younger these days. I do believe it's your exotic suntan and much longer hair. You look very pretty.'

He gave me a toothy grin and I noticed one of his teeth was missing.

I stood up and grabbed my handbag.

Rather than feeling overwhelmed I was in fact now feeling rather underwhelmed by it all.

I had absolutely nothing that I wanted to say to this man.

'But Lorraine, please, we need to talk. I need to explain. I want to apologise to you.'

My eyes darted away from Charles's silly grin into the other room where I could see our boys playing pool while also keeping watchful eyes on us. Seeing me up on my feet, looking like I was about to leave, I could see that Lucas was frowning.

Josh caught my eye and slowly shook his head.

I sat down again and took a sip from my orange juice.

'I don't want an explanation Charles, but I will accept your apology.' I said to him calmly.

'Lorraine, I'm sorry for what I did. I apologise for hurting you.' He said writhing in earnest.

A silence hung between us as he waited for my response.

'And?' I prompted.

'And for betraying you.' He obliged.

'With my best friend' I extended on his behalf.

He nodded. 'Yes. That too. I apologise, and I hope somehow you can forgive me.'

He lowered his head and his eyes and I saw his lower lip was trembling.

I'll admit that I felt oddly satisfied by this display of remorse.

'I accept your apology, Charles.'

'You do? Then you also forgive me, right?'

I laughed at this seemingly preposterous assumption. Apology? Yes. But forgiveness?

'Charles, I have just realised something.' I said to him.

'What? That you still love me? Because I still love you, my Lorraine!'

'What? No. I have just realised that all the emotions and all the angry words that I'd saved up to throw at you in this moment are no longer needed. Life has moved on for both of us. Immeasurably. I'm not your Lorraine anymore, Charles, and I don't love you. I haven't for a very long time. I'm my own person now, thank you very much.'

I stood up, kissed Charles on the top of his balding head and wished him a merry Christmas.

I walked away not feeling wretched but feeling free. Really and truly free.

There was a lightness in my step. It was like I was walking on air.

I burst out of the pub door and stood outside. A blast of icy air took my breath away.

It was still raining and so I started to dash back to the car, gasping and fumbling in my bag with cold fingers for the keys, when I heard Lucas shouting me. 'Mum! Stop! Wait!'

I turned and smiled at him to make it clear there should be no animosity between us.

'Mum, I know Dad is truly sorry. He regrets everything. He needs you to forgive him.'

I looked at my disappointed son, who'd obviously had every intention of reconciling his parents. 'Look, my darling. Your dad and I love you and your brother very much and we appreciate your efforts. But we are divorced. There can be no reconciliation. You have to understand, it's no longer about what your father did but rather that I've moved on and now love someone else.'

Lucas nodded. 'Okay. You know Josh and I just want you to be happy, don't you, mum?'

I reached out to touch his face and I kissed him on the cheek. 'Thank you. Likewise. It's what I want for all of us. Now go back inside. It's freezing out here. I'll see you soon.'

I watched my son walking back into the pub. The collar of his jacket tugged up against the shards of freezing rain, his hands rammed into the pockets of his jeans. I was proud of my sons for trying. And, thanks to their intervention, I had got the angst about seeing Charles again over and done. How strange that when it came down to facing him, expecting bitterness and angry words, what I'd actually felt for him was sympathy. It had been the same with Sally, in the end.

And, of course, I feel I now have closure at last.

Chapter 8

It's now the middle of December. Our little artificial tree, that I'd dragged from the loft a couple of weeks earlier, is now decorated with baubles and lit up with tiny lights. It's snowing outside. Not the magical slowly fluttering kind of white snow that lays deep and crisp and even and looks ever so pretty on the ground, like a traditional Christmas card. This was the blowing a blizzard kind of messy brown snow that turns into slush as soon as it contacts wet urban tundra.

So today, once again I'm housebound, and getting seriously fed up with my own company.

Consequentially, I've taken to cyber-stalking Damion and Gloria Goldman.

It's all in the name of research and in preparation for the plan to get Ethan's island back.

With no sign of a copy of the lease from Ethan's lawyers, I've now decided that negotiating or sweet talking or even pleading with them into handing over the island is back on. It's amazing really, how all this personal and business stuff about them is freely available on the internet. So, it's not like I'm doing anything questionable or illegal.

And I'm finding every click to an article or a feature about their lives is quite fascinating.

Clearly, the Goldman's are a Golden Couple. They are often referred to as 'The Goldmines' and they have their discerning fingers in many rich pies and their names on many affluent boards. Interestingly, as well as the technology company in Silicon Valley and the casino complex in Las Vegas and their Trump-esq tower in New York, they also have a portfolio of super-exclusive hotel resorts throughout Europe that they call The Goldman Collection.

It's this upmarket 'collection' of hotels that has my utmost attention.

Because in a recent online interview for GQ Magazine, I read that Damion has said that he intends to "expand our luxury hotel enterprise globally over the next year" starting with an exclusive flagship resort on a recently acquired private island hideaway to be opened in time for the next holiday season. When pressed in the article, he refused to name the actual location of the island but went on to refer to the venture as 'the best kept secret in the Caribbean'.

I can only assume he's referring to his dastardly development plans for Waterfall Cay.

He then claimed not just to be building a hotel resort in the traditional sense but creating a 'retreat par excellence' with a superlative marina for the mooring of world-class superyachts as well as an extensive waterpark featuring a

Perspex tube slide into an aquarium filled with marine life, a zipwire ride through the rainforest canopy, and an exotic zoo of animals from all over the world. There were boastful hints of his multi-million-dollar budget, his impressive conglomerate of 'big-name' shareholders and how he is now under 'extreme pressure' to open this new venture on time.

In my mind's eye, I can see all the industrial cranes and the power drills at work to develop the marina, where the beautiful lagoon and the untouched coral reef once were. My thoughts darkened, as I imagine a modern multi-storey hotel complex being constructed alongside an ugly array of waterpark slides and swimming pools that would form a tragic scar on the surface of the tiny island. My heart aches with pity for all the island's creatures that will lose their perfect habitat and their lives. I shudder with fear for those so called 'exotics' that will be imported into the Goldman's new zoo.

My brow is furrowed as I stared at the screen at Damion Goldman's smiling airbrushed face.

Like Ethan, Damion is an incredibly handsome man, but he also looks fearsome in a way that Ethan never could. It was in the mouth, I decided. Damion's lips were set to stoic by default. In contrast, Gloria's lips were red and plump and glossy and set into permanent camera-ready smile. I see she is a keen Instagrammer with an impressive 2M+ followers and her own hashtag. At first glance, I assume her popularity is simply down to her model looks and great fashion sense, but to her credit, she also seems incredibly active on the charity fundraising circuit. Her great #passion is with #humanitarian work.

It's on her IG feed that I see photos of her looking pious while posing with little children at a school project in Africa. Then looking even more glamourous wearing a khimar headscarf in a desert somewhere while helping to set up a healthcare facility.

Maybe, on second glance, there is more to #GloriaG than a pretty face?

I realise that I'm starting to admire her even though I'm trying very hard not to like her.

I thought back to that fateful day on Waterfall Cay, when she'd caught me off guard with her familiarity over Ethan, and with her perfect model figure and her long vibrant red hair.

But, unexpectedly, she'd also been unpredictably friendly towards me.

She'd cast a wry smile and a covert roll of her almond-shaped grey eyes in my direction as her husband and Ethan had rallied strong words at each other. It was as if she'd found amusement in the two of them almost coming to blows in front of us. For some reason she came over as a woman's woman. And an ally rather than a rival?

Just as I pondered this thought, a new Instagram photo of Gloria suddenly appeared.

In it she was wearing her underwear – designer lingerie of course – pouting suggestively into a full-length mirror while holding up two strategically placed gowns. *Which #StellaMcCartney shall I wear to my fundraiser in the Bahamas? #Gloria #Art4Humanity #ChristmasChildren*

Clearly, the fashion designer had sent her a whole rail of gowns to choose from to wear at the fundraiser she was attending soon. Did I groan? Did I actually have pangs of dress envy?

Wait a minute? Gloria Goldman was attending a Christmas children's charity fund-raiser in the Bahamas? My mind started whirling with possibilities at the potential in this information.

A couple of internet clicks later, I'd found out that she was due to attend an art exhibition and a charity auction at the Atlantis Hotel on Paradise Island in the Bahamas and it was happening tomorrow night. I caught my breath as Plan A began to fully form in my head.

What if I was to go there and meet up with Gloria for a heart to heart chat over Waterfall Cay? What if I could persuade her onto our side? What if I could get her to talk to her husband?

Surely, she would want to play a part in bringing these two estranged brothers together?

And, it would be easier and far more conducive for me to speak with Gloria in the Bahamas than to travel all the way over to California on the slight chance that I'd get an invitation to speak with both her and her husband at their home. Plus, it was half the flight time and distance away. Why not? I have the time. I have the inclination. It's not like I had any other plan right now. And it's not like anyone here would mind me flitting off for a few days.

I could simply say that I was going to do some Christmas shopping in the Bahamas.

Who knows what might become of it?

I quickly checked to see if there were any event tickets still available.

Yes, there were. But they were eye-wateringly expensive.

I checked my bank balance online to assess my financial situation. I had a good nest egg of savings because Charles had wanted to buy my half of our house for cash when we divorced. I'd been careful about dipping into it and knew this money was meant to last me a long time and at the very least until I could claim an old age pension. Going to the Bahamas and to Gloria's function would certainly put quite a large dint into it.

But it was going to benefit an important charitable cause.

It might bring Ethan and Damion together again as family.

And, it could be the only way to secure Ethan's island dream.

Imagine! How could I even put a price on such a prize as Waterfall Cay?

Click. Click. Click. In no time at all I had arranged a flight to Nassau, I'd bagged a room at the Atlantis hotel, and secured a ticket for tomorrow night's charity art exhibition.

I felt a great rush of excitement as my heart began to beat faster and adrenalin surged through my body.

Wow. This was going to be a new adventure. A thrilling new assignment.

A high-stakes mission to save Waterfall Cay island and return it to Ethan.

Oh, and I was definitely going to need a new dress.

Chapter 9

The Bahamas

As my flight touched down on New Providence Island, Bahamas, I gazed enthusiastically out of the plane's small oval window to see clear blue skies and bright sunshine. Once again, I was leaving an airplane with just a small carry-on bag and wearing light clothing and a pair of flip-flops, only this time I was escaping the cold and grey of London for a few days.

I whizzed through immigration and got a taxi from outside the airport building to take me along the winding coastal road towards downtown Nassau. My driver, an older gentleman called Joseph, spoke in a wonderful deep local drawl and told me he'd been born and raised in Nassau. Then he enthusiastically regaled me with which particularly rich and famous person lived in which particularly fabulous house behind the tall fences and electronic gates on West Bay Street. 'Look, that's Tiger Wood's house. This one's Oprah's. An' here is where Tom Cruise lives!' Then he pointed out each and every one of the big five-star hotels and exclusive vacation resorts on the famous stretch of sand along Cable Beach. I suppose he must think tourists like to know these things. I peered out at the vast green expanses of the Royal Blue golf course, after which he pointed out to me the colourful and popular fish fry restaurants at Arawak Cay. 'The best fish fry in the Bahamas!'

Then on our way into downtown Nassau, we jostled with expensive cars with blacked-out windows driven by chauffeurs and with colourful reggae-blasting Jitney busses driven by determined looking dreadlocked Bahamians. Then, I was treated to a spectacular view of the harbour and the glittering bay, where enormous modern cruise ships, looking like giant shopping trollies, entered and departed, and where the iconic silhouette of the original and world-famous Atlantis Resort dominated the skyline.

I was filled with a sense of excitement and anticipation.

'Which one you stayin' at Ma'am?' Joseph asked me, as he glanced through his rear-view mirror at my reflection. Traffic had drawn to a standstill because we were caught up in a bottleneck in the road, after which, all roads led across the arched bridge to Paradise Island.

'Atlantis!' I repeated to him.

'Yeah, well, there's five hotels at Atlantis. There's Beach, Coral, Royal, Harbourside, Reef, and the Cove. Which one you at?'

'Oh, I'm not sure.' I quickly tapped at my phone to check my booking information.

'I'm axin', Ma'am, as they've each got different entrances an' different expectations.'

'I'm at the first one you mentioned. The Beach Tower.' I told him. 'Is that one the best?'

'Nope. The Cove is the best.' He replied, as if already anticipating a cheap tip.

I realised of course, to my dismay, that Gloria was sure to be at The Cove.

As we headed over the high bridge onto Paradise Island, I had an elevated view of the entire ocean themed resort of Atlantis. Although vast and sprawling, I could see it was built around the marina and the famous waterpark and a maze of walkways and bridges and interconnecting pathways. So, maybe it doesn't matter so much at which hotel I stay?

I know I should be feeling tired from my early morning wake up and from my long flight, but I'm actually feeling energised, by the ambient temperatures and sunny skies and the happy holiday and touristy vibe in the hotel reception area. It's amazing what sunshine and warmth can do for a person's mood as well as for those achy joints. I'll admit to feeling a soreness and stiffness in my bones from pretty much the moment I arrived back in the UK and now miraculously it's all gone. I joined the queues of people, mainly families, checking in.

There's no welcome glass of champagne, considering the price of the rooms here. However, after checking into my room and finding it was neat and basic and clean and that my view from my small balcony overlooked a swimming pool and palm trees and the beach, I was satisfied.

I decided to take a walk to scout out the venue for this evening's fundraiser.

I double-checked my ticket to see that, of course, it was all happening at The Cove.

My hotel was at the far end of the resort in an L-Shaped block. I walked outside into hot sunshine and followed a winding path that took me past a busy swimming pool and a sunbathing terrace where every sun lounger looked to be taken. I passed a popular coffee shop and a bustling bar until I'd left the undefined confines of my hotel and was now on the trail towards all the other hotels in the complex. Including those huge imposingly and impressive ones with the arched connecting bridge that you see in all the brochures for Atlantis.

I crossed paths with lots of people wearing swimsuits and carrying towels who were either heading towards or from the water park. Soon, the path I was taking had me walking along the side path of a meandering lazy river in which people were floating in large inflatable rings. I passed several more bars and pizza places and doughnut stalls that all looked and smelled tempting and then I stopped at an impressive giant-sized glass wall in what looked to be the entrance to a cave. Perring through the glass, I came face to face with several reef and nurse sharks, who were all swimming around a clear underwater tube passing through the middle of the tank that had guests sliding through it at great speed. Sourly, I wondered if this was the kind of thing that Damion Goldman had in mind for his waterpark on Waterfall Cay?

Continuing on, I walk across a wobbly swinging rope bridge and cast my eyes over a huge freeform lake with an area primarily for motorised water-sports. People were zipping around on jet skis. There was also a man-made sandy beach there full of sun-worshipers. To my right, a separate area of lake had a huge amount of manta rays swimming around in shallow waters.

Having seen sharks and manta rays swimming in the wild and now having seeing them in captivity, I would under any other circumstances have felt uneasy and upset, but I do know that this aquarium here at Atlantis is one of only two in the western hemisphere with a dedicated programme of expert staff and marine scientists whose practices and research techniques have helped in the study of migratory patterns of many different marine species.

Ethan has told me all about it and so I assume he might have even funded it.

After fifteen minutes of walking, it starts to feel like an awfully long way over to the other side of the resort. My new rubber flip-flops, bought hastily at Gatwick on the way out here, have already started to fall apart and have given me blisters between my toes. Ouch!

I finally arrive at The Cove exhausted and red faced and hobbling.

I plonk myself down in a comfortable chair at a

designer-inspired sanctuary of a poolside bar and order an iced-coffee from a smartly dressed waiter. The pool here is absolutely gorgeous. It's a place of quiet ambiance and serenity with willow furniture and chic looking cabanas complete with a butler service and classy looking people. The centre of the pool even has an island with palm trees and there's waterside mattresses for extra decadent dipping and lounging. My taxi driver had been right. Each of these hotels here were progressively nicer and obviously more expensive. And, until I'd seen this one, I'd been very happy with my original choice. What was it that Buddha said about the grass being greener?

For your peace of mind do not overrate what you have received or envy others.

Here, beautifully sun bronzed people clad in designer swimwear and expensive looking sunglasses are reclining on sumptuously padded sun loungers or gliding through the azure blue water towards the swim up champagne bar. I watch them all keenly through my bargain-bin sunglasses and keep a look out for any woman who might have long red tresses.

I sit for a while, observantly sipping on my eye-wateringly priced iced-coffee.

But only having spied blondes and brunettes, I eventually decide its time I headed back to my own more modestly appointed hotel. But, before doing so, I saunter over to the grand foyer.

It was, of course, the epitome of luxury in marble and

gold and with miraculous looking suspended-in-mid-air crystal water features. At reception, I enquired about the location of the charity fundraiser event being held later this evening.

'It's being held in the Grand Ball Room, Madam. Would you like to buy a ticket?'

'Oh, I have a ticket.' I laughed. I don't know why I laughed. I guess I'm feeling a little intimidated by the grandness of everything and the slightly shallow and scathing looks I've just received from a fellow resort guest, now standing near to me with an obvious opinion on my lack of designer apparel. I think I'll be glad to retreat to my side of the resort after all.

'Can you please tell me if Gloria Goldman has checked in yet?'

The receptionist tapped her keyboard. 'I'm afraid, we don't seem to have a Gloria Goldman.'

Another more mature looking receptionist, having been eavesdropping on our conversation, sidled over to me with her already arched eyebrows raised. 'Erm—do you know Ms Goldman personally, Madam?' she asked me purposely.

What do I say to that? I do kind of feel like I know her; as we've met once.

'Yes, of course. I'm soon to be her sister-in-law.' I answered boldly, laughing again.

The two women looked as astonished as I felt.

Where on earth had that come from? What was I thinking? Why was I lying?

Only it didn't actually feel like a lie. It felt more like an actual possibility.

I smiled and drummed my fingernails nervously on the marble countertop for a few moments. Until I realised my nail polish was chipped and then I resorted to clenching my fists.

'She's staying in one of our private villas.' The more mature one said, while picking up the house telephone. 'Shall I call a butler to take you over there in the buggy, Madam?'

Eager to meet with Gloria, I was just about to agree to this when I remembered that I was hot and sweaty and still wearing the clothes I'd been travelling in and that my hair was in a crazy humid frizz. 'Oh, please don't bother her. I'll see her later this evening. Thank you.'

I hobbled away, carrying my flip-flops, to leave the cool sophisticated opulence for the fiery heat outside. But I soon perked up once I discovered that the crowd of people I suddenly found myself standing amongst were all in a queue for a complimentary shuttle service running between all the hotels and I didn't have to walk all the way back on my blistered feet after all.

A few moments later, I was on the shuttle bus and being whisked via the lobbies of all the other hotels in reverse order, to the shopping mall that was right next door to my own hotel.

I went straight into the nearest boutique.

I wanted to look the part tonight. I needed to look like I

was the sort of person who could appreciate expensive art and afford it too. I also needed a pair of comfortable shoes.

In the boutique, an assistant fussed over me as I tried on a few dresses until I found 'the one'. I knew it was the one for me the very first moment I slipped into it. It felt just right. Made from gossamer light silk fabric with a classic halter neck design, the gown was backless all the way down to the small of my waist. It floated over my hips and shimmered under the lights of the shop like the blue and green and silver scales of a mermaid's tail.

I looked at my reflection in the full-length mirror and smiled.

The assistant smiled too. 'Madam, that gown is perfect on you.'

'I'll take it!' I said and then also took a pair of kitten-heeled slippers that were perfect too.

I then stopped off at the nail and brow bar. My hair I could wash and manage myself, because I would certainly be wearing it up tonight in an attempt to look sophisticated. I did however splash out on some very nice toiletries and a new perfume from the cosmetic store. Oh, and a double expresso with a caramel shot from the coffee shop to boost my flagging energy levels, before heading back to my room for a caffeine-fuelled pampering session.

By the time I reappeared, the sun was setting over Nassau.

The daytime skin-searing temperatures had settled into a pleasant and relaxing ambience.

I took the complimentary shuttle bus back over to the ballroom at The Cove, stopping along the way to drop off and pick up men, women, and children, dressed in swimsuits and carrying towels. I smiled and blushed as I garnered a few flattering comments from my fellow passengers. It's amazing what a new dress and a slick of lipstick can do for one's confidence.

When I arrived at the Cove, a young woman in uniform on the door checked my ticket and then stared at me for a considerable moment and then she also kindly complimented me.

'Madam, your dress is—well, what can I say? It's just—wow!'

I was thrilled and did a little twirl. 'You think so? Do you like it?'

'Yes. It's beautiful. Really beautiful. I love the way it catches the light!'

She's a fresh faced and pretty girl in her early twenties. A student, I imagine, working her way through college by helping out at events like this one. On a minimum wage too and so relying on tips and goodwill. I quickly decide that she might be a lot younger than me, but she was certainly around the same height and dress size. I decided to offer her my dress.

'Would you like it? Only, after tonight, I certainly won't need it again.'

'Really? Seriously? Oh, my goodness. Thank you. This is incredible. Yes, I'd love it!'

I made a mental note to remember her name from her badge.

'Then, I'll leave it in a bag at reception for you tomorrow Jennifer, with your name on it.'

I walked confidently into the ballroom to see waiters shimmying between guests and offering flutes of champagne or platters of tiny delicious looking canapés. I picked up a drink and advanced into the throng to mingle and to try and look like I belonged. I scanned my eyes over the attendees for the one feature that would make Gloria Goldman stand apart from all the other women in the room; her vibrant red hair. There were other redheads of course, those with various shades of ginger or auburn tones but Gloria was a red head with attitude.

Gloria's hair was the colour of fresh blood.

And suddenly, I saw her. She was in a long black lace Stella McCartney dress, standing in the centre of a group of men and women and laughing and tossing back her hair.

She looked like the star in her very own vampire movie.

I immediately spun around on my kitten heels and retreated in short steps.

I knew I couldn't possibly approach her while she was in the midst of her posse.

I'd have to wait until I could catch her alone and we could talk privately.

I hoped it might eventually lead to a meaningful conversation.

I hadn't come all this way for nothing. I also had to consider that she might not remember me. Just because she'd made an impression on me did not necessarily mean it went both ways.

I moved away to stand behind a pillar so that I could be discreet in continuing to watch her, as she worked the room like a social butterfly, flirting from guest to guest and flitting from painting to painting. The art on the walls, each with its own pistol packing bodyguard, was impressive. Not that I'm an expert, but I did spot a Vettriano. I'm guessing it's not a print.

I also managed to engage in a couple of arty-type conversations with a couple of friendly-types of people, so not to completely adopt the personality of an unsophisticated wallflower.

I also enjoyed another glass of champagne. Then someone wearing a smart tuxedo appeared on the stage with a microphone. He thanked everyone for coming along to support the foundation and asked people to 'dig deep' before introducing their 'esteemed chairperson' who was of course Gloria Goldman.

Gloria swept onto the stage to rapturous applause and she gave a short speech.

Her voice was clear and confident and her words well-chosen and warmly presented.

She thanked all the people who had helped her to bring the event together to raise funds for children born with life-threatening and deformative conditions caused by mosquito borne viruses. I, and everyone else in the room, applauded her heartily as she handed over the microphone to the auctioneer who kicked off the sale.

'The first item this evening is a highly collectable watercolour by a sought-after artist. An investment for the future. Shall we start the bidding at $10,000?'

The immediate hail of responses faded into the background as I made my way across the room to where Gloria was making her way off the stage. When she reached the bottom stair, I was standing right in front of her.

'Hello, Gloria. I don't know if you remember me? I'm Lori. I'm Ethan's friend.'

She stared blankly at me for a moment and then I saw her red lips part and the corners of her perfectly made-up eyes crease into a friendly smile. 'Yes, of course. We met on the island. How wonderful to see you again, Lori. Are you interested in buying some art?'

'Erm, no, actually. I came here to speak with you about a matter of some importance.'

Her eyes sparkled with curiosity. 'Does it have anything to do with Ethan?'

'Yes. It does.' I held my breath hoping his name was the password to her attention.

'Okay, Lori. I'd love to chat but I'm working tonight. It's my job to sell paintings.'

'Tomorrow, then?' I suggested.

'Yes. If you ask at reception, they'll escort you over to my villa. Say, around 10a.m?'

'Great. I'll see you then. Good luck tonight with your fundraiser.'

She thanked me and I watched her gracefully launch herself into the room, saying: 'Ah, Sir Gordon, how lovely to see you. Have you picked out a painting you like yet?'

The following morning at 10a.m. sharp, I was back at The Cove, after being sat on a bus jam packed with almost naked people carrying towels and floaties and wishing that once again I'd had the foresight to stay there too. I remembered to leave the dress and the shoes that I'd promised to Jennifer with the receptionist, who then quickly and kindly arranged for me to be whisked over to Gloria's residence in an electric golf cart.

I sat next to a smiling butler who was wearing white shorts and a short sleeved pale blue shirt. We whizzed along a winding yellow stone path that looked like it was paved with gold and after a few minutes we came to a halt outside a villa that overlooked the beach.

Not just any piece of beach, of course, as this patch of white-sand paradise was easily as heavily guarded as a G7 Summit Meeting.

'Hello?' I shouted into the open doorway and was soon greeted by Gloria herself.

She rushed towards me wearing a long flowing sheer white dress held together at her narrow waist by a gold rope belt. She looked like she was gliding across the polished Mediterranean terrazzo tile floor towards me like a Greek goddess in her temple and with her arms open wide in welcome. In my white cotton shorts and a pale blue blouse, it's a wonder that she hadn't confused me with one of her staff, but she was warm and friendly and kissed me on both cheeks.

'Lori, how lovely to see you again. Do come inside. Join me for some tea on the terrace.'

She led me through the villa and outside again, through a billowing white cotton drape and onto the terrace, where there were several big comfortable lounging sofas and a small private swimming pool.

'Please, make yourself comfortable. I'm sorry we couldn't talk last night. I was kept so busy; I didn't even manage to grab a glass of champagne all evening. Can you believe it?'

I sat down on a squashy sofa and looked around me at the fabulous villa and its beautiful terrace with pots of tropical flowers and opulent outdoor furnishing and the exquisite tray containing a tall glass jug of iced lemon tea and matching tumblers on the low coffee table.

And, I thought to myself, what a far cry all of this was from just a couple of days ago when I'd been standing outside a supermarket on a cold and dismal dark winter's day, to this heavenly scene. 'And I trust it was all a great success?' I enquired.

She rolled her eyes with joy. 'Yes. It was fantastic. Surpassing all my expectations!'

I watched her as she poured our tea steadily. The sharp morning sunlight catching both the crystal glass jug and the huge diamond ring that Gloria was wearing, sending shards of light in all directions. This morning, without any make up on her face and with her blood red hair worn loose and tousled, Gloria, whom I know from my research is much the same age as me, looked much younger and even prettier than she had last night.

'I'm intrigued.' she said. 'Do tell me — how is Ethan?'

'He's in the Antarctic, actually.' I felt a little agitated that she'd mentioned Ethan so quickly but also quite pleased that we could get straight down to the reason I was here. 'We can only assume that right now he's happily counting seals and penguins.'

Gloria giggled, showing a glimpse of small and perfect dazzlingly white teeth.

'So he's still off trying to save the world?' she concluded.

'Gloria. I'm here because I want to talk to you about Ethan and Waterfall Cay.'

She passed me a glass of iced lemon tea. 'Okay. I'm listening.'

'You and your husband are planning to build a hotel resort on the island.'

'Yes. But let me tell you straight away that Ethan is quite wrong about us stealing the island from him. That's just ridiculous. We've acquired it legally and authentically. I'm afraid he must just have sour grapes about it!'

'On the contrary. Ethan says his brother intercepted his agreed deal. Illegally.'

'And do you have proof of this?'

'Erm, no. I don't.'

'Then why are you here? And why is Ethan in the Antarctic, if it means that much to him?'

'Ethan doesn't know I'm here. I've come to ask if you'd be willing to collaborate with me in convincing your husband to stop his development on the island and to relinquish the lease.'

Gloria looked horrified. 'You're asking me to turn against my husband in favour of Ethan?'

'No. I'm simply asking you to speak to your husband so that he can appreciate that Ethan, his brother, has set his heart on having Waterfall Cay as his principle home. Our home. The island is very special to both of us.'

I saw her eyes drop quickly from my face to my finger in search of a ring.

'I heard he'd divorced Marielle. Are you and Ethan — getting married?'

I ignored the question. 'Look, we really want it back!'

Gloria started laughing. Her laughter sounded like a peel of tinkling bells.

'And, in exchange for what, exactly?' she questioned.

'In exchange for a reconciliation with his brother. Think of it as a peace offering.'

Gloria looked surprised and suddenly fell silent. Her next words came out in a sigh.

'You mean like a white feather?'

'More of a golden chalice, actually.' I retorted. 'One that could reconnect them as family. If Damion gave the island back to Ethan, no matter how it was obtained, it's a gesture that could bring them together as friends and brothers again. Don't you see, the fact that they are both interested in this island, is a perfect opportunity to reunite them.'

'Lori, it's a wonderful sentiment and it would be amazing if you could pull it off.'

My heart soared. 'Then will you help me?'

But then she shook her head despondently. 'No. I can't get involved. But I wish you the best of luck because I too would love to see them reconciled. All the time I've known them they've been sworn enemies. So, unfortunately, I don't expect Damion will want to hear about a white feather or a golden chalice. And, you say, Ethan isn't even aware of your plan?'

'But they are family. Brothers. Have you any idea what caused this terrible rift?'

Gloria shrugged her delicate shoulders. 'What can I say except that it's complicated? I do know Ethan had just finished high school and Damion had just completed his master's degree when their parents died. There's quite an age gap between them and they've never seen eye to eye. So afterwards they both went their separate ways.'

I pondered this for a while. Sibling rivalry could explain an awful lot.

'I just know that Ethan isn't a quitter.' I told her, my tone now betraying my anguish. 'He fights the good fight every single day with governments and bureaucrats and yet for some reason, he'd rather relinquish the island, than fight Damion.'

Gloria raised her perfectly arched eyebrows. 'And do you think they should fight over it?'

'No, not physically. But it's clear to me that Damion wants the island for business reasons and Ethan has set his heart on it for very personal ones. I feel so strongly that Ethan has the stronger case and he shouldn't give up on the island or indeed on his brother. Family is family!'

Gloria nodded and smiled sweetly. 'Yes. I absolutely agree with you. I too wish they would try to understand each other. They are both grown men for goodness sakes. But they are polarised. And, try as I might, I really don't see how I can help you or they can be persuaded.'

'I only know Ethan. But you said earlier that you know both of them?' I ventured.

She stared at me for the longest time without speaking but her eyes spoke volumes.

I prompted her further. 'I recognised that you already knew each other on the beach a couple of weeks ago. And you said that it had been a long time since you'd last seen each other?'

Unexpectedly, Gloria reached out and took my hand in hers, as if she was trying to comfort me and to soften the blow of me hearing something I might find either traumatic or distasteful.

'Lori, if you're going to marry Ethan, then you probably do need to know that I knew him a long time ago and before I met Damion. And, maybe, you'll also appreciate why I can't help you.'

'Go on — tell me.' I whispered to her in both dread and encouragement.

Gloria took a deep breath. 'Other than when we all met on the island, the last time I saw Ethan, was fifteen years ago at a high-profile fundraiser in Boston. It was the last time Damion and Ethan saw each other too – at a chance rendezvous – that almost cost me my marriage.'

'Your marriage? Oh, my goodness. Do you mind telling me what happened?'

'Ethan and I first met in New York many years ago. We were young and were together for just one wonderful summer before we went our separate ways. I'd just started modelling and working between London, Paris, and New York. Ethan, at that time, was just starting to get famous for his conservation work – some of it controversial as it was the early days of campaigning for things like the ozone layer – and he was incredibly busy setting up his foundation and starting to travel all over the world. I suppose I never expected to see him again.'

Gloria paused to sip her tea and I saw that she was now trembling.

'Please, do go on.' I coaxed. I was quite breathless with anticipation.

'When I'd only been married to Damion for a few months, we bumped into Ethan in Boston. I couldn't believe it. But I was excited to see him again. I did the introductions. I was justly proud of my new husband, and I honestly thought that these two handsome Scotsmen would enjoy each other's company, at what was otherwise a rather tedious event. It was only then that I discovered my favourite ex-boyfriend and my new husband were brothers.'

I almost choked on my iced lemon tea.

Gloria now looked much paler than she had a moment ago.

'Well, as you might imagine, it didn't go down so well.' She told me. 'Especially when it later became clear how much the two of them hated each other. It was terrible. Awful.'

'And what an amazing coincidence.' I stammered, imagining the awkwardness. 'Only, how was it that you didn't realise they were brothers? After all, they both have the same last name?'

Gloria shook her head. 'But they didn't. Ethan was using the name Ethan Jones.'

I was suddenly sat bolt upright at her making this point. I immediately cast my mind back to the terrible quarrel I'd once had with Ethan when we were on an assignment in Malaysia when I thought he'd deliberately lied to me about his name. I too knew him as Ethan Jones.

The discovery that he was really Ethan Goldman had almost ended our fledgling relationship. But he explained to me how he'd been using an alias in order to disguise the fact that he *was* the Goldman Global Foundation and not just someone working for it. I remember how some of the other volunteers at the time liked to call him 'Indiana Jones'.

'Well, if it makes you feel better,' I confessed to Gloria. 'I fell for the same trick. I'd had no idea who he was when I first met him either and I had assumed he was Ethan Jones too.'

Gloria sighed heavily. 'You can just imagine what happened when Damion found out that I'd slept with his brother. Even though it had been many years before and long before we were married. It caused us terrible problems in our marriage. When the extent of their rivalry came to light, I really thought I'd lost Damion forever.'

I was so shocked by this that I didn't know what to say. I just sat there with my mouth open.

Gloria continued. 'Luckily for me, my husband loves me. He eventually agreed to marriage counselling. But I had to work very hard over a long period of time to persuade Damion that I'd only ever loved him, and that I'd never been in love with Ethan. In turn, during our counselling, I discovered the root of the deep-seated rivalry with his younger brother and he actually cried while telling me his parents had loved Ethan more than they'd ever loved him.'

'Really? How heartbreaking. But how can this possibly be true?' I asked.

Gloria shrugged her slim shoulders and looked sad. 'Well, it was substantiated when both parents died. Apparently, they left everything to Ethan. Damion never got over it. He's deeply hurt. However, like you, I'd like nothing more than to see an end to their rivalry.'

I was stunned. I knew from snippets of information garnered from Ethan that his Scottish parents had become incredibly wealthy from investments they'd made during the early days of North Sea offshore oil and gas production. Is that where all of Ethan's money came from?

And why didn't he want to share it with his only brother?

Seeing how sad Gloria looked I tried desperately to put a positive spin on things.

'But Damion is now incredibly wealthy too. Except he's a self-made man. That must be far more satisfying for him, surely? And, I imagine his disappointment over not inheriting, has helped to shape him into the successful man that he is today?'

'Oh, yes.' Gloria immediately agreed. 'I'm sure it's the prime motivational force behind his incredible work ethic. It's just a shame that Damion only ever measures his success against Ethan's. Last year, for example, Damion made the cover of *Time* magazine. He was listed as number one in the T100 and the most influential man in America. Damion came home that day, with a copy of the magazine and a bottle of champagne. He was triumphant. It was like he'd just conquered the whole world. Then, on the TV news that same night, we hear that Ethan has just been knighted by the Queen of England.'

Gloria suddenly looked at me with great concern, as if she feared she'd been far too candid.

'Oh Lori, please tell me that you will keep this information to yourself? Just between us? This is highly confidential. If you are trying to help Ethan, then believe me, I want to help you. I also want you to succeed in bringing these two brothers together for the benefit of all of us. But I can't be seen to be a part of it. I do truly love my husband. But he really can be quite ruthless when it comes to giving out second chances to anyone – especially to me and certainly to Ethan – and so I'm afraid I might lose him forever if all this gets stirred up again!'

I stared at her in awe and felt incredibly grateful for her honesty.

'I promise you faithfully, Gloria. I will keep all you've told me in complete confidence.'

She then smiled and looked more relaxed. 'I feel I can trust you, Lori.'

We finished our iced tea and then Gloria's phone pinged with a message.

She apologised to me, saying it was about last night's auction and she had to make a call.

'Then I must head off.' I said to her. 'I'm flying back to London later today. Thank you for everything, Gloria. Especially for being so candid with me. I came all this way to meet you with high hopes and good intentions and I'm so very glad I did. Let's keep in touch but of course discreetly. It's clear that your husband loves you very much and that you love him. I suspect, from what you've said about him that he does have a forgiving side, but to be honest I'm feeling far less optimistic now about my chances of getting the island back for Ethan.'

We swapped phone numbers and Gloria embraced me and kissed me again on both cheeks.

It was hard not to like her. She seemed generous, kind, charitable, and unpretentious.

All something of a refreshing surprise when faced with my assumptions of her.

'I hope we can meet again, Lori. But under easier circumstances next time.'

'Yes. I hope so too. Happy Christmas for when it comes, Gloria.'

I started to walk away when she called out to me once more.

I turned and hesitated. I saw her expression had recovered to one of strength and resolution.

'Lori, if you're still determined to get the island back for Ethan, there's really only one way.'

I caught my breath in anticipation. 'Okay. I'm listening.'

'You'll have to play Damion at his own game. Find a way to take it back!'

Chapter 10

I took a taxi back over the bridge that connects Paradise Island with Nassau Town and then I found a nice traditional style Bahamian café in which to have lunch before heading out to the airport. I needed time to think about everything that Gloria and I had talked about. I also needed to come up with another plan to take back the island as she had so bravely suggested.

I'd perhaps have to devise a plan as ruthless as Damion Goldman himself.

But how could I possibly take on a man like that?

Was it an impossible task?

After all I've done and seen over this past year, I do know one person can make a difference.

I know that actions speak louder than words. That fortune favours the brave.

I sighed. It irritated me that I still hadn't received a copy of the lease to Waterfall Cay.

I really felt that it might still hold some vital clues on how I could proceed.

I ordered a conch salad and checked my phone again.

No messages from my boys or my mum today and nothing from Ethan.

Okay, so absolutely no one is missing me at all and no news is good news.

I believed that my trip to Nassau had been worthwhile, in both meeting Gloria and in helping me to understanding Ethan's estranged relationship with his brother, but it also felt like I had more questions than answers and that I was going home empty handed. Then, for some reason, I did something I never normally remember or ever bother to do.

I checked my email spam folder on my phone.

And there it was – a copy of the lease that had been delivered to me – over a week ago!

My heart pounded in my chest as I clicked on the PDF attachment.

In the time it took for the file to open, I hoped and prayed that there might be something – anything at all – that everyone else had somehow missed but that I might immediately spot.

Something I could use against Damion Goldman to take back Waterfall Cay.

Inside the document, I found a long and convoluted text with all sorts of numbered paragraphs listing conditions and responsibilities of the 'lessor' and the 'lessee'.

I read it repeatedly. I'm no legal expert, but as my eyes read and my brain computed and my heart continued to pump adrenalin faster and faster around my body, I began to understand how to go about undoing all of Damion Goldman's plans.

Clearly, I needed to file an application as a conscientious objector with the government of the British Virgin Islands, that would specifically result in a protection order being granted on the island. It didn't even look too difficult to obtain.

On the BVI government website it stated that the protection of an indigenous species was the primary reason listed for applying for protected status. Second on the list was for the protection of an endangered species. Ideally, of course, I knew I should try and find both.

Surely, that couldn't be too hard in a tropical rainforest on virgin territory?

I imagined myself lurking in dark damp caves in search of a rare bat or becoming entangled up in a giant web looking for an elusive spider or scrambling around on the ground in pursuit of an indigenous iguana. But then my mind fluttered back to the time at the waterfall when Ethan had explained to me about how the largest butterfly in the world had once been found on Waterfall Cay. It had been a long time ago – and he'd also said it was extinct – but what if it could be rediscovered? What if the giant butterfly was not extinct at all but had simply migrated elsewhere? Like what had happened in the Galapagos Islands on that TV programme I'd seen?

Then all I had to do was find it and bring it back to be reintroduced to Waterfall Cay.

Surely that would be a cause for celebration and a reason to establish a protected sanctuary?

Not that it would be easy of course, once Damion caught wind of it.

Ethan had already warned me that Damion was corrupt in his business dealings.

He'd insisted that Damion would have seen to it that his planning permissions and permits were all in order. But from what I've just read, unless he's got support on the ecological board, there's no way he'd be able to rally against an official protection order issued by the islands governing body. Was this the one and only thing in this lease that he'd underestimated? The one thing that could quickly and effectively shut him down?

Any delays or a shutdown that affected his construction plans would likely impact the ability for the resort to open at the start of the new season – which in turn might affect profit projections and annoy his shareholders – causing them to have no choice but to pull out on him.

I imagined the whole scenario to be like a chain of tumbling dominos.

An official form needed to be completed by the applicant or 'petitioner' together with a statement or 'petition' supporting the protection case. A testimony by an expert was also required to be attached to the petition. After which, the application would be considered 'as a matter of urgency' and a decision promised 'by the next monthly ecological board meeting'.

I felt like yelling 'eureka' and I'm suddenly and totally convinced my plan will work.

I was sure that this – Plan B – was the best way to take back the island.

Not that I know much about butterflies. But I'm sure it's possible to find someone who does.

I've learned from Ethan, who knows a lot about everything but who would never claim to be an expert in all things, that when in doubt you must delegate. You find a qualified expert.

So, as I ate my lunch, I did some internet research into butterflies of the Caribbean and the first thing that popped up was a butterfly exhibition currently on the island of St Lucia.

See Butterflies from all over the Caribbean flying freely in our Botanical Gardens.

Attend talks by an expert lepidopterist and learn about the lifecycle of a butterfly!

This felt like fate to me. What if I was to go over to St Lucia today, instead of flying back to London? Then I might narrow down my search. Plus, I'll have access to consult with butterfly experts, all while having a lovely time on the island of St Lucia!

I rattled off a text message to my mum and to my sons.

Extending my trip for another few days to take in another exhibition. See you at the weekend!

*

St Lucia is a lush verdant gem in the island chain known as the Windward Islands in the Lesser Antilles of the Caribbean Sea. It is probably most famous for its dramatic twin mountains known as the Pitons and it's smouldering sulphuric volcano as well as its beautiful natural rainforest interior and incredible palm tree lined white sand beaches. It's also famous for its tikki bars and rum punch and is known as a luxurious rather than a budget destination.

Using an internet booking site, I managed to book a couple of nights of accommodation, at a very reasonably priced boutique hotel overlooking the Pitons, in the small town of Soufriere on the west coast. Importantly, it's just a short walk away from the botanical gardens hosting the butterfly exhibition. With another few clicks on my tablet via the internet, I also had a late afternoon flight out to St Lucia from Nassau.

I headed out to the airport feeling excited that my trip had been unexpectedly extended and in anticipation as to what I might achieve while on an island that I'd always dreamed of visiting.

St Lucia looked beautiful as we circled before descending into the international airport.

On arrival, I stood in a line to pass through immigration but as I only had hand luggage, I breezed past all the people at the carousel having to wait for their bags, and quickly found the bus station and a local bus to take me to Soufriere.

One of my very favourite things about travelling and

arriving somewhere new is that feeling of being wide-eyed with amazement at seeing a place for the very first time. Tropical places smell so interesting and local roads seem far more exciting to travel along when you really don't know what's around the next bend. Then, when the route reveals itself, you see colourful and interesting looking people and amazing scenery and strange new objects and building and plants and trees and varieties of birds that you might have never seen before. It's the very essence of travel and adventure and of feeling alive!

The bus I'm on right now is an old one and the road ahead is steep and winding and narrow.

The driver revves-up the engine in anticipation of the next steep hill. It sounds like it might explode. At the hairpin bend, I can hardly bear to look at the sheer barrier-less drop over the side of the mountain or to look to see if there is a vehicle coming towards us from the opposite direction. But I do look and I cringe and I jump in my seat as horns blare and engines scream.

When we arrive in Soufriere, which in colonial times used to be the capital of the island (now replaced by Castries in the north west) I get off the bus in the town square with its neatly clipped grassy area and stone fountain, and I feel like I've already had an adventure.

I follow the bus driver's helpful instructions to find my hotel.

He assures me it's a two-minute walk up the street and he points a finger towards some pretty painted French colonial style buildings and a Caribbean catholic stone-built church.

'Walk straight on past the Church o'the Assumption,' he tells me. 'An' you'll see it on the left-hand side.' It was a bit of an uphill hike and more like ten minutes than two minutes.

But, despite the heat and feeling slightly breathless in the heavy humid air, it was more than worth the trek when I saw the view from the top of the street. The main feature was of course the magnificent twin dormant volcanic spires on the coastline that rear up from the sea as verdant jagged peaks. The Pitons. The sunlight and the shadows catching these peaks from my vantage point showed them off to their very best. It's a world-famous UNESCO view that I've seen so many times on many photographs and brochures and all those pictures seemed to have been taken from this very same spot where I stand. None, however, do it justice.

The hotel owner I meet is a lovely woman whose actual first name is Lovely.

She pronounced it Lover-lie and said it was spelt in the same way but without the hyphen.

Miss Loverlie, a small lean woman with a kind smile, insisted on carrying my bag – a small backpack I'd bought in Nassau containing the few possessions I had – and showed me to my room. It was a small square room with a private bathroom. There was a double bed and simple wooden furniture, all painted white and clean looking. I went straight to the open French doors and gasped at the view again in amazement.

'How do you ever get anything done around here with this view?' I asked her.

Miss Loverlie laughed. Her long dreadlocks shook and the beads at the end of each of them clacked together. 'Oh, you get used to it, an' realise it ain't goin nowhere!'

I spent the last hour of the afternoon, after a refreshing shower and a small meal of Caribbean bean stew and plantain, sitting on the upstairs terrace and sipping a glass of chilled wine while watching the sun go down over the Pitons. I took a photo and sent it to Ethan and to my boys with the hashtag #NoFilter as it certainly needed no enhancements.

The next morning, I was up early to have breakfast before venturing further uphill to the botanical gardens. Miss Loverlie gave me a map and brochure that explained how the botanical gardens were a privately-owned estate that included an area of tropical rainforest, a nature trail to a waterfall, and the old and renovated sulphur springs wellness spa with its luxurious and therapeutic bathing pools. As the butterfly exhibition was on all day but the talk by the expert didn't start until the afternoon, I decided that my first adventure of the day should be to head along the nature trail to see the spectacular waterfall, fed by a river coming directly from the dormant volcano.

I joined a walking tour. It was obviously going to be a tame experience to walk along a well-maintained nature trail path to the waterfall. Compared of course to hacking through the jungle with Ethan and his machete and leaping from boulders and crossing rushing rivers. But the nature trail here is a major draw for tourists on the island. Plus, I was curious to know if the waterfall was anything like as beautiful as the one on Waterfall Cay.

Our guide was a local man called Melvin and he was welcoming and wonderfully knowledgeable about the nature trail. I was joining a couple of American tourists and a Canadian family on the tour. Melvin escorted us along the pathway through the gently swaying palm trees, pointing out glistening tropical ferns and flowering banana plants, and he explained how the trail that we were walking along was of historical importance. It was once used by slaves who harvested coconuts. He also alerted us to the many colourful island birds, including many types of tiny and colourful hummingbirds, who were feeding at various succulent tropical flowers along our route. We ambled along in the gentle morning heat and humidity, taking photos and craning our necks up into the tall palm trees in the hope of seeing the famous green parrot that was indigenous to St Lucia.

When I caught Melvin's attention, I asked him if he knew anything about butterflies.

I also told him that I was looking forward to attending the exhibition and talk later today.

'I know more about birds than I do butterflies,' he kindly explained to me. 'But, when we get back to the gardens, I can introduce you to Dr Tomas Remington. He's one of the world's foremost lepidopterist. He's giving the talk this afternoon on the lifecycle of the butterfly. He's very passionate about his subject. I'm sure he'll be happy to answer your questions.'

We continued with our hike to the waterfall, which I was so excited to see. This particular waterfall on St Lucia is described as a 'waterfall of many colours'. The reason for this is apparently quite unique. The falls are fed by natural rainwater mixed with rich minerals from the sulphur springs. These minerals: copper, magnesium, iron, and calcium, all stick to the rockface in many layers over time and this is what gives the illusion that the waterfall is a constantly changing kaleidoscope of colour. It's magical and spectacular!

We aren't allowed to bathe in the pool below the falls, as it's purely a visual attraction.

So, I take some photos, hoping to capture all the rainbow colours, and then I join the party who are heading back to the gardens and to the luxury spa to indulge in the therapeutic waters and the mineral-rich mud treatments. I long to lounge about in the spa too, but instead I happily followed Melvin over to the conservatory, where *The Butterflies of the Caribbean* exhibition is being held and where Dr Tomas Remington awaits us.

Melvin escorted me inside the high domed and impressively constructed conservatory.

The atmosphere inside is warm and humid just as it is

outside but here the free-flying butterflies can all be safely contained within the walls of fine mesh. All the flora and foliage in the exhibit, Melvin tells me, has been specially selected and brought here from all over the Caribbean to suit the particular diets of the varied species of caterpillar and butterfly.

When we find Dr Tomas, I must wait for a while to meet him as he is indisposed at the top of a very long high ladder. I gaze up to see that he is precariously balanced and holding a butterfly net in one hand and the top rung of the ladder in the other and he is cursing like, well I was going to say a sailor, but perhaps more like a pirate.

'There is a lady here who wishes to meet with you Dr Tomas!' Melvin yelled to him.

The ladder wobbled a little and the cussing ceased. 'A lady? Me? Are you sure?'

His voice is high and doubtful.

'Yes. She wants to talk to you about butterflies.' Melvin assured him.

'Okay. Well, tell her I'll be down just as soon as I catch this fucking butterfly.'

I stifled my giggles because I could see Melvin's eyes were wide with embarrassment.

Dr Tomas came down the ladder very quickly a moment or two later using a sliding technique that suggested he had either previously trained with the Circus de Soleil or he was very well practiced with going up and down ladders.

He looked a little perplexed to see me standing right in front of him and I was a bit surprised myself.

Perhaps because he's tall, dark, and ridiculously handsome.

I suppose I expected a butterfly expert to be someone geeky-looking with his glasses perched half way down a long narrow nose and with messy hair and baggy overalls on a lean nondescript body. Dr Tomas is quite the opposite. He's wearing tight skinny jeans, slung low on his narrow slinky hips. His cotton t-shirt bears the words 'without change there would be no butterflies' and it looks a size too small stretched over his rippling gym-honed torso.

He stares at me for a moment, with his surprised but also slightly bemused looking dark brown eyes. When he eventually blinks, his eyelashes look like small dark butterflies fluttering on his sculptured cheekbones. I see he has two small colourful and fluttering butterflies in his net and that he also has an intricate tattoo of fluttering butterflies down his forearm that finishes with one larger one on his hand. Interesting.

'Is that its common name then – the fucking butterfly?' I ask him innocently.

At first, he looks a little embarrassed, but then his perfect lips curl into a smile.

'Oh, no. You see, I was catching these butterflies while they were actually copulating.'

I try to keep a straight face. 'Ah, I see. So you were being scientific?'

Dr Tomas raised his dark and perfectly shaped eyebrows knowledgably. 'Yes, indeed. You see, the caterpillar's only aim in life is to eat and then once it metamorphoses into a butterfly, its only aim in life is to have lots of sex.'

'Yes, Ma'am,' Melvin collaborated. 'That's a word scientist around here use all the time.'

I was reminded of the time that Ethan took me into the jungle at night when we were on a small island in the Andaman Sea, just off the coast of Thailand, to witness the call of the Tokay Gecko. Otherwise known as the fuck-you lizard because 'fuck-you' is exactly what its call sounds like. It's both shocking and hilarious to hear it shouted en mass from the undergrowth.

'I'm Lori, by the way. It's nice to meet you Dr Tomas.'

'Oh, please drop the doctor. I only have a PHD. I don't save lives. My friends call me Tom.'

We shook hands and smiled at each other.

Melvin, having satisfactorily introduced us, went about his own business.

'So, how can I help you Lori?' Tom asked me, as we walked over to a catchment area in which he released the two small butterflies captured in his net.

'Well, I'm here to find out more about butterflies and their habitat and their life-cycle. But I'm also here to ask you about a specific variety of giant butterfly. I'm hoping you might be able to help me to track it down.'

As soon as I mentioned giant sized butterflies his interest was certainly piqued.

'How very interesting. We have a *Pterourus Homerus* here that I can show you. That's a Giant Swallowtail native to Jamaica. We also have the *Morpho Menelous*. That's the Giant Blue Morpho. Are you studying the giant genus specifically, Lori?'

'Well, it's more like research. And, it's very interesting that you have the Blue Morpho, as it's the Green Morpho butterfly that I want to find.'

'Really? Then I can only wish you luck, because as far as I know, it's extinct.'

'That's what I've been told too. But are you at all familiar with the research of Alfred Russel Wallace – the nineteenth Century biologist and explorer?'

Tom looked delighted. 'Yes, absolutely. He's a hero of mine, actually.'

'Mine too!' I enthused, suddenly feeling all geeky and collaborative. 'I recently saw a TV programme about the research that Wallace did in the Galapagos Islands. It was about the migration of indigenous species over incredible distances. It's inspired me to hope that the Green Morpho could perhaps be rediscovered elsewhere in the Caribbean and then re-established back to its original home on a small island in the British Virgin Islands.'

Suddenly, Tom's eyes were sparkling and he had the biggest grin on his handsome face.

'Well, my goodness. That's a great theory you have there and a really interesting quest!'

'And, I was wondering if you had any information on

where I might start looking for the Green Morpho? Or, if you have any contacts in the butterfly world who might be able to help or know of any similar research being done, or indeed of any recent sightings?'

'Okay, Lori. Leave it with me and let me make a few phone calls. I'll get back to you later today. In the meantime, let me show you around the conservatory here and take you through our *Stages of Life* butterfly exhibition. I think you'll find it very interesting.'

I happily agreed to the private tour and I was feeling so relieved that he hadn't simply dismissed my theory as impossible rubbish and that he actually wanted to help me.

We entered the main exhibit area and walked together side by side along a winding pathway that was meant to replicate a tropical Caribbean rainforest. The air in the conservatory was still and warm and heavily scented with the varieties of tropical flowers that provided the caterpillars with their favourite food source. 'Caterpillars are very fussy about what they'll eat.' Tom told me. 'Many species will only settle for one or two specific plants in their diet. It's one of the reasons many have become so endangered.'

'So, if I'm hoping to find the Green Morpho, what plant should I be looking for?'

'They love one particular kind of tropical creeper. It's called the *Clitoria Ternatea*.'

'The clitoral *what?*' I gasped. 'Noooo! You just made that up!'

I suddenly caught a terrible fit of giggles. I couldn't stop laughing.

Tom looked delighted. 'No. I assure you, the flowers are the shape and form of a woman's genitals, hence the Latin name. But of course it's more commonly known as the Butterfly Pea, and where you find IT you will surely find THEM!' He enthused.

I could hardly wait until I could tell Ethan about this, he'd think it was absolutely hilarious.

Joking aside, I had to admit that this was really useful information.

Exactly the kind of thing I needed to know for when I found the giant green butterfly.

The first part of the *Life Cycle of a Butterfly* exhibit showed examples of the egg stage of the lifecycle. There were lots of shrubs and plants and vine leaves with the undersides of their leaves covered with tiny textured butterfly eggs. Tom pointed all these out to me and I marvelled at them. I thought each looked exactly like a shiny drop of dew and yet inside there was a tiny fertilised beginning of a new butterfly. At the next stage, where the caterpillars had hatched and emerged from the eggs, we stopped so that Tom could reach up and pluck a caterpillar from the underside of a succulent and fleshy green leaf.

We were stood underneath a large tree that was feeding lots of chomping caterpillars.

'Look here,' he said. 'You can see this one is shedding its skin in order to grow bigger.'

I peered at it and tried not to look disgusted. I really wasn't so keen on caterpillars.

All I saw was a wriggling, furry, and horrible looking maggot that gave me the shivers.

'Typically, this will happen up to five times and just look at all those tiny body hairs!'

I shuddered. The fat ones with lots of hairs, I decided, were even more nausea inducing than the smooth soft and squidgy ones. I took a step back. It was incredibly hot and humid in this part of the exhibit area and it was suddenly hard to breathe. I was starting to sweat profusely and my breathing had quickened. I was starting to feel horribly dizzy.

My heart was racing. My skin was burning hot, but I was also feeling icy cold.

What was happening to me? I started to worry that I might vomit.

And, in front of delicious Dr Tom, that would be *really* embarrassing.

Then the unthinkable happened. The most awful thing. The stuff of my nightmares.

At first, I didn't realise what was causing the feeling of pitter-patter on my head and on my shoulders and my bare arms. I thought that maybe the sprinklers had come on because of the heat. I turned my eyes away from the small hairy yucky squirming creature cradled in the centre of Tom's palm and then noticed that there were more of them on the ground and all around us.

Instinctively I touched my hair. What was that?

Droplets of condensation from the tree above perhaps?

But caught between my fingers was another of the wriggling green and hairy beasties.

I immediately threw it down on the ground and raked at my hair and found more.

On the ground there were now hundreds of them.

It had started to 'rain' caterpillars.

In horror, I shook my head and rubbed my hair and stamped my feet and started screaming.

I carried on screaming and doing this 'rain dance' until Tom grabbed me firmly and shook my shoulders while yelling my name loudly until I stopped screaming and stamping.

Then I stood there in front of him shaking and sobbing and in something of a complete mess.

'Lori, look into my eyes. Come on, focus. Lori, breathe deeply and look at me!'

I did as I was told while Tom counted to five slowly and deliberately until I was calm.

'Oh my goodness. What just happened? What have I done?' I gasped in horror.

All around us there were sticky squishy squashed dead green caterpillars.

'You had a panic attack.' Tom told me. 'Have you ever had one before?'

'No. Never. I didn't know what was happening to me. It was awful.'

I was shocked. I was appalled. I was full of apologies and totally and horribly embarrassed.

Again, fearing I might vomit, I turned and fled outside through the nearest emergency exit door and sat down on a bench outside with my head down and my arms wrapped tightly around myself until the sick feeling subsided. How excruciating. I knew I was averse to caterpillars.

I knew I didn't like them at all. But I hadn't realised until now that I had a real fear of them.

Even if they do look revolting and creepy – like Ethan once said to me – it's not as if they bite or they are poisonous or anything. My fear is stupid and totally unreasonable.

Tom came outside and sat with me. We didn't speak for what felt like forever.

I'd just murdered hundreds of his children. I suspected that he hated me now.

'Lori. I think the best way to handle this is for you to go back inside and face your phobia.'

I looked at him in amazement. Was he mad? Did he not see what just happened in there?

He stood in front of me and held out his hand. 'Come on. You must do this.'

I took a deep shuddering breath as he took my hand in his and spoke to me softly.

'I mean, how are you supposed to re-establish a population of Green Morpho in the British Virgin Islands, if you can't tolerate them at the caterpillar stage? Besides, I still must show you what I personally consider to be the best bits of the exhibition. That's the silken cocoons. And, if we're really lucky, we'll get to see a new butterfly drying its wings for its very first flight. You don't want to miss that, do you?'

I was suddenly tearful and so touched by his care and his forgiveness that I felt obliged to do as he suggested. And, of course, he was right. How was I supposed to complete my mission to get the island back for Ethan, if I couldn't stand the sight of a little caterpillar, let alone a giant one? So I stood up on my wobbly legs and followed Tom inside.

Maybe this time I was more prepared, I don't know, but I forced myself to be brave and I did manage to control myself and to do the deep-breathing thing and to hold a caterpillar in my hand. I didn't like it. But I did it. After seeing the caterpillars in the silken cocoon stage and watching a butterfly slowly emerge to dry its wings and then to be surrounded by a myriad of fluttering beautiful butterflies including the impressive Giant Swallowtail and the (commonly found) Giant Blue Morpho that was so big that I held it across both of my outstretched hands, I was feeling recovered and entirely grateful to Tom, albeit, still very embarrassed.

He seemed to have forgiven me, even if I hadn't yet forgiven myself.

He told me I didn't need to attend his talk this afternoon, as I'd had the private version of it.

'Go somewhere and relax, Lori. Go to the beach. I'll

make a few calls this afternoon,' he told me as I was leaving. 'I have colleagues dotted around in various places in the Caribbean doing research on various projects. I'll ask about for you. Let's see if I can find out any news on the possible whereabouts of your fabled Green Morpho.'

We shook hands formally and I thanked him again and gave him my phone number.

Then I made my way back down through the gardens and out of the black wrought iron gates and down the street to my hotel room for a lie down and a nap to recover from my ordeal.

It was during this quiet time in my room, and while reflecting on what had happened to me in the conservatory, I realised it had been exactly what I thought had happened to me as a child.

The subconscious mind worked in strange ways. Was my aversion to caterpillars actually a real fear? Tom had called it a phobia. Was he right?

If so, then finding the giant sized Green Morpho, would be even more of a challenge.

I checked the time. It was 4p.m. here and so 8p.m. in London. I knew my mum would be home.

She was happy to hear from me and I listened to how busy she'd been all day. I asked her if she'd seen the boys and Zoey. She said she hadn't. And this weekend coming, she knew they had Christmas parties to attend, so she didn't expect to see them this weekend either. She asked me how I was getting on with my exhibitions, so I explained about being at the butterfly exhibition and how seeing caterpillars everywhere had freaked me out.

'The strange thing is that I remembered something about being trapped in our old garden shed with lots of caterpillars. Do you know if that really happened to me when I was young?'

'Ah, the caterpillars in the bucket!' Mum chuckled on recalling the event. 'Yes, you were only about six or seven years old and we came tearing out the house because you were screaming like a banshee and trapped in the shed. But the door wasn't locked and you had taken all those awful little creatures inside there with you. It took us ages to calm you down. What a terrible scare you'd given us and yourself!'

'Well, I suppose that kind of explains a few things.' I remarked with a shudder.

Chapter 11

I must have dozed off for a while lying on my comfortable bed in my hotel room. My mobile phone ringing woke me up. It was Tom. He said that he'd just spoken over the phone to a friend who was a zoologist on another island here in the Caribbean and he had a bit of information that might be of interest. Suddenly, I was wide awake.

'Oh, wow, that's fantastic. Can we meet somewhere to discuss it?'

I was just about to suggest a cocktail bar somewhere for a drink.

'Lori, let me take you out to dinner tonight. I know an amazing restaurant in the hills.'

I was rather taken aback, especially after what had happened today.

I was still cringing and thinking he must have the impression that I'm a crazy woman.

Neither was I normally up for accepting dinner dates from handsome men whom I don't know very well. But it's an enticing offer and I am feeling hungry and a restaurant on St Lucia in the hills does sound rather amazing. Plus, he has 'a bit of information' for me.

'Erm, thank you, Tom. That sounds very nice. I'd really like that.'

'Then I'll pick you up at six-thirty.'

'Okay, I'm at the Loverlie Island Hotel.'

And, once again I find myself in a situation, whereby I have nothing suitable to wear.

For a moment, I have a pang of regret about leaving my beautiful dress in the Bahamas.

Then, on second thoughts, it could be a tad too dressy for a casual Caribbean restaurant.

Having spotted several small boutiques around the town square area when I'd first arrived, I grabbed my purse and headed out in search of something light and casual to wear while having dinner with Tom. Not that this is a date. This is just having dinner with a new friend.

I walked down the narrow street towards the square, passing small colourful houses and friendly local people, who either nodded graciously or waved politely as I passed them. As I walked passed one house, I saw a young woman there with a little girl sitting on her lap.

They are sitting in the open doorway and the woman is braiding the little girl's hair.

She calls out to me. 'Hey, lady, come here. Come inside. I can tell you your future!'

I stop and turn and smile. What an extraordinary gift?

I'd absolutely love for someone to be able to tell me my future.

I laughed. It would solve all my problems for sure.

If I knew exactly what my future looked like, then I was sure to be less stressed about my choices and less anxious about making all the wrong decisions. The little girl is bright eyed and beautifully dressed and her hair is decorated with colourful beads and ribbons. But the woman's dress is worn and her expression is worn too. Her eyes gave me such a soulful look that I nod my head and I understand. It didn't matter to me if this was a hoax or a scam or the real deal.

This woman is just looking for a way to feed her family tonight.

'I can tell you where to find your fortune or the man of your dreams!' She assured me.

I walk towards her. 'Okay. Do you read the tea cup or the cards?'

'The tarot. I have a special gift passed on to me by my mother and my mother's mother and her mother before her. They were all able to see the future in the cards. My daughter will also have this gift. I charge only ten dollars for a reading. That's a very cheap price.'

The little girl smiled and nodded her head and all her beads and ribbons shook.

I was ushered inside the small room, sparsely furnished but spotlessly clean.

I sat down on the chair opposite the young woman,

who took a pack of tattered looking tarot cards from a silk cloth wrapping. She handled them very carefully and began to slowly shuffle them. 'As you can see, these cards are very old. They once belonged to my great great grandmother who brought them here from New Orleans. Before she owned these cards, they belonged to Marie Laveau, the witch queen of New Orleans. They have very special magic in them and I warn you that they only ever speak the truth.'

It was a lovely story and certainly added depth to the reading.

She studied me intensely as she shuffled and lay out four cards in a spread on the table. She then looked down at the cards and gasped, seemingly taken aback by what she saw in them, or rather she made a great show of being impressed by them. She touched each one lightly with the tips of her fingers. The first card depicted a noble man dressed in armour and riding on a chariot and carrying a sword aloft in his hand.

'Unlike many others who come to St Lucia, you are not a tourist here. You are like the man in The Chariot because you are on a special journey. You are on a quest of great importance. You are looking for something and you seem very determined to find it. This card is one of great bravery.'

'And do I find what I'm looking for?' I asked her, by way of encouragement.

I had intended on staying visibly sceptical or at least

as quietly detached as possible, because of course many 'fortune tellers' get their insights by reading the subject in front of them, rather than the cards on the table. But I couldn't help myself. I was suddenly super excited because she was saying all the right things to me. All the things I wanted to hear.

It gave me a weird kind of hope that she was a genuine fortune teller after all.

She cast her eyes down to the next card. But, from where I was sitting, it didn't look at all promising. This card showed a tall tower with lightning strikes hitting it and flames shooting out of it and someone falling out of it head first onto rocks. Oh dear. Gloom and doom and perhaps even death. I felt my mouth go dry in my anticipation of her telling me something like: *If I were you, lady, I wouldn't even think about getting on an airplane anytime soon.*

She looked at me intently again. 'Your quest of great importance will be a challenging one. The Tower shows both challenge and change –but if change is what you seek –then you will be very successful.'

'So, this is a good card? It looks kind of scary to me.' I told her.

'There are no good or bad cards in tarot. But there's a warning here. It'll be much harder than you think to achieve your goal. You'll need lots of determination to bring about the change.'

I nodded in understanding. I agree. Because nothing good comes from something easy.

The third card now under her scrutiny is a King. He's seated on a throne while holding a stick. The stick has leaves growing out of it and so I feel this card must be some kind of omen.

'The King of Wands is powerful and successful. He is honest and trustworthy.'

This card, I decided, must represent Ethan. I waited to be told more with bated breath.

'You must look for a person of high authority and seek their advice. This will help you.'

Suddenly, under a wave of realisation, I suspect she might be referring to Tom!

The next card she considers is one that shows a naked woman dancing with various creatures around her and the four elements of fire and water and air and earth. The card is marked: *The World*. 'This is a major Arcana card and one that symbolises your ultimate success. The World card assures you that you will indeed achieve the changes that you want and as a result your world will be changed for the better. It shows fulfilment and a satisfactory ending but also a new beginning.' Then she sat back and smiled at me. 'That will be ten dollars, please.'

I thanked her and gave her a twenty dollar note, waving my hand to show that I wasn't expecting ten dollars back. She tucked the note straight away into her bra for safe-keeping.

On my way out, I handed over five dollars to the little girl who looked delighted.

From the corner of my eye, I saw her mother quickly claiming it from her.

I trust to buy her food rather than sweeties.

In a small boutique at the corner of the street, I found a light cotton wrap dress with a batik frangipani flower design. It caught my eye immediately. I tried it on and loved it and bought it together with a pair of colour coordinating flip-flops.

Then, back at my hotel, I quickly showered and washed my hair.

I was all ready and dressed for 6 p.m., so I wandered upstairs to the open terrace where there was a bar called *Sundowners*. I ordered a cocktail and for the second time I felt privileged to watch the sun going down over The Pitons. As well as the famous peaks, I also had a clear view of the street from the terrace, so I could sit on my stool and sip my drink and watch out for Tom's arrival at the same time. At six-thirty exactly, a motorbike roared up the street and stopped outside The Loverlie Hotel. I looked down and watched the rider with interest.

I saw that it was indeed my King of Wands.

And he was obviously expecting me to ride pillion!

I slurped the last of my drink and hurried down to meet him.

Tom was smartly dressed in dark trousers and a short-sleeved cotton shirt with a collar. He gave me a kiss on the cheek and he looked me up and down, not in a lustful way in my opinion, but by way of admiration and assessment. 'Lori! Hey, nice dress. You look wonderful!'

'What you really mean is can I get my leg over your bike in this dress?' I laughed.

He handed me the spare helmet he was carrying.

'Hold on to me nice and tight!' he instructed as I hitched up my dress and swung my leg over the seat. I wrapped my arms around his waist, and we sped off down the street. The vibration from the roaring engine reverberated right through my body. Tom's body felt warm and hard and strong beneath his shirt and I felt completely safe with him as we speeded around the bends and along the winding uphill road. He was a competent rider and it was so exhilarating to be on a motorbike. It also felt like a wonderful respite from the oppressive heat of the evening to have a blowing wind to cool us down. It was so much fun. I haven't done anything quite like this since I was a teenager when I defied my mother by accepting lifts from boys with motorbikes.

It was quite dark as we reached the restaurant. The Tropical Parrot was a low stone building perched at the top of the hill and it looked so pretty and so lush in its jungle setting. Strings of twinkly lights had been wrapped around the trunks of the palm trees that lined the path to the entrance and along the outside trellises too. There were tubs of tropical flowers everywhere.

It looked quite magical. With our helmets placed aside, we walked down the twinkling pathway to a cacophony of croaking tree frogs, and into the restaurant to be warmly greeted by the Maître d'. The place was busy and at each table sat well-dressed couples chatting intimately together over a candle, a sprig of fresh tropical foliage, extravagant food and a bottle of wine. Soft music with a reggae vibe played in the background and the atmosphere was filled with subtle chatter and flavoursome aromas as waiters whisked past us carrying plates aloft, leaving a trail of delicious wafts in their wake. We were led over to a little table for two on the outside terrace, where the atmosphere was warm and sultry and, dare I say it, very romantic.

I was relieved to have made an effort with the dress as this was certainly not a casual venue.

It also looked to be expensive and, as this absolutely wasn't a date, I had full intentions of offering to split the bill. We were cordially seated and given a wine list.

'Red or white? Which would you prefer Lori?' Tom asked me.

'You choose. I really don't mind.' I replied. He was being such a gentleman and I didn't want to risk the fifty percent chance of disappointing him if we were sharing a bottle.

He ordered a dry white Bordeaux and I thought that a fine choice.

I glanced around and saw that another couple on a table not too far from us had ordered lobsters and they were just being served. My taste buds immediately sprang into action. Seafood and lobster are my favourite food in the world. I was reminded of a time I was on an island off Malaysia called

Langkawi, where I ate the most amazing seafood. I also thought about Ethan, wearing his dive gear while carrying a lobster up the beach that he'd caught for our Christmas dinner last year. Perhaps my sexiest memory out of many sexy memories that I have of him. I gave myself a mental shake back to the present and decided that I really should apologise again to Tom for what had happened today.

'Tom, I have to say that I'm still terribly ashamed, quite mortified actually, about what I did to your wonderful exhibit today. I'm truly sorry. Honestly, I'm not normally such a wimp.'

He looked at me sympathetically and then shrugged. 'Well, luckily, all the caterpillars that you stamped on were a common variety. So at least you didn't make any extinct.'

I didn't know whether to laugh or cry at remembering the green squishy carnage.

Fortunately, the sommelier came over with our wine and the waiter with the menus.

We tasted the wine and perused our menus while the waiter poured our drinking water.

The atmosphere seemed quite tense in our silence. Unless it was just me feeling that way.

'The grilled caterpillar with mango salad and the turf and surf for me.' Tom decided.

His eyes were shining at me in great amusement as he closed his menu.

I stared at him in horror

The waiter looked confused. 'Sir?'

Tom was laughing so hard that people were starting to look over to see what was happening.

I told him that he had a very warped sense of humour but then I had to laugh too.

'Sorry, Lori. I couldn't resist seeing your face. Of course, I meant the grilled shrimp!'

'I'd also like the grilled shrimp to start and lobster thermidor to follow.' I said decisively.

Then, in the soft twinkling lights and flickering of the candle, I asked Tom how long he'd been a butterfly guy.

'Professionally, for twenty years. But I've been interested in butterflies since I was a little boy growing up in Puerto Rico, where we have many beautiful varieties. The process of metamorphosis is so fascinating to me. The fact that a small grub can become such a lovely flying creature is nothing but a miracle. These days I work as a consultant. I've been touring with the *Butterflies of the Caribbean* exhibition all this year. It comes to a close this month, so you came here at just the right time, Lori.'

While he's talking, I'm listening but also guessing he might only be a few years younger than me but then his Latino good-looks and his dark tousled hair, together with his rather naughty sense of humour, give him the dangerous aura of someone much younger.

I decided that if I wasn't in love with Ethan, I'd have found Tom incredibly exciting.

'Why don't you tell me about your quest to find the Green Morpho?' he asked me curiously.

I took a sip of my wine while I wondered exactly where I should begin.

'Well, we know that in the nineteenth Century, the Green Morpho was once indigenous to an island called Waterfall Cay in the BVIs. When its numbers dwindled, to the extent that it was classed as endangered, an attempt was made by Alfred Russel Wallace to create a sanctuary on the island. But it was too late and the butterfly became extinct. I'm simply hoping to rediscover it.'

'This is fascinating and your research is of great interest to me, Lori. Only, I'm surprised that I've not come across your work before, especially as it concerns Wallace?'

'Oh, I'm not an expert. I simply have a theory. And, as I explained to you earlier today, my theory is that the Green Morpho has simply migrated elsewhere. If this is the case, then I'm hoping it can be re-established back to its original home and that a protection order can be petitioned to protect its future there.'

Tom gave me the same sparkly eyed look of amazement that he'd given me earlier.

I was thrilled. I was also amazed. I could hardly believe that I was doing this.

In explaining my plan to him, it made it feel real and viable and actually achievable.

'And, this island in the BVIs, Waterfall Cay, is it special to you in some way?' He asked.

'Yes, it's special to me. But not as special as it is to the Green Morpho.' I answered him while feeling determined to keep the conversation in the vein of conservation and within his realm of expertise. We sipped our deliciously chilled wine and gazed out at the uninterrupted views from our table of the twinkling lights of the town and the harbour below us and across the calm and dark inky waters of the Caribbean Sea. The rhythmic croaking of tree frogs and chirrup of crickets from the flowery foliage filled the sultry and humid air.

'This restaurant, it's amazing. Thank you for suggesting it.' I said, feeling more relaxed.

'You're very welcome. I've wanted to eat here since I arrived on the island. But I didn't want to dine alone. As you can see, it has an intimidating reputation as a couples place.'

It certainly makes me feel better that Tom had a reason, other than a misplaced romantic gesture, to bring me here. Especially when seeing all the romantic couples around us has my thoughts wandering thousands of miles to the cold and distant Antarctic and then back again.

My longing for Ethan right at that moment feels like a physical stabbing pain in my heart.

I imagine him here with me, smiling and laughing and talking and holding my hand, kissing my fingers. I was so taken up that tears filled my eyes and I stifled a little sob. I can't help it.

Then, I realise Tom is saying something to me although his voice sounds far away.

I see he looks a bit panicked and he sounds a little fearful. 'Lori, are you okay?'

Poor Tom. Maybe he thinks I'm about to lose it again right here in the restaurant?

I smile to reassure him I'm fine. 'Tom, I'm truly grateful for your understanding today.'

He looked relieved. 'Oh, it's fine, really. You were actually very brave today. Going back in, after what happened, it took some gumption. Panic attacks are more common than you think. I know that because I have panic attacks myself on occasion. I too have my fears!'

I looked at him incredulously. I would never have guessed.

'Is that how you knew what to do and to say to calm me down?'

He nodded and smiled. 'Yes. The controlled breathing and counting really helps.'

'I called my mum today.' I told him.' She confirmed that I'd had a traumatic experience involving caterpillars falling on me when I was young. I'd forgotten. Or, maybe I'd thought it just a childhood nightmare. But, as it did happen, I suppose it explains my reaction.'

'I made some calls today too,' he told me, cleverly switching the subject to one he possibly found more agreeable. 'And I have news of a possible sighting of your giant butterfly.'

'Oh my goodness! Really? That's fantastic! Where?'

'A friend of mine was doing research on the island of

Luminaire. He was deep in the interior, when he said he saw a giant green butterfly that might possibly have been a Green Morpho.'

I gripped my starched napkin in excitement. 'Oh, that's amazing. Did he get a photo?'

'No. He said he only saw it briefly. But it had a large wingspan – easily over six inches across – and it was an iridescent green colour. Only afterwards, he thought he might have been mistaken. He warned me that it might have been a common Blue Morpho, reflecting the green environment. But it's worth checking out, just in case, don't you think?'

'Luminaire?' I queried. 'Just north of Puerto Rico. Is that right?'

'Yes. It's a small island between Tortola and Puerto Rico. Not too far away from the British Virgin Islands, so you could be right.' Tom continued. 'Natural migration could be a reason for it being there. Or, equally, the Green Morpho could have been taken there by traders and managed to get free and survive on the island undetected. Luminaire is kind of off-grid these days because of its active volcano.'

'I need to go there as soon as possible!' I gasped.

'Do you intend on gathering up all the giant caterpillars by yourself?' Tom teased.

I tried not to shudder while imagining me filling a bucket full of giant wriggly creatures.

'Yes, of course. If it's the only way to re-establish them to their original island home.'

Our appetiser came. It looked delicious. Plates of plump grilled shrimp on a dressed salad.

'Have you ever been to Luminaire before?' Tom asked me before taking a bite of his shrimp.

'No. But it has a rainforest. So conditions must be very similar to Waterfall Cay. You?'

'Yes. I've been there. It's a nature reserve. You should bear in mind that it's a very undeveloped island and not the easiest of destinations to reach. There's no direct route. You'd have to get from here to Dominica and then over to Tortola, before connecting to San Juan on Puerto Rico, and then take a ferry boat over to the island.'

I took out my phone and quickly looked up transportation from St Lucia to Luminaire.

He was right. There are no direct scheduled flights. I clicked through the options. All of them entailed flying via several other islands, with long waiting times in between, before eventually arriving on San Juan. Then, inconveniently, the final flight arrived far too late in the evening to catch the last ferry boat.

'There might be another way.' I said, clicking onto an island charter website. 'I could charter a flight and fly there directly. Because, it now seems that due to the increased popularity of the hiking and nature trail on Luminaire, there's a new airstrip on the island.'

Again, I was kind of astonished and amazed at my own words and resourcefulness.

And also, my unashamed raiding of my own bank account.

Years ago, when I'd been married to Charles, even though we had our own travel agency, I would never have considered chartering a flight for a client if a scheduled plane wasn't available or matching up with an itinerary. But since I've been with Ethan, who often charters planes as a matter of convenience, I've learned to explore all the alternatives and options.

'Charter a plane? That sounds expensive.'

I shrugged. 'Probably no more expensive than taking three separate scheduled flights and a boat. And look at the time that will be saved. I could be there in two hours instead of two days!'

Tom looked a little perplexed. 'But, of course, you'll also need a permit.'

I wondered what on earth he was talking about. 'A permit? Why? I have a passport.'

'I mean a special zoological permit that gives you permission to collect flora, fauna, or invertebrates from any of these islands. You can't just go there and help yourself!'

I looked at him inquisitively while he thought to arm me with this new information.

'And do you have one of these special permits?' I asked him curiously.

He was grinning at me again. 'Yes, indeed I do. Because I'm a certified zoologist.'

'Does that mean you are offering to come along and help me find the Green Morpho?'

He was laughing loudly now and he pretended to mop excess sweat from his brow.

'Phew. For a moment there, Lori, I thought you'd never ask!'

'Then we'll leave tomorrow!' I enthused, thinking this was going to be quite the adventure.

Especially, if my tarot reading was anything to go by.

Chapter 12

Luminaire

I couldn't sleep. I'd been awake most of the night. I was too excited about my next adventure to close my eyes. I was either too hot or too cold and the air-con unit in my room far too noisy. My mind was busy thinking about butterflies and islands and Ethan. I was also a little worried about Tom. Well, maybe not worried, as much as a little concerned about him.

I sincerely hoped that when it came to light about me going on a nature trail and to a remote island with another man, with whom I would be spending two days and one night in close proximity, that it wouldn't be misconstrued by Ethan. Not that Ethan was a jealous man.

But I know how I might feel if he were in the same situation with another woman.

And, it was undeniable, that Tom was a very sexy looking and handsome consort.

But, as far as I was concerned, Tom was my expert and guide and nothing else.

I just hoped that Tom felt the same way. And that he didn't think I was leading him into a romantic getaway by inviting him along. Although, technically, he'd invited himself along.

I do trust my instincts, however, and I certainly didn't get any untoward vibes off him.

So, I'll have to assume he's a gentleman.

Besides, I need him not only because he knows the island terrain but because he has the permit and, also because he's an expert in butterflies. I'll also need him later, to write the expert's verification statement, on my petition for protected status on Waterfall Cay.

I went back to imagining the nature trail on Luminaire. Tom said that the rainforest was dense and verdant and lush, lit with streams of diffused sunlight pouring through the ancient treetops. It sounded so similar to Waterfall Cay that I was convinced it was where we would find our prize. I tossed and turned until the glow of dawn started to creep over The Pitons. Then I gave up trying to sleep and checked the time on my phone. It was 6a.m.

I'd arranged to meet Tom at 7a.m. at a supplies warehouse on the road to the airport.

We were going to need camping equipment as there are no hotels at all on Luminaire.

But before then, I had to let my sons know where I was going.

I'd made a firm promise to them a while ago, that I'd always let them know my plans.

It was 10a.m. in London. When Josh answered my call, he was finishing his coffee break in work and Lucas was on a train heading into the city. Hardly conducive to a proper conversation.

But I did manage to explain to them that I was going off grid for a few days.

'I'm heading to a small island today and I doubt I'll get internet or a phone signal.'

'Why are you going there, mum?' Josh wanted to know.

'If it's remote then it could be dangerous!' Lucas warned.

'I'm going on a nature trail. But don't worry, I have an expert guide with me, so I'll be fine!'

A bit of internet research informed me that Luminaire is known as 'the natural island' in the Caribbean because it is so undeveloped and untouristy compared to its neighbours. It was so named by Christopher Columbus, when he came across it at night under a full moon, with its volcanic form surrounded by a heavy white mist and lit from within by millions of synchronously twinkling fireflies.

In the fourteenth Century, it was a trading station and a sheltering place from storms, offering respite to the Spanish treasure fleets after a long journey over the Atlantic from Europe and while heading into San Juan on Puerto Rico.

Sir Frances Drake too, was known to have used the island as a resting place. He'd used the busy trading centre as a supply point during his voyages. These days, the island is uninhabited, mostly because of its active volcano, but hikers and botanists and zoologists have been visiting it in droves since a nature trail was established on the island: a wild and undulating segmented path that extends for one hundred miles around the island.

Other than that, the island doesn't attract tourists because the air there is sulphurous – it smells like rotten eggs – and because unlike most other Caribbean islands, there are no white sand beaches along Luminaire's fringes because the sand is volcanic and coarse and black.

The only settlements are long abandoned villages and ruined eighteenth Century French settlements. The old fort and its ramparts, that once vigilantly guarded the sweeping bay, is said to be overtaken by rampant vines and sleeping sloths and wild monkeys.

The interior consists of dense and in places almost impenetrable rainforests.

In the centre of the island there is a steep misty mountain peak and below that there are sharply sloping hills, wild river rapids, dramatic waterfalls, and impassable mangrove swamps.

I thought it sounded amazing. I'd asked Tom, at which point along the trail he thought we might find our butterflies. He told me that his friend, who had actually been on Luminaire looking for iguanas not butterflies, had seen what he thought to be the Green Morpho in the third segment of the trail. Tom said it would take us almost a full day of hiking to reach that segment from the airstrip. Of course, we'd also have to allow the same amount of time to return.

I downloaded a map of the island and a hiking guide to the trail segments on my phone.

I saw that the trail in section three led through an elevated area of rainforest terrain and then up to a plateau with sulphur springs and hot spas and a volcanic basin known as 'the boiling pool'. After that, the trail consisted of rocky areas of cliff face with caves and pools and waterfalls and then an undulating segment of lush mountainous and with fast flowing rivers and ridges that promised incredible views of the sulphurous lake. I was excited but had to admit to being also a little intimidated by the scale of the challenge that lay ahead.

Ultimately, I was so glad that Tom had offered to accompany me.

Our taxis synchronously arrived at the supply depot on the main highway at 7a.m. The sun had only just risen but it was already incredibly hot. It was also incredibly humid. As I expected the day to get even hotter and sweatier, I was suitably dressed in a cotton vest and shorts and on my feet, I wore my newly acquired colourful rubber flip-flops. In stark contrast, Tom was dressed in sturdy lace up boots and grey and black combat trousers and a long-sleeved grey t-shirt. I suddenly realised I must have made a big wardrobe mistake.

Inside the depot, we bought hiking backpacks. Tom said we needed to cover up as much as possible to protect ourselves from mosquitoes, leeches and ticks in the jungle conditions, so I had to buy some sturdy boots, socks, long trousers and a long-sleeved top, together with a set of waterproofs – as apparently it wasn't just a rain forest in name only – as well as things like tents, sleeping bags, water filters and other camping gear for our overnight stay.

Then we headed into the supermarket next door and bought our food supplies.

'We need to buy easy to carry essentials and quick to prepare hi-energy foods.' Tom told me. I agreed. I was already overwhelmed by the sheer amount of stuff we'd have to carry.

I got out my credit card and really hoped this mad cap venture wasn't going to be in vain.

Tom also had a duffle bag with him full of scientific stuff like collecting boxes for caterpillars and butterfly nets and all sorts of other paraphernalia that he said we might need.

I popped a bottle of wine and some chocolate biscuits into our trolley.

Tom made a tutting sound and shook his finger at me in disapproval.

Reluctantly I put them back, deciding this trip was going to be more challenging than I thought, and we headed off to the airport with our fully laden backpacks and me in a little sulk.

At departures, I went to check us in for our flight.

We were invited to wait in the private charters lounge and told our pilot was on his way.

It was then, to my alarm, that I spotted a large warning notice about travel to Luminaire.

It said that all travel and transportation to the island at this time had been suspended.

When I pointed this out to Tom, he looked troubled and immediately made a call on his mobile phone to someone he knew who happened to be an official in San Juan, on Puerto Rico.

He had an animated conversation in Spanish. I waited anxiously and then once the call was over, he took me aside to tell me that they'd cautioned against all travel to the island at this time, because parts of the trail had been closed due to damage caused by the last hurricane.

'Some of the trail is still impassable. Bridges are down and there have been landslides.'

I was gutted with disappointment. Suddenly, just like that, and all my plans were in shreds.

What was I to do? If we couldn't go to the island, then we wouldn't find our butterfly.

It was the one and only lead and sighting that we knew about.

Without the butterfly, I wouldn't be able to file a protection order for Waterfall Cay.

Was this the challenge the tarot cards had warned me about?

If so, then how could we possibly get around it? When it now seemed impossible.

'However,' Tom continued to say. 'I told them who I was and that I needed to go there today with my assistant for important research and they were suddenly open to negotiations.'

He gave me a broad smile and looked rather pleased with himself.

'Really. Are you famous or something?'

He shrugged. 'Sure. I'm the famous butterfly guy from Puerto Rico!'

I laughed. 'Ah, yes, of course. So how did you negotiate?'

'I explained how we only needed access to Segment Three from the airstrip.'

'And that's not affected by landslides and broken bridges?'

'No. It's okay. So, they gave us permission to go.'

I sighed with relief. Without Tom's influence we certainly wouldn't have got permission.

He was certainly proving to be my King of Wands.

'That's good. Because I'd promised my boys I wouldn't go anywhere inherently dangerous.'

'Your boys?' Tom queried. 'You have kids?'

'Yes, Josh and Lucas. But they aren't kids anymore. They are grown men.'

Tom studied me for a moment. 'So, Lori. Are you married?'

I looked at him and blushed, wondering if this might be a loaded question.

If so, then it is best answered now. Lines had to be drawn and our situation made clear.

'No. I'm not married. But Tom, I want you to know that I do have a steady boyfriend. Only, I think it's best mentioned now, so that we can focus on finding butterflies.' I told him firmly.

He gave me the biggest of smiles and looked relieved. 'Me too!'

I laughed in a spluttery kind of way, 'You have a boyfriend? You're gay?'

He laughed loudly and enthusiastically at my wide-eyed surprise.

'Yes, and yes. Only, I thought it best to mention it, so we can focus on finding butterflies.'

I blushed from head to toe. Had he been worried about me making a move on him?

Oh, how excruciatingly embarrassing. Maybe he thinks I'm some kind of cougar?

All passengers for Luminaire, go to Gate One.

Your aircraft is ready for boardin'. All aboard for Luminaire.'

We went through the gate and onto the hot tarmac and then I saw the plane I'd chartered.

And I realised at once exactly why I'd been able to secure it for such a reasonable price.

It was a single engine, four-seater, Cessna. It was an old one too with more than a couple of patches of duct tape holding things together. Despite this I couldn't stop myself from grinning.

Tom looked to be rather less enamoured. 'This is our plane?!' he gasped.

I nodded enthusiastically. 'Don't worry. I've flown in a Cessna before and it was fine!'

I was referring to the time I'd flown across Borneo to Sandakan with Ethan, to the base for our visit to the Orangutan orphanage that Ethan's foundation, the Goldman Global Foundation supports.

It had been one of the most special and most wonderful days of my life.

'Of course, I'd been terrified at first.' I admitted. 'When I first saw the plane, I thought it looked too small to take two passengers and all their luggage and far too beaten up not to crash!'

Right now, I see Tom is having all those same thoughts.

I'm pleased to see that our friendly pilot, who introduces himself as Captain Edward, really does look the part. He's dressed in smart dark trousers and a white short sleeved shirt with epaulets and he has a pilot's cap on his head. It does evoke a certain professional confidence.

The last Cessna pilot I'd met had worn tatty shorts and hadn't even bothered with shoes.

Captain Edward greets us with handshakes before suggesting that Tom might like to take the co-pilot seat next to him 'because he looks strong and capable'.

I find this a little offensive. I mean, don't I look strong and capable, too?

I can see Tom is now suffering from the intense heat. He's sweating rather badly.

Walking outside from the airconditioned lounge had been like hitting a wall of heat.

I see perspiration rolling down his face from his forehead and his shirt and underarms are now soaked with dark damp patches of sweat. But I'm feeling a bit miffed, because I'd wanted to sit in the front, in the co-pilots seat. I climbed into the cramped space in the back of the plane and prised myself into the small seat. Captain Edward passed me our backpacks. I put them onto the seat next to me and arranged Tom's butterfly nets so that they didn't keep whacking me on the head. Then I secured everything with the seat belt.

'At least we do have seatbelts.' I yelled to Tom. 'During my last Cessna experience, my seatbelt fell apart during take-off. Of course, I can laugh about it now!' And I did.

But Tom was still outside the plane looking terror stricken.

Captain Edwards was talking to him, but Tom was vigorously shaking his head.

Then I realised that something was going on here and it wasn't good.

Oh, my goodness; he was refusing to get into the plane.

Straight away I realised, if Tom didn't come, I wouldn't be able to do this on my own.

For a start, I didn't have the necessary permit. I'd also be on an island totally on my own while there was a travel ban in place. I wouldn't have a clue what to look for or where I should look. I don't know anything about the plants that the Green Morpho caterpillars likes to eat.

Without Tom's help, how would I go about collecting them without killing them all?

I squeezed my way back out of the small space in the rear of the plane to speak with Tom.

I could see that he was trembling like a leaf. He was as white as a sheet and his breathing was fast and heavy. I suddenly realised what was happening. Tom was having a panic attack.

Oh my gosh—he was afraid of flying.

'I'm sorry, Lori. I can't go in that plane. I was going to tell you this morning, I'm afraid of flying, but then I thought I just might be okay if it turned out to be a big plane. But I can't possibly go in that small one. I just can't. I'm sorry.'

'Listen here, son,' said Captain Edward. 'This is a very safe plane and I'm a very safe pilot. I've been flying aircraft for thirty-five years and I've only ever crashed once!'

He folded his arms across his chest as if he was terribly offended by all the fuss.

'You've crashed once?' I repeated.

'Yes. But the plane is fixed and I'm still alive, aren't I?'

'Come on, Tom. Let's go inside and out of this heat and we'll get some water to drink.'

So we went inside and I bought water and we sat down and I held Tom's trembling hand.

'Tom, remember yesterday morning, when I had my panic attack?'

He nodded and sipped his water.

'Well, it was you who gave me the confidence to face my fear, so I know you've got this.'

After a minute or two, he stood up. 'Yes. You're right, Lori. I will do it. I can do it.'

'Now for your safety briefing.' Captain Edward said to us once we were all safely strapped in. I nodded at Tom and thought this was most reassuring. This at least showed Tom that our captain was genuinely concerned for our wellbeing. The last time I'd flown in a Cessna, the pilot hadn't bothered with a safety talk at all. Except, I do think that Captain Edward's cockpit manner could do with a less serious tone. For both our sakes, I wish he wouldn't glare at us so intensely and use the words, crash, emergency, and survival, quite so much.

'If we should crash into the sea, then our chances of survival very much depend on you both acting very quickly and following my instructions to the letter. In such an emergency, I will shout out specific clear instructions to you. You will obey me immediately and without question. Do you both understand?' His delivery was quite terrifying.

His description of an emergency made it sound like crashing was a foregone conclusion.

Tom once again looked as pale as though all the blood had been drained from his face.

But we both nodded our heads and shouted: 'YES CAPTAIN.'

Captain Edwards then went on to tell Tom how, in an emergency situation, he should go about removing his seat cushion and collapsing his seat to allow access to the window exit. And then how exactly he should pull on a lever that would release his side window so that we could all climb out of it to escape into the life raft. When in real life, of course, there was no way in Hell that either of us would ever fit through that tiny window or I'd be able to climb over either of these two big men, especially if they were both rendered unconscious in this hypothetical crash. I'd be trapped in a sinking plane.

We both did a bit of deep breathing while the tiny plane taxied down the runway.

I felt terribly guilty for giving Tom a false sense of security.

We were going to die after all; and it was all my fault.

The front propeller was now whizzing around so fast that it had become invisible.

I couldn't help but to wonder if it was still there or had it already fallen off?

Then, with the engine screaming at fever pitch, we soared into the air.

I looked down from my side window and saw only deep dark blue mesmerizing water.

I distracted myself by trying to pick out the shapes of large sharks, whales, or pods of dolphins. After a while, with the constant drone of the engine providing some comfort, I began to relax. But could see that Tom had yet to stop gritting his chiselled jaw and grinding his perfect teeth. Just as I was starting to get cramp in my legs and my eyes were aching from seeing nothing but blue water beneath us and blue sky all around us, we flew over Puerto Rico and Tom put aside his sick bag, to point out all the landmarks below that he knew so well.

'Look there's my village. That's my old school and you can see the football field!' he yelled over the noise of the engine. Thank goodness, he was okay and had started to relax at last.

Then, after more blue water, an island appeared on the horizon and I caught my breath.

I can only imagine how it might have looked to Christopher Columbus under a full moon back in the day when the world was new, but today, in the morning sunshine, it looked truly magnificent with its volcano standing tall through a swirl of mist and with a dense green forest at its base. Our plane circled the island before making its final approach onto a small airstrip.

When the plane came to a full stop, Captain Edward flicked switches with a flourish and pulled on levers to power down the plane. 'Welcome to Luminaire. Please remain seated until the doors are open.' But a second later Tom was out. He'd grabbed the emergency door handle and practically thrown himself out of the plane and onto the hot dusty ground.

Meanwhile, I had to wait until I was helped from my seat and hauled out feet first.

Once we were outside, the first thing that struck me was the awful smell.

The hot humid air being blown across my face was infused with the smell of rotten eggs.

'Phew, that really stinks!' I remarked. 'No wonder this place is uninhabited.'

'Yep, but it's surprising how soon you adapt and get used to it.' Tom warned me. 'A couple of hours and your senses will be dulled and then you just won't be able to smell it anymore.'

I held my nose and doubted that very much.

We pleaded with Captain Edward not to forget to return for us.

'I'll be here at 6p.m. tomorrow. But, if you are not here, I won't wait!' He warned.

'We will be here. Just please don't forget us.' We begged.

Just to be sure he did remember us, I plied him with the promise of a generous Christmas tip when he came back and then I kissed him a fond farewell on both cheeks. Both Tom and I, in dread of desertion over the holidays, then made a great fuss of watching him leave and waving him off, knowing that we were alone on this island for two days now no matter what.

Loaded up with our heavy backpacks and an assortment of camping gear and other necessities, Tom and I set off walking inland along a narrow grassy path through a forest of tall bamboo. I had a kettle and a frying pan tied to my pack that clanked together as I walked making me sound like a rather annoying one-man band. Tom walked with his two butterfly nets waving in the air like he was making a distress call and he carried his separate pack too containing all the special plastic boxes we would need to use to transport our precious cargo of collected caterpillars. As I walked, I was acutely aware that there was no one other than us on this island. The only sound I could hear was a warm breeze whistling through the bamboo canes. It sounded eerie. Like unseen people whispering: '*watch out – we see you – watch out.*'

If Josh and Lucas knew I was here, then I'm sure they'd be sending in the marines.

If Ethan knew the full extent of what I was doing here, then goodness knows how he'd react.

The route, which we hoped would bring us out at the start of segment three, seemed to have been carved out of the bamboo by a staggering drunk armed with a machete. I was in the lead position and the tall canes on either side of us made it impossible to see very far ahead.

Occasionally and confusingly, the trail opened and went off in many other directions.

Tom said these narrow diversions could have been made by animals.

I wondered what kind of animals. Gorillas, lions, tigers, giant snakes?

Tom suggested monkeys, armadillos, racoons, large iguana, or wild pigs.

I kept referring to my map to get my bearings and as bamboo forest became rainforest terrain, not for the first time did I start to have very real doubts about whether this crazy plan of mine was actually a good idea after all. Here we were, on an island, just the two of us, intending to be here overnight without anywhere to stay or without any bathroom facilities.

The thought of the latter stopped me dead in my tracks.

No shower or flushing toilet—for one night and two days!?

'I've just realised something!' I said to Tom, stopping so suddenly that he bumped into me. 'We have no contact with the outside world here. There's no internet. No cell phone service. What if something happens to either of us? Like an emergency? How on earth will we get help?' My voice was so high and so shrill, it caused a commotion amongst a flock of nearby birds who all took off at once, causing me to immediately dive for cover into a big prickly bush.

Tom replied. 'Well, I have a radio. I guess we could use the emergency frequency.'

'Really? A radio. Oh, that's okay, then. Good job!'

I wondered why I hadn't thought to bring a radio.

Maybe it's because normally I'd always left that kind of thing to Ethan?

I carried on walking, checking the map and guide that I'd downloaded onto my phone.

'I just realised something else.' I said to Tom in an equal

panic. 'I have both the map and the guide on my phone, but we are going to be here for two days and the battery on my phone only lasts for half that time. What will we do? There are no electricity or recharge points!'

'I have a solar powered charger and a USB cable. So, we're fine.'

'But what about at night? When it's dark? Did we remember to bring torches?'

'Lori, haven't you ever been camping before?' Tom asked me in all seriousness.

'No. Never. The closest I've come to it is staying in a wooden hut on a beach.'

'Well, that sounds a bit like camping, I suppose.' Tom noted with a shrug.

'Not at all. I had an en-suite bathroom and an electricity generator.' I admitted in dismay.

We'd only managed to hike for an hour or so and the stink of rotten eggs in the air was starting to make me feel rather queasy. My backpack seemed to be getting heavier and heavier.

I didn't like to complain (and I was determined that I wouldn't) but my new boots were already rubbing on my heel. I really wished I was still wearing my lovely new and comfy flip-flops instead. When we came into a rocky clearing, I was so glad to stop and rest, because my back was bent over and aching to compensate for my heavy load and my shoulder muscles were silently screaming with pain. I plopped myself down on a rock and immediately disturbed a small black scorpion. It jumped onto my foot and ran across my boot and then made off to hide under an adjacent rock. I was glad not to be wearing my flip-flops, after all.

'Okay, so this is where we join the trail at Segment Three.' Tom informed me. 'It's a good five-hour hike to the plateau, where we'll find the sulphur springs and the hot spa pool.'

'Oh, yes. That's sounds truly wonderful!' I breathed. 'Let's camp there tonight!'

No doubt, after today's endeavours in searching for our butterfly and all the resulting aches and pains and blisters we are sure to suffer along the way, I really fancied putting up my tent and then spending some time wallowing about in skin rejuvenating mud. I then imagined myself floating in a cleansing therapeutic spa pool afterwards. It would be even better than the natural spa on St Lucia and so worth an exhausting five-hour hike.

But Tom didn't agree. 'Actually, the sulphur springs here are unlike those on St Lucia. Here they are simply cracks in the earth's crust that allows steam and toxic fumes to escape. Plus, the spa pool is not for swimming. It's actually called The Boiling Pool because it's full of bubbling sulphuric acid.'

I bit down onto my lower lip and held onto my already aching disappointment.

'Then where do you suggest we camp tonight?' I asked him.

'We should camp in the rainforest. It'll be far safer there.' Tom suggested.

'But there might be snakes and spiders!' I objected. 'Rainforest is the same as jungle!'

'Yes. I expect you're right. But we'll light a fire and that might warn them off.' Tom replied casually, as he set off to follow the path ahead, now that it was his turn to take the lead.

I tried to keep my mind on the positive and my eyes focussed on looking for butterflies as we made our way through the rainforest, which wasn't easy as the ground was slippery and riddled with tree roots and vines. I actually fell over a couple of times. The landing was soft, but it was really hard to get back to my feet again with my bulky backpack on, so I rolled about in the mud much like a hermit crab in an ill-fitting shell, while Tom marched ahead.

If Ethan had been here, he would have stopped and helped me to my feet.

If Ethan had been here, he would have insisted on carrying half my heavy stuff.

If Ethan had been here, he would have held my hand and escorted me along the way.

We eventually stopped in another clearing and rested for a while. Tom got out his little gas camping stove and his coffee pot and brewed a ridiculously strong expresso coffee that he served to me with a chunk of cake. He said the sugary cake and the caffeine would help to boost my flagging energy levels. I suppose that at least he'd noticed I was flagging.

We soon set off again, now like giant tortoises lumbering along with our shells on our backs.

Along the way, we spotted several different types of butterflies fluttering about but they were all small yellow ones. Nonetheless, it was very exciting to see butterflies here. I listened carefully as Tom identified them all and informed me of their common and Latin names.

'Let's hope we can find the Green Morpho very soon!' I said to him optimistically.

'Yes. I hope so too. If only for identification purposes. Lori, you should remember that our prime objective here on this island is not to collect butterflies, as they are far too fragile to transport. Instead, we must focus our search on finding the Green Morpho caterpillars. The best way to do that is to look out for and find the one and only flowering plant that our fussy Green Morpho caterpillar chooses as its food source –and that's *Clitoria Ternatea* – the Butterfly Pea.'

'Ah, yes. Because where you find IT you will surely find THEM!' I recalled him saying.

Chapter 13

As we walked, I remarked to Tom on how the strong sulphurous smell had disappeared again. Interestingly, he said that it was actually still here, but we'd simply adapted to it as these levels of concentration. We were now deep into the tropical rainforest. It was dense and dark and surprisingly noisy, as all around us, up in the trees, behind the trees, in the bushes, were ominous grunts and screeches and high-pitched calls. We trudged slowly along what was supposed to be an established trail in this segment, but some parts of it were so overgrown that it was hard to know which way was right or wrong.

When we were unsure Tom took out a compass and double checked our heading.

Eventually, we could tell that we were getting closer to the sulphur springs, because the smell of rotten eggs had returned and the air once again had become heavy and pungent.

Tom rummaged through his backpack and produced two cloth facemasks for us to wear.

'The sulphurous air here is not dangerous, but these might help, if the smell bothers you.'

We plodded on, but I could still smell and taste the sulphur in the air and on my tongue.

Then we came to a place where the map showed a definite two-way split in the route.

We consulted the map on my phone. It showed there was a choice of going steeply uphill to the bubbling volcanic activity on the plateaux or to carry further on along a level heading through the rainforest and to the last third of the segment.

'I say we carry on.' Tom said staunchly.

But, for the last hour or so, I'd been racked with sharp stomach pains and I was suddenly desperate for a bit of privacy. I could feel a surge of volcanic activity happening deep in my belly and I suspected it might have been caused by the really strong coffee I'd drank earlier.

I squirmed as my insides bubbled and groaned and I really needed to go.

But where do I go? It's not like there are any rest rooms here?

'Tom, I really want to see the bubbling pool. I think it'll be very interesting.' I said with some urgency. 'Why don't you wait here while I just go and get a quick photo?'

'That's not a good idea, Lori. The air there is toxic and the crater is weak.'

I squirmed again and was just far too embarrassed to admit what was going on.

'No. I absolutely insist. I'll be quick. I really want to see that crater for myself.'

'But it's incredibly dangerous. Last year, a guide lost his life when he fell through the crust into the boiling mud. We really should keep going. If we increase our pace, we can set up our camp and get a fire going before it goes dark. I don't know about you but I'm starving.'

'Then you go on ahead. I'll catch up.' I said, crossing my legs at the crossroads.

Tom turned to me in frustration. 'I really don't advise it.'

I stamped my foot in pain with flatulence but realised it looks like utter petulance.

'Buddha says 'to travel is a better thing than to arrive' so I want to see those sulphur springs!'

Tom raked his hair in exasperation. 'That wasn't Buddha. It was Robert Louis Stevenson!'

'Really? Are you sure?'

'Yes. If you are going to quote Buddha, you could at least get it right.'

I bit down on my lower lip again as another wave of cramp hit me right in the guts.

'Then go!' He said dramatically, waving a dismissive arm in the air and then removing his backpack and taking out his drinking water bottle. 'I'll wait here. If you're not back in ten minutes, I'll know you've become unconscious from breathing CO2 gasses, and I'll have to endanger my own life to come and rescue you!'

I ran along the uphill path, huffing and puffing and

sweating and wishing that I'd at least had the good sense to leave my backpack with him. I was feeling compelled to rush, not only because I feared having an embarrassing accident, but also because he'd only given me ten minutes to relieve myself before he was coming up here to find me.

When I eventually got to the ridge at the top of the hill, I stopped to catch my breath in the smelly air and to find a safe spot to stoop. Ahead of me lay a huge flat area of ground that was pocked with hollow craters and pools of bubbling yellow mud. It looked like the surface of the moon. I spotted a small raised ridge that might provide me a bit of added privacy and I headed over there quickly while discarding my backpack and whipping down my trousers.

As I stooped, I looked across to the middle of the crater and saw what had to be the infamous 'boiling pool' – a steaming and burping and blisteringly hot mud pool – certainly not anything like spa facilities. This place was more like Jurassic Park than any Caribbean island I'd ever known. All around were craters and jagged cracks in the ground with steam escaping from them. Having now seen this place for myself, I'd started to believe Tom's account about the place being unstable – it looked like the volcano could erupt at any time – and I could imagine how a man could easily fall through this fragile crust to his death. It all looked entirely possible and very scary indeed. I quickly tidied myself up and tip-toed as close as I dared to the boiling pool to get a photo. Then I turned around and held my phone in the air to get a selfie with the bubbling crater in the background – thinking my boys would be impressed and intrigued by this lunar-esq landscape – when I heard a noise behind me coming from a nearby crater just a few steps away. It sounded like a squeal and then a whimper. It sounded like the cry of a child.

I tucked my phone away and went to investigate. What I actually found in there was a monkey. It was lying on its back at the bottom of the crater and it was a pitiful sight. It was hard to know how long it had been in there. I look down and all around and wondered how it might have become trapped? It whimpered again in a plea for help when it saw me standing there. 'Come on Monkey. Get up. Climb out.' I told it in an encouraging tone.

But it just lay there, limp and lethargic, with sad wide eyes, and in a crater only about four feet deep. Not too deep or too hard for a monkey to climb out and to escape from. Maybe it was in shock or simply too afraid to help itself? But I could hardly go away and leave it there.

I was going to have to go in there and get the poor creature out myself.

I decided to test the strength of the bottom of the crater first to see if it would hold my weight. I dropped in a heavy stone, not too close to the monkey obviously, who had started whimpering again. It seemed to be solid enough down there, so I climbed in and slid towards the little chap. He looked at me with such grateful eyes and so I bent down to lift him gently into my arms and to cradle him securely like a baby. I murmured soothing sounds to him about how I was going to get him out and make him better. And, I was just about to stand up and start to make my way back when I suddenly felt really dizzy. Then everything went totally black.

When I woke up sometime later, I saw Tom's face full of concern.

'Lori, can you hear me?'

'Monkey?' I groaned.

Tom was shouting now. 'Yes. I have the damned monkey. What on earth possessed you to do that alone?' His voice was full of panic and disbelief. 'When you didn't come back after twenty minutes, I came to look for you. I found you unconscious and holding onto a monkey in the bottom of a crater!'

'What happened to you giving me just ten minutes?' I asked him in a croaky dry voice, while trying to sit up. 'Ouch, I have a pounding headache. What happened?'

'The craters up there are filled with toxic gasses that are heavier than air and seep through the ground and accumulate inside the bowl. You could have died!'

'Oh my goodness. You did warn me about toxic gas. I thought you were exaggerating.'

When I saw that Tom had saved the little monkey too I was most relieved.

But Tom was clearly angry and disappointed with me and who could blame him?

'Here, drink some water and take a painkiller. We need to keep going.'

After a reasonably short time, I recovered, and we set off again. Tom said we were now well behind schedule and so he kept up a hasty pace and remained uncommunicative as we hiked.

Even though he was marching way ahead of me, I could just tell from the way he was stamping his feet as he walked, that the expression on his face must be set to livid.

He'd been further aggravated by my refusal to leave the monkey behind.

'But it's just a baby!' I implored him.

'Exactly. There will be a mum and a dad and a whole family troop out looking for it.'

But the poor thing is clinging to me like a dependent child and is so adorable.

I insisted on carrying him until he recovers. He's still quite lethargic in my arms.

I made a carry sling for him with a sarong that I had with me and he settled into it.

As we walked, I kept thinking about how stupid I'd been not to listen to Tom.

We'd only been on the island a few hours and he'd already saved my life.

I really did need to stop being so stupidly impulsive.

Like Tom, Ethan would have been appalled with me today. He'd have called me TSTL.

This was the acronym that we used to describe some

of the less able rookies who managed to slip through the selection nets and join the GGF conservation programmes.

TSTL: Too Stupid To Live.

We whacked our way along what remained of the overgrown trail path. Tom was ahead swinging his machete back and forth and I used a stick to tap the ground while keeping my eyes meticulously on where I was stepping because every branch and vine in my path looked exactly like a snake to me. When we stopped for a short break and a drink of water in a clearing, we were suddenly invaded by a troop of small monkeys. They must have been following us discreetly, but despite Tom's warning, these were not the same type of monkey as Monty – as I'd named my new friend – so they can't have been related to him.

Monty has black hair and a flat white face and a long tail. But this troop were smaller with brown fur and they had yellow and grey flecks around their black faces. There was at least a dozen of them. They looked cute but as soon as we'd opened our packs, they came in thick and fast to snatch anything they could get their thieving hands on.

One stole a butterfly net and ran up a tree with it. Another grabbed a full box of breakfast cereal bars from Tom's pack. I immediately shut my pack and sat on it while holding on firmly to the holdall with our caterpillar collection boxes in. Then I watched in both horror and amusement as Tom flew into a complete panic. He was waving his arms and screeching and swearing. Not so much like a pirate but like a dramatic drag queen. He fought furiously for a while with a monkey who had grabbed an item of clothing from his pack and I watched as a t-shirt with 'I'm a social butterfly' on it was reduced to shreds.

Only when it was beyond repair did Tom actually let go.

'I really hate monkeys!' he told me adamantly, as Monty, who was a much bigger primate than these naughty little rascals, bravely chased the last of them away.

When we reached the place that Tom had decided was the best place to camp for the night, we hurried to get our tents up before darkness fell. We each had the same type of small one-man tent. We set them up next to each other in an open area for safety and so we wouldn't have to deal with continual drops of water or anything else that might fall on us from the trees.

Tom had his tent up in no time at all and while I was still looking at the instruction leaflet.

It's not that I'm totally useless, but it's now almost dark and a helping hand would've been appreciated. Especially as he knows I haven't ever put up a tent before. Of course, this example once again makes me appreciate how much Ethan does for me when we are on our expeditions.

Ethan is old school when it comes to being a gentleman. He still opens doors. Offers his seat. Insists on opening the wine and pouring it too. I suppose I've just got used to that kind of support. Oh, how I miss him and dearly wish he was here right now. I tried to imagine what he was doing right at that moment. Maybe he was erecting a tent in a snowy blizzard?

I stropped about cursing loudly until my tent looked something remotely like Tom's.

Tom had set about lighting a fire and putting the kettle on to boil.

I did feel better and more appreciative towards him when he handed me a mug of tea.

We sat next to each other in front of the fire on a log but soon discovered it was crawling with fire ants – so called because their bite is painful and burns – and we'd jumped up and leapt about slapping ourselves silly to knock off the tiny offending creatures. Then we rolled away the log and we were now sitting primly on two hard rocks on opposite sides of the firepit.

Not for the heat of it but certainly for the light and comforting ambiance it gave out.

Of course, I'd first had to check that our stones weren't harbouring anything like a snake.

The surrounding forest is in full shriek as dusk falls and as the birds and animals claimed their perches or other resting places for the night and the nocturnal ones did their waking up rituals. I cradled little Monty in my arms and fed him a mango. Now that he'd been cleaned up a bit (I'd brushed the mud off him with my own hairbrush) he looked so cute with his shiny round expressive eyes and he clearly loved being groomed and cuddled.

When I'd thought Tom was looking the other way, I fed Monty some cake.

For some reason, cake had been allowed in our supplies as it was 'high energy'.

Whereas, in my expert opinion, so was wine and chocolate.

'And don't feed him our supplies!' Tom snapped at me. 'And, by the way, your hairbrush is now so full of fleas it should be thrown in the fire!'

The little monkey hissed at Tom and showed him some incredibly sharp teeth in response.

I tucked Monty into the sarong hammock I'd made for him and rocked him to sleep. During this time, Tom informed me that this island is not quite uninhabited after all. It is apparently home to 'tribes of rabies-carrying primates' who all came here on the first trading ships.

He claims that they move around the forest in organised raiding parties.

And again, he warned me that Monty's family troop were likely to be out searching for him and when they find him, they would surely attack us thinking we were his kidnappers. As a result, he assured me he would be keeping his machete close to hand all night.

After the kind of day that I'd had, I was thinking I could do with a nightcap about now.

If Ethan were here, I told myself, he would certainly have produced a bottle of wine. Or at the very least, a bottle of rum, for which he'd have cracked open a fallen coconut and made me a cocktail for sundown. I glanced over the flames of the fire at Tom and willed him to at least produce a hip flask. He didn't. So, I tugged off my boots, squeezed out my sopping wet socks, and saw that I had a large angry looking burst blister on my heel. A little sob escaped my throat.

Tom looked over at my foot. 'You need to clean that before it gets infected.'

He handed me the first aid kit. When he saw that I was out of socks, he redeemed himself as a gentleman by kindly giving me his last dry pair, insisting the pair he'd worn today would dry out overnight by the fire. He remarked on the scar I had on the top of my foot and I explained how I'd once cut myself quite badly while on an island in the Andaman Sea just off Thailand and how everybody I met had warned me about it getting infected.

'Of course, in the heat and humidity, my foot soon turned a grizzly-looking green.'

'What did you do? That can be a really serious situation.' He asked me in concern.

'Oh, Ethan came to my rescue. He cleaned my foot, administered antibiotics, and pain relief in the form of a cold beer.' I smiled sentimentally at the memory.

'Is Ethan the boyfriend you've mentioned?'

I nodded. 'Yes. He might be my husband if I decide to accept his proposal.'

I don't know what made me blurt that out so suddenly. I suppose it's something to do with feeling vulnerable and being out here on an island and so far from everyone else. In many ways, it feels like we're castaways here. There's always the worry that we might be if Captain Edwards didn't return as promised. I fixed a clean dressing to my heel and frowned not with pain but in anxiety.

'And so, will you marry him? Tom asked me bluntly.

'I'm really not sure.' I answered him honestly. 'I'm still thinking about it.'

Tom shrugged. 'In my experience, you either know or you don't. It's usually that simple.'

I shook my head. 'My life is not simple. It's very complicated.'

'You follow the teachings of Buddha, don't you?'

I laughed. 'Yes. I try. Only you corrected me earlier over a quote.'

Tom laughed. 'Don't feel bad. I've often heard people quote John Lennon and credit Buddha. One of my favourite Buddha quotes is: "time decides who you meet in life, but your heart decides who you want in your life". It tells us to trust our heart. Maybe that will help?'

I looked at Tom as he poked at the fire with a stick and orange flames leapt up.

The damp air around us glowed and felt warm and ambient against the darkening forest.

I saw him grinning. A coy grin. As if he too was considering sharing something with me.

'What? What is it? Come on, tell me!' I begged.

'I'm getting married myself soon.' He told me proudly.

'Oh, wow, congratulations! So where is the lucky man right now?'

'He's in Mexico. I'm going there for Christmas and we're getting married on the beach.'

'That sounds so romantic. I wish you both every happiness.' I said to him sincerely.

'So, Lori. How long do you have to make up your mind?'

'I have until New Year's Eve when Ethan promises to return from his latest expedition.'

'Not long, then. I think we should talk it through. Tell me why you are hesitant?'

'No. I can't.' I tried to laugh it off and make light of it.

'Why not? Come on, Lori. I'm a very good listener. I promise you that what you say on this island stays on this island. Imagine how much better you'll feel once you've made a firm decision. Because right now, if you don't mind me saying, you seem a bit uptight about everything and I guess that now I know why. This is important. Is it not?'

'Thank you, Tom. Yes, it is important. But it's a long and incredibly complicated story.'

My voice sounded breathless and exhausted just thinking about it all.

'That's okay. We have all night and no TV. I'm all ears. Start at the beginning.'

So, slowly and surely, I told him about my life and all that had happened over the past year.

Every. Single. Moment.

I told him what had caused me to leave my family and

my home. My journey through Thailand. Meeting Ethan. Volunteering at a turtle sanctuary. Travelling around the world on a conservation ship. Missing my family. Dashing back home thinking I'd lost my mum. The guilt. The awful feeling that I'd abandoned my sons. Then I told him about how everyone already had their Christmas plans in place.

'Which despite me being there, didn't include me.'

How everyone was far too busy to see me or each other for more than a few minutes.

'I honestly felt like I had to make appointments to see my own family.'

And, of course, I told him about Waterfall Cay and eventually, I got to the part where two complete strangers end up being the only two people on a Caribbean island that smelled of rotten eggs in search of an extinct species of butterfly.

Tom listened to my story in silence and by the end of it he seemed quite stunned by it all.

'Oh, I'm sorry, Tom. I really didn't want to burden you with all of this!' I wailed.

'Actually, I'm kind of honoured that you've included me in your mission. I had no idea what you were dealing with or the events had brought you here. But now I totally get it. But, as you've confided in me, Lori, I'm going to offer you some advice.'

'Okay. I'm listening.'

'I think you're being way too hard on yourself.'

'You think so? Really?'

'Yeah. You can love your family from near or far these days.'

'Because love knows no bounds?' I offered.

'No. Because there is the internet and with it there are ways to message and to see your family any time and it's all free wherever you are in the world. Obviously, not here, but this is the exception. And you've already proved to yourself that within half a day – or a day at the most – you can jump on a plane and be there for them. Your family won't love you any less because you choose to be happy. Trust me, I know. And you aren't choosing him over them. And, if they don't realise that straight away, then give them time and they will surely come around.'

Tom was like my sounding board. The angel and the devil on my shoulders personified.

'Maybe it's not just my family.' I admitted to him and perhaps finally to myself.

In talking this through with Tom I knew I had touched on something far deeper.

'Maybe it's because over the past year I've lost and found myself. I've discovered, perhaps for the first time, who I really am. I'm not just a wife and a mother. Not anymore. I'm me. I'm Lori. And, during the process of finding myself, I have made a promise to never lose sight of the person I truly am ever again. I suppose that is what makes me hesitant to marry again.'

Tom smiled at me reassuringly. 'I know exactly what you mean. I've had those same fears. Losing my identity.

Living my life for him instead of for myself. All of that.' But then he shook his head and adopted a dreamy expression. 'But I now believe that being acutely aware of who you are and what you can bring into a marriage, means you can go into it as a partner, not as an acquisition. It's important to respect each other as individuals.'

Tom was clearly a very soppy and romantic soul.

'Maybe. All I know is that there are things in this life I still want to achieve and they amount to more than just being married to the great Ethan Goldman. One of those things is taking the island back.' I reiterated, reminding Tom of the important task at hand.

'I agree. And now, more than ever, knowing what I know about why we are really here, I too want us to find the Green Morpho, so we can go and slap a protection order on that island!'

We both stared into the flames again and focussed our thoughts on our plans for a full day on the island tomorrow. 'There's a waterfall to tackle tomorrow.' Tom explained to me. 'We'll have to climb up the side of it. But, as it's part of the established trail, I'm expecting there to be some ropes and climbing supports to aid us. I should warn you that it still might be tough.'

'If it gets us up to the part of the segment where your friend thinks he saw our butterfly, then we'll do it.' I said, my voice sounding just as determined as I was feeling right at that moment.

'Yeah, that's where I believe we have our best chance of

spotting the Green Morpho and finding our Butterfly Pea plants full of caterpillars and in the cocoon stage of their metamorphosis. We should have packed up our camp and be ready to go at first light.'

'Yes. Because by around midday, whatever stage of the trail we have reached, we really should be prepared to turn back to meet with our flight out of here at 6pm.'

Tom nodded. 'My fear is not getting back to the airstrip in time.'

I stared into the flames of the fire and realised my fear was going back empty handed.

Chapter 14

I woke just before it was light and lay in my tent in darkness, tucked up in my sleeping bag, with the sounds of rainforest all around me. Tree frogs chirruped and geckos clicked. I imagined the high-pitched squeaks were probably fruit bats and the loudest calls were monkeys. Branches creaked overhead, but conversely; I didn't feel afraid.

Zipped up in my small tent, I felt safe. I felt like a butterfly wrapped up in a cocoon.

I sincerely hoped that when I emerged from my cocoon today, that we'll find our Green Morpho and a butterfly pea plant full of chomping caterpillars. That the tarot would have been right and, despite all the challenges we will face today, that we would have found our prize.

As the first rays of diffused jungle light hit my tent, I heard Tom moving about. Then I heard the sound of his tent being unzipped and him making his way into the jungle to relieve himself. I crawl out of my tent and do the same thing only in the opposite direction. On my way back, I manage to collect some bananas and stuff my pockets with ripe mangoes for our midmorning energy snack. It sounded like we might need extra energy today, as I reminded myself that this section of the trail consisted of steep terrain, dense forest, and fast running rivers that cut across our path on our way to the island's waterfall and our journey's end.

I was just contemplating this when I heard an unearthly scream. It was undoubtably Tom.

I ran back through our camp with my heart pounding as the screams kept coming and I leapt over branches and vines and jumped through bushes until I found myself dashing into a clearing where Tom was hysterical and doing some kind of frenzied dance.

His partner in the dance was Monty, who had taken possession of Tom's machete.

It seemed the faster Monty wielded the weapon the more Tom screamed and leapt about.

I didn't mean to laugh but it was so very funny. Monty didn't look to be threatening Tom. He looked to be having fun. But, of course, poor Tom didn't appreciate the game and he was quite terrified as he danced about with his arms and legs flailing in the air.

'Help! Do something Lori. Save me!'

'Here Monty.' I said gently. 'Here ... have a banana!'

I threw one onto the floor and it landed between them. Monty immediately stopped swinging the heavy machete and turned and looked at me and then the banana. Remembering how last night, Monty had loved sucking the mango, I repeat my call and threw a mango into the same spot. I looked to Tom's terrified face and nodded to him in collaborative sympathy.

Poor Tom was dripping with sweat and was a quivering wreck.

Then to much relief, Monty dropped the machete and walked on all fours over to the fruit.

He picked it up and grunted at me as if in thanks and then sat quietly peeling the banana.

I went over to pick up the machete and, also Tom, who had sunk down onto his knees.

'Thank you, Lori. I honestly thought he was going to chop me up into pieces with my own machete. I put it down for just a moment and then he just appeared and grabbed it and started swinging it about. It was the scariest thing. You saved me Lori. You saved me!'

'Well, now that we have saved each other, we should both be a bit more careful in future.'

I looked at Monty, who bared his teeth in a smile and showed me his half-chewed mango.

We ate our own breakfast of cereal bars and cake washed down with tea for me and coffee for Tom. Then we packed up our camp and set off to tackle our next challenge that morning, which was to cross a log bridge over a narrow rushing stream and scarily deep rocky crevice.

'You go first.' Tom instructed. 'Why me?' I wailed from the muddy embankment.

The logs that had been lashed together to form a bridge

were covered in moss and lichen and looked so wet and slimy and so slippery underfoot. To fall would have been a catastrophe.

With Monty in my sarong sling and clinging to my front, on Tom's instruction and with his constant reassurance, I inched my way across each log. I held onto the straps of my backpack as if it were a safety parachute. Tom had attached a rope around my waist and he was holding onto the other end of it. Once I'd safely reached the other side with Monty, it was Tom's turn.

I threw the rope back to him and attached the other end in a double knot to the trunk of a tree. I knew there was no way I'd have been able to support his weight if he slipped and fell into this ravine. Tom made the crossing easily, putting my terrified efforts to shame.

He leapt confidently onto the bridge, tip-toed gently across it, then leapt off it again to land beside me with all the grace and flourish of a prima ballerina. He was a sight to behold.

When I told him this, he looked even more pleased with himself.

We carried on trekking through the sweltering forest. The going was steep and slick and the air all around us was heavy and dripping and steamy. It was so uncomfortable and exhausting to be so hot and sweaty and to be carrying all this equipment. We kept our eyes open for the flowering foliage of the butterfly pea. Occasionally, we saw butterflies along the route, but they were not the

Green Morpho. So far, they've all been the tiny yellow 'sulphurous' ones.

Tom pointed out various shrubs and plants that some of the other caterpillars liked to eat.

I tried to be objective and calm as he turned leaves to reveal hairy wriggling specimens.

The forest here was so overgrown that in some parts we literally had to hack our way through using Tom's machete. Occasionally we separated to broaden our search area but then we had to be extra careful not to get lost. After about an hour, we decided to move onward and upward to our next challenge, as we were closing in on the last leg of the trail and we were getting close to the waterfall. Enthusiasm fuelled us once we heard the rumble of fast flowing water.

Thankfully, the falls didn't look too imposing. It was a narrow stream of water falling from the higher level of the rainforest in one twisting opaque streak, like a white horse's tail, into the sparkling pool far below. Although, in the rainy season, this would certainly have been a considerably larger and much faster flowing volume of water. In December, it was the dry season, and we could see how the previous season's fierce flow had carved out deep smooth dry rivulets at each side of the falls. Tom pointed out that these dry flumes could be used as guided pathways to assist our climb to the top of the falls.

But, before we made the climb, the pool of cool fresh water was far too tempting to overlook.

I had my swimsuit on underneath my outer clothes in

anticipation of being able to take a dip at some point today – and my first wash in almost two days – and I couldn't get my combat gear off fast enough. Tom also quickly stripped down to his boxer shorts. In the swirling pool beneath the falls, there were lots of the same type of translucent fish that I'd seen on Waterfall Cay. I took this as a very good sign. I was sure, if we were to find our butterfly anywhere, then it would be close to this beautiful cascading waterfall.

For a few moments, I lay back in the cool silky water with my arms and legs splayed, and I stared up into the rainforest high above me where the trees were drenched in mist. I tried to imagine seeing the Green Morpho here in flight, as if to manifest it in reality.

It was a wrench to have to leave the pool and get dressed so soon, but we were conscious of the passing time, and we simply couldn't afford to allow the morning to escape us.

I climbed the falls first, leaving Monty behind. He sat quietly watching us with a concerned expression on his face as I clamoured over the smooth slippery wet limestone flumes and rocks at the side of the waterfall. Until I got half way up a chute and wedged between two boulders and ended up getting stuck fast. Tom came up behind me and ended up giving me a push and a shove up to the next level by gripping both his hands onto my bottom.

It was hardly a dignified assent but at least I knew he wasn't enjoying himself.

We continued step by careful step until we eventually reached the top. At this higher level, the rainforest was even more lush and looking up into the treetops and forest canopy, I could see colourful parrots in the trees and lazy lima snoozing on branches. To my surprise, I also spotted Monty. Somehow, the clever and agile monkey had managed to follow us and was now sitting high up in a coconut palm. 'Monty. How did you get up there?'

He shrieked and kindly threw me down a coconut.

I had to jump out of the way as it hit the ground and split open with a splat. The coconut water was lost but I did have immediate access to the wonderfully moist and tasty coconut meat inside. 'Well, thank you Monty!'

Tom and I searched the whole area meticulously. We found ourselves ambling along the side of a narrow gorge of the river. But there were still no butterfly peas and no butterflies.

Not one. Not even the small yellow ones.

Time was not our friend today and I was now feeling totally despondent. I tried to rally my mood by thinking about the tarot card reading again. I thought about Ethan and Waterfall Cay and about Damion and Gloria Goldman. And then I wondered what the heck I was doing here? Was I completely crazy? It was just a few days to Christmas and I really should be back in London. And, thinking of London, and how cold it was there, I wondered how I'd ever begin to adapt to being back in the freezing cold UK again after all the sunshine and incredible heat of here in the Caribbean. I took in a deep breath of forest air and considered how the air smelled sweet and damp and earthy and how strange that I could detect no sulphur in it.

Yet, it must still be here just the same as before?

How amazing it is that our senses can adapt so well?

And suddenly, I realised that I'd used and heard that word *adapt* so many times over the past twenty-four-hours. 'Tom— remember yesterday, when I said the smell of rotten eggs had gone because I couldn't smell it anymore?'

'Yeah, that's right. Our senses had adapted so we hardly noticed it anymore.'

'Only, it got me thinking about how the Green Morpho might have adapted to being here on this island. We have been looking for the Butterfly Pea all this time but there is none to be found here. So, what – in your expert opinion – might be its next preferred source of food?'

I held my breath in anticipation and Tom looked up at me with a sparkle in his eye.

'Lori, I think you're onto something! I would guess that if the Green Morpho has adapted to whatever is the closest pea plant genus on this island. Then the new food source would be ...'

'Yes?' I begged him in encouragement.

'*Entada Gigas*. It's more commonly known as Monkey Ladder. It's a strong vine that grows like a snake through the trees and the pea pods that hang from it are huge. Its ripened seeds are large and brown and shaped like a heart, so they'll be easy to spot on the ground!'

'A vine that looks like a snake?' I repeated.

We separated to cover and comb through the area of dense rainforest at the top of the falls.

The trees and plants here were all very different from those we'd come across previously on the trail. Sunlight was diffused here, not just through the tree canopy, but through a cloak of hanging mist. At this elevated level, on the sloping sides of the island's volcanic cone, the rainforest looked luminous and magical. I could see the sun climbing ominously high in the sky and knew that when it reached its highest point, we would need to leave here to head back along the trail, or we wouldn't be able to reach the airstrip in time for our flight out tonight.

My heart and my optimism were soon down in the dumps again though, when I simply couldn't identify or find anything that fitted with Tom's descriptions. No large brown heart-shaped seeds on the ground and no snake-like vine with hanging pods in the trees. I retraced my steps feeling defeated and headed back to the falls using the sound of water as my guide.

I shouted out for Tom at the place we had parted as he was nowhere to be seen.

But then I suddenly heard him shouting back to me. His voice sounded like a distant echo through the rumble of water. I peered down from the top of the falls and saw that he was far below and standing with Monty on the dry flat rocks at the side of the falls with our gear.

'How did you get back down there so fast?' I yelled to him.

'I jumped!' he replied.

'You've got to be joking!' I breathed. 'In your boots and your clothes?'

'No. I took them off and threw them down onto the dry rocks over here!'

I looked hesitantly at the distance between me and the rock and then the pool below.

'Come down here Lori. I've got something to show you?'

'What is it? What did you find?'

'Monkey Ladder! He yelled back. And I saw he was wearing the biggest of grins.

'Really? You found it?' My hesitation over jumping the falls was immediately forgotten and I was soon scrabbling out of my boots and throwing them over the edge and looking for the best route down. 'Use the water like a flume. It's easy. It's just like being at a waterpark!'

And I remembered the waterpark at Atlantis in the Bahamas and seeing people using the tall flumes there. At the time, I'd thought they must be stark raving mad to do for fun what I was considering doing right now. I'd seen them suspended at the top of the waterslide, leaning back with their ankles crossed and their arms hugging themselves, before—whoosh!

A moment or two later, I was balanced precariously on the very edge of the terrifying drop that led directly into the steep twisting natural flume. Cool rushing water swept around my bottom and my legs and with one brave forward flick of my hips, I found myself being swept away and carried down into the cascading fall and deep swirling water far below.

When I came up in the pool I was whooping and laughing. I'd done it!

I dressed quickly and followed Tom and an enthusiastic Monty into an area of the rainforest that we'd certainly explored before. But at that time, we hadn't been focussed on anything growing higher than ten feet off the ground. We'd been looking for a shrub and now we were looking for a hanging vine. We tipped back our heads and craned our necks into the high canopy above us as we stumbled through the overgrown forest floor. The trees here were tall and varied with straight trunks that seemed like beanstalks into the heavens. There were some tall thin swaying coconut palms, tropical pines with sharp ridged bark and high branches with what looked like razor-edged needles. There were also some huge ceiba trees and it was these that looked to be draped with a vast woven net of green leafy vines and from that netting hung long black pods from ribbon like vines. The Monkey Ladder.

I stood and marvelled at it with so much adrenalin coursing through my veins that I felt euphoric. Then suddenly, I saw movement in those high misty heavens, and I scrunched up my eyes to try and focus. Birds? Bats? Or—dare I suggest giant butterflies?

'There! Up there! Do you see?' I yelled, pointing upward in excitement.

Tom has spotted them too. I wasn't just imagining them after all!

'I see them! But I can't tell what colour they are from here. Are they blue—or green?'

Tom quickly produced a small pair of binoculars from his pack and peered through them urgently. I saw that his hands were trembling slightly as he looked through the lenses.

'Green! I'm sure of it! They're green!' He was practically screaming now.

He turned to me and his expression was ecstatic. 'We found them! They are here!'

He threw out his arms to scooped me up in a tight embrace and at the same time he was leaping about with joy. Monty started screeching and I began weeping. I couldn't help it. Great gulping sobs of utmost relief. But also anxiety. How on earth were we to reach them when they looked to be hundreds of meters in the air? It seemed the Green Morpho caterpillars had adapted so well to life here on this island that they'd become airborne acrobats.

'But how are we to reach them when we don't have enough rope?' I questioned.

Somehow, Tom didn't seem to be as fazed by this dilemma. He picked up a long length of tough dried root that lay on the forest floor. 'We can make a sling and a ladder out of these roots.' He pulled on it, trying to snap it and failing, to show me how suitable it was for the task.

'But Tom, how will you reach the tree canopy? I just don't see how this can work!'

'I can easily make the climb.' He told me stoically.

I knew Tom was adept with ladders. I remembered seeing how agile he was on the day we met, but how he could possibly fashion a sling and a ladder right now with no tools?

'You can't do this alone. Not with only an hour before we have to leave here!'

But Tom wouldn't listen and he set to work. Using long lengths of the root, he showed me how to cobble together a makeshift length of rope and something that resembled a long flexible ladder. He explained. 'On an island in Thailand once, I watched a local man climb a tall palm tree to reach the coconuts at the top and he kindly gave me a lesson in how it was done using the ridges in the trunk as an anchor points for a sling. I think I can shimmy up the trunk with my equipment bag and the ladder slung across my body to reach the vines.'

He straddled the nearest coconut palm and demonstrated the technique to me.

It looked impressive, but it also looked difficult and incredibly risky and dangerous.

Unheeded, Tom began his brave climb. I held my breath and watched as he made slow progress up the tall narrow trunk. He was trying to be careful and measure each move he made but he'd already slipped once and ripped his trousers and I could see a bloody gash in his knee.

When he was around ten feet off the ground, I suddenly had another idea.

'Wait! Stop! I know someone here who could easily do the climb!'

Tom peered down at me looking quite exhausted and perhaps now willing to listen.

Perspiration poured from his brow and ran down his face. His breath was fast from exertion and from his efforts. I threw a glance at Monty, who was sitting watching us with great interest.

'You mean Monty?' Tom asked me from his vantage point.

The monkey was getting accustomed to his name and grinned at us.

'Yes. I saw him climb straight up a palm tree earlier. It was no problem to him.'

Thankfully, realising this was a far better plan, Tom came down and we set to making a harness for Monty from a synthetic rope in our backpack. Then we attached a length of vine rope to his harness and in turn attached this to the ladder he would take with him up the tree.

When he was ready, we pointed up the tree to the coconuts at the top and he immediately scampered up it. I feared the makeshift ladder would be too heavy for him to drag behind him but, just like he'd managed to wield the heavy machete, he seemed to manage it quite easily.

I cajoled Monty with lots of praise and encouragement while Tom kept hold of the end of the rope. When Monty reached the top, leaping around in excitement and in the process secured his end of the rope to the strong palm fronds at the top of the tree. I yelled to watch out for falling coconuts. Tom grabbed his pack containing the caterpillar boxes and the ladder and began to climb. Tom's upper body strength is impressive and soon he was up at the top of the tree with Monty and releasing the helpful monkey from his harness.

'Come on, Lori! Get up here quickly. We have work to do!'

I too began to climb the swaying creaking rope ladder. This was no time for fear. I clambered up slowly and purposefully and kept my eyes on Tom and Monty as I ascended. I felt like Jack climbing the beanstalk into the high heavens. Tom waited anxiously until I'd reached him in the canopy. Then we used our combined body weights to bend the top of the tree slightly and sway towards the strong leafy vines of the Monkey Ladder.

I reached across to a thick branch of the adjacent tree and tied our safety ropes onto it.

I worked quickly and was silently thankful for all the hours that I'd spent aboard ship with Ethan, as he'd patiently demonstrated to me repeatedly, how to tie strong knots.

'The caterpillars are reddish-brown with small patches of lime-green on their backs. The eggs are small and pale green.' Tom told me, but I didn't need reminding. They also had stinging hairs and secreted a rancid smell if they felt threatened. I didn't look down.

We'd come all this way and this was my quest. I wasn't quitting now.

I reached across to the Monkey Ladder leaves closest to me and visually checked them.

Some did have holes in them indicating caterpillars had been munching and others had the tiny eggs stuck on their undersides that looked like tiny shimmering drops of dew.

Oh, mum and Josh and Zoey and Lucas and Ethan, if you could only see me now.

I was going to have to crawl along an adjacent horizontal branch to get to where I needed to be and so with my latex gloves on and access to my collecting boxes, I inched along the branch, almost jumping out my skin after coming across a small sloth, who might have been more surprised than me to find a human in his tree. It leapt away, making me grab the branch with both hands and shredding holes in my now useless gloves. I gathered myself and, finding the branch sturdy, I continued on until I was around six feet or so away from Tom.

I checked the thick hordes of leaves and vines growing all around me and saw they in turn were covered in many reddish-brown caterpillars with small patches of lime-green on their backs. I asked Tom to pass me a collection box and then started to harvest them and a quantity of their food. I worked quickly and meticulously, turning over the leaves to examine the undersides and plucking off their eggs and all the happily munching caterpillars together with those sleeping and metamorphosising in their silky cocoons.

Then suddenly, amongst the vines, I saw something and I froze with fear. It was a snake. A big one. It looked to be sleeping on the branch. I couldn't speak and neither did I want to move in case I woke it.

I turned my widened eye balls in Tom's direction to try and alert him.

'What's up?' He yelled, his voice projecting through the space between us.

I had no choice but to move my arm in a slow and undulating way as if I was playing a game of charades. I was attempting to indicate 'there's a snake on the branch'.

'A snake?' Tom yelled.

'I wobbled my eyes and groaned. 'Yes!'

'What colour is it? How long? Any distinctive markings?'

All very difficult questions to answer only in slow mime.

'Shhhhh' Tom suddenly urged with his finger to his pursed lips. 'Did you hear that?'

'What? Hear what?' I hissed in horror.

Had the snake woken? Was it preparing to attack me? Am I going to die a horrible death?

'One and one is two. Two and two is four—' Tom whispered ever so quietly.

'What on earth are you doing?' I wanted to know.

'Ha-ha! It's an Adder!' Tom laughed so loudly that he rocked the branch back and forth.

'This is not the time and place for your sick sense of humour and silly jokes!'

Then the snake started to move away.

I suspected it had been disturbed by my trembling and Tom's vibrations along the branch.

'Joking aside, it's a racer snake. It's passive and none poisonous.' Tom assured me.

With my heart banging against my ribs I continued my mission to collect eggs and caterpillars and chrysalises. Oh Ethan, if you could only see me now!

Then a giant Green Morpho butterfly fluttered past me, it's large wings iridescent against the canopy of green. I gasped and caught my breath. My mesmerised eyes widened and every hair on my body rose with excitement. It was so beautiful. When I looked across at Tom, I saw that he was grinning from ear to ear and giving me a big thumbs up sign.

Chapter 15

Back to Tortola and Waterfall Cay

Just after noon, we started to head back to the airstrip to meet with Captain Edward. As we passed by the area below the plateau, where I'd first found Monty, he'd suddenly leapt from my arms and went his own way. We can only assume that he recognised the way back to his family. I watched him go and wondered if he could ever know how grateful we were to him?

Thanks to Monty, we had ten containers of healthy-looking caterpillars in various stages of growth, several large bags of foliage for them to munch on and lots of leaves with eggs attached. We'd also collected some of the precious chrysalises with the caterpillars inside them completing their metamorphosis into the giant Green Morpho.

Edward arrived right on time as promised and flew us straight onto Tortola as arranged. It was a short flight of just thirty-five minutes. I could tell that Tom was feeling just as exhausted as I was and that he was more relieved than afraid to fly this time. Not to mention starving.

We seemed to have lived for two days on cake alone.

After landing on Tortola, we took a taxi over to the marina, where Ethan and I had initially hired a motorboat on the day he'd introduced me to Waterfall Cay. I left Tom to check us into an adjacent hotel and to check on our precious cargo of Green Morphos in their various stages of development while I went to see the man in the Panama hat.

As I didn't have a clue how to drive a motorboat and neither did Tom, I had to ask Mr Panama Hat, whose actual name was Jorge, if he'd be willing to rent out his boat to us complete with a driver for a departure first thing in the morning. He agreed to drive us himself and produced a card machine. I am guessing that my bank card was steaming.

Back at the hotel, Tom and I agreed to meet up in one hour in the waterfront restaurant.

We were both ravenously hungry, thirsty, but far too sweaty and filthy from island rainforest and pungent aromas to consider sitting down to eat yet. My entire body ached and was stiff and sore from two days of walking, climbing, gripping onto tree branches and from the tension brought about by the fear of falling and the fear of failing to complete our mission.

Even taking one flight of stairs up to my room seemed to take all the energy I had left in me.

Only the thought of being able to shower and wash my hair enticed me to make the effort.

My room was small and clean and had a balcony with a beautiful view over the bay. I eyed the bed and wished with all my heart I could just lie on it for a moment, but I knew that if I allowed myself that luxury, I'd have crashed and starved to death in my sleep.

After a hot water shower, I wore the only clean thing I had in my pack.

It was the dress I'd bought on St Lucia. Although, I feared it would likely be holding onto an undetectable only to me pungent sulphurous smell. Just before I went downstairs, I texted my sons and my mum to tell them I was just back in the land of wi-fi and would call them later.

I doubted I had the energy to speak coherently until I was fed. I'd already decided on something considerable for my dinner like a double cheeseburger and fries and a pudding that contained a high percentage of chocolate.

Tom was already in the restaurant when I got downstairs. He looked so unlike jungle Tom.

He was ridiculously handsome now that he was clean and his hair, still damp from the shower, was combed back off his forehead. He was wearing chino shorts and a t-shirt that had 'born to be a butterfly' printed on it that looked impossibly white against his darkly tanned skin. The restaurant wasn't busy, but I saw that a few of the women and several of the men were busy eyeing up Tom. I greeted him with a kiss to both sides of his smoothly shaven face and sat down. Picking up the menu, I was hopeful that service would be reasonably fast.

Our waiter introduced himself as Anthony. As I ordered my burger and fries and a chocolate cheesecake, he poured us water as a matter of course. I gulped down a whole glassful straight away without stopping to breathe. 'Whoa, someone is thirsty!' Anthony remarked.

'Yes. Very. Can we also have two cold beers please too?'

'Two bottles of local beer coming right up!'

After our meal, lethargic with food and dizzy with tiredness, Tom and I parted company for the rest of the evening with a reminder to each other to set our phone alarms for an early start.

We had to be on the move as soon as the sun came up.

I lounged back on the blissfully soft bed and mulled over my thoughts about the past couple of days. Knowing the final part of the plan was the most crucial and our timing tomorrow had to be perfect. Firstly, we had to reach Waterfall Cay and trek to the waterfall to rehome the Green Morpho caterpillars and cocoons and eggs. Then we had to be sure to get back to Tortola and file our petition. I'd checked the government website to see a notice that they closed at 4.30p.m. tomorrow. It was going to be another gruelling race against the clock kind of day.

Too tired to hold a proper conversation, I quickly messaged my mum and my boys again, saying that it was late here and I was going to bed. I did explain that I would call them tomorrow evening from the airport with my arrival time back in London.

I'd looked quickly at flights to see that I had a couple of options with different airlines.

Before I could sleep, I had to draft out my petition statement, knowing that time would be of the essence tomorrow. Tom had also promised to draft out his expert statement before he went to sleep. I knew I had to be factual and practical in my plea as it wouldn't do to be emotional. I decided on three succinct paragraphs. One that detailed the historical value and presence of the Green Morpho on the island at the time when Wallace had first identified the species. Then noting the fact that the giant butterfly had been previously declared as endangered and then falsely reported extinct. Followed by the rediscovery and the second chance being offered to the world to save and preserve the Green Morpho on Waterfall Cay, as classed and identified by world-renowned expert and lepidopterist Dr Tomas Remington.

Then I slept like a proverbial log until my alarm went off at 5.30a.m.

Jorge was waiting for us as we arrived at the marina. He was stocking the boat with a cool box filled with drinking water, sandwiches and fruit for our picnic lunch. He asked us if we'd like champagne too, but we declined. I explained to him that the trip was of a scientific nature and that we also required his discretion as we were dealing with a rare species. He agreed and didn't ask any awkward questions. Probably because he knew Ethan and I worked together.

So Tom and I brought onboard our precious Green Morphos and Jorge steered us out of the bay and headed out down the straits. We enjoyed the warm sun on our skin and the fresh wind in our hair, but we could hardly relax. I could see that Tom was anxious and fretting over the condition of our precious cargo. It had been many hours since we'd taken them from their original home and we hoped our efforts to rehome them wouldn't take too much longer.

After almost three hours, once we'd passed the Dog Islands and I could see Mosquito Island emerging on the horizon and Necker Island in the far distance, I knew we'd soon spot Waterfall Cay off our port side. Tom remarked, just as I had the last time I'd made this journey, that these islands seemed to be at the very end of the world.

Finally, we slipped quietly into the small heart shaped bay and secured the boat.

Tom and I hurried to get our boxes ashore while Jorge relaxed back on the boat.

Tom and I traipsed through the rainforest towards the waterfall. It felt strange being back here without Ethan. I'd explained to Tom that the site where we were rehoming the Green Morpho was at the opposite end of the island and away from the beach area, the lagoon, and all the construction works. Like the experienced hikers we had become, we made good progress along the track that Ethan and I had previously trekked and we reached the waterfall, breathless and sweaty and quite exhausted.

As I was myself, Tom was in awe of the incredible setting. As we entered the lagoon, the emerald pool looked so amazing and enticing, that we had to resist the temptation to throw ourselves into it because we had our important work to do. Tom had to scout around the waterfall area to assess the very best place for us to rehome our charges while I unpacked our boxes and equipment. When he came back to me, he said he'd found lots of Butterfly Pea plants growing in the shaded area at the back of the waterfall and we immediately set to our task of transferring our chomping caterpillars – several hundreds of them – but still only a tiny amount of the ones we'd seen on the vines on Luminaire.

Once they'd all been happily rehomed, it was the turn of the chrysalises, which were still attached to the foliage they had woven themselves onto. We hoped that when they woke up from their sleep, they wouldn't even know they had just been airlifted to another island. Ditto the eggs that were still all attached to the undersides of the same leaf their mothers had chosen for them. All we needed now was for the butterflies to hatch.

Tom estimated it might perhaps be a day or two before those in their cocoons began to emerge. When our task was completed, only then did we go for our well-deserved swim.

'I can hardly believe that we actually managed to pull this off!' Tom exclaimed in surprise.

'What? So you really *did* think this plan of mine was crazy?' I laughed, splashing him.

'No, not crazy, but it was certainly daring. I can see why you want to live here. It's idyllic!'

'While we're here, I'd like to show you what's going on at the other side of the island.'

I was also curious to see how far Damion's plans for his hotel and resort had progressed.

So we made our way back to the boat, where we found Jorge happily fishing and eating sandwiches, and we stowed away our specimen boxes. Then we headed over to the beach and lagoon area using the route that I knew would bring us out right at the top end of the beach.

'We can use the boulders below the headland to spy on the Goldman's construction site.' I told Tom. And so, when we got there, we both squatted down and ducked our heads and peered out from our rocky hiding places to be completely shocked by what we saw.

There were construction workers everywhere. Noisy machinery was being moved from the jetty that crossed the reef to the footprint of the resort, where building materials were stockpiled and cranes swung shuttering into place and cement machines noisily churned the toxic concrete sludge to be poured into the sand and to provide the foundations to the building and swimming pool. The difference in what I'd seen here last time and now was heartbreaking.

'This is happening even faster than I thought possible!' I breathed.

'Yes. We really need to get back to Tortola and file those papers.'

I nodded. My throat felt tightened by all the turmoil and the intensity of my emotions.

We had clear seas until we reached Virgin Gorda, then frustratingly, we had to slow right down because we got caught up in a Christmas pageant taking place in the straits. There were so many sailing yachts and power yachts and catamarans, all being driven by people wearing Santa hats and sunshades and with their boats decked out for the upcoming holiday.

It took us more than an hour longer than expected to clear the straights.

When we finally reached the harbour at Road Town and tipped Jorge to watch our stuff, we made a dash in a taxi to the government buildings. I'd been continually checking my watch and had estimated that we would arrive back mid-afternoon and with an hour to spare on closing time. Time enough to complete the paperwork between us and file our petition.

But to our despair, despite what had been on the website, the offices were shutting earlier.

'Sorry, but you'll have to come back next week.' The woman closing declared.

'Please, this is important. Can you just give us the paperwork we need to pursue our claim?'

I quickly explained what is was that we needed. My tone was of desperate begging.

Luckily, we were dealing with someone who believed in Christmas spirit and who willing to give us the time of day and we were given the guidance booklets and a wad of forms to complete. 'Getting an indigenous species documented is straightforward. The board is very keen to favour and support new petitions. Just pop your completed paperwork through the letterbox on the door an you'll be informed of their decision after the next board meeting in January. Thank you and happy Christmas.'

I calmed myself and gritted my teeth. 'Thank you and Merry Christmas.'

Tom led me back to the waterside café. We sat in the shade and drank iced coffee.

'For some reason, until I saw the pageant today, I'd completely forgotten about Christmas.'

'Yeah, it had kinda escaped me too, but it is just a couple of days away.'

'So it's likely to be at least a couple of weeks, possibly more, before we hear anything.'

Tom shrugged. 'Think of it this way. It could work out in our favour. It might be ten to fourteen days before the application is processed, but in a butterfly's life cycle, that's plenty of opportunity for our Green Morphos to establish themselves and for all the pupa to hatch. Come on, Lori. Cheer up. We did a great thing. We found a species that the world thought was extinct and we returned it to its natural habitat to survive and to hopefully thrive. We should celebrate. It's Christmas!'

Of course, he was right. We must wait. We must be patient.

The paperwork looked pretty straightforward. I completed a statement that defended the petition and provided evidence to warrant both a wildlife preserve and a protected habitat on Waterfall Cay. Tom finalised his witness statement confirming the sighting of the indigenous/endangered species and stated his formal qualifications as a credible expert in his field. An hour later and we had posted our petition and our mission had been accomplished.

We stood staring at the letterbox for a while and then we turned to each other.

'Well, it's been an amazing adventure.' Tom said to me.

'I don't know how to thank you.' I said, feeling quite overwhelmed and lost for words.

'No need.' He assured me.

'So when do you fly to Mexico to join your fiancé?' I asked him.

'I've already booked a flight out this evening.' He told me with a dreamy look in his eye.

I smiled. 'Good. I'm going to jump on a flight back to London. I want to offer both you and your soon to be husband my heartfelt congratulations. But I don't actually know his name?'

Tom laughed. 'No. That's because when we talked, I realised my fiancé and yours have the same first names, and I thought it might just confuse things.'

'You are marrying an Ethan, too?'

'Arh and, so it seems, are you!' Tom remarked.'

I laughed. 'Yes. I've decided that I'm going to marry my Ethan. If I send you an invite, will you and your Ethan come to my wedding?' I asked him.

Tom nodded eagerly and wiped away a tear. He really was a very soppy and romantic soul.

We travelled to the airport in the same taxi together, connecting on Facebook and Instagram and swapping email addresses. 'Lori, promise you'll let me know as soon as you hear anything. I'm happy to come back and assist. Just let me know and I'll be on the next flight.'

'You're willing to get on another plane for me?' I laughed.

He rolled his eyes in defeat. 'Yes. Because I really want this to succeed as much as you do.'

Chapter 16

London UK

As my plane touches down in London, I'm cuddled into my scarf and smiling to myself. Having had this time to just sit and contemplate life for all these hours, looking down at clouds and swathes of blue ocean as I've crossed the Atlantic today, I'm filled with hope and excitement.

I'm feeling calm and rational and thinking positively again.

My time with Tom in the rainforest on Luminaire has been illuminating to say the least.

Tom's right. My love for Ethan doesn't have to compromise my newly found freedom. My separation anxiety from my family has been real, but clearly, they haven't missed me too much.

They'd simply been concerned and naturally worried for me and I for them.

I know my family is happy and living their busy lives. It's such a relief not to have to worry.

As for my mum – well, of course she's getting older – but we are all getting older.

And what I wish for my mum is also what I wish for myself.

Love. Purpose. Independence.

My mum has lots of friends and family who love her. She is more purposeful than most people half her age. And, of course, continued independence is a blessing for as long as it lasts.

I love my family and I love Ethan. I find purpose and independence through travel.

So fear and anxiety and guilt no longer have a purpose or a place in my backpack.

Through technology and transport, I'm able to love my family from near or far.

I'm not going to beat myself up anymore or compromise on anything.

I've decided I want it all. I'm going to take back Waterfall Cay. I'm going to marry Ethan.

And I'm going to embrace every single adventure in life that comes my way.

And all that starts today.

I walked off that plane feeling as light as air. It's the weekend. Lucas and Josh and Zoey have all said they'll come around and spend some time with mum and I this evening. We're going to have a meal together and I expect we'll open our gifts ahead of the Day itself because, of course Josh and Zoey, are spending Christmas in Cornwall with her family and Lucas will be with his dad. I don't mind now. I'm over my disappointment. I'm over myself. I've decided I'm going to join mum serving lunch to those less fortunate on Christmas Day.

Once again, Josh and Zoey are here to meet me and to take me back to mum's house.

Our conversation is happy and chatty and, although I'd been away for a whole week, there's a casual enquiry as to what I've been doing back in the Caribbean. But I didn't go into any details. I just explained how I'd wanted to see an interesting exhibition about butterflies and had travelled on with a friend to a couple of other islands. They didn't ask me anything else.

I can only assume it sounded incredibly dull compared to the party scene in London this week and their own busy plans for the holidays.

On Christmas Eve, with shopping done and gifts wrapped and preparations complete, as darkness fell, our suburban street was festooned with fairy lights and Christmas decorations. Plastic reindeer and inflatable snowmen wobbled about on frosty front lawns and model Santa Claus's climbed up rope ladders hanging from the icy guttering of the houses. All the neighbours were being jolly, despite not really bothering with each other too much all year and were offering neighbourly invitations to pop in for a mince pie and mulled wine.

Inside our little house, the artificial tree that I'd dragged from the loft a couple of weeks earlier, was decorated with baubles and lit up with tiny lights. Christmas cards where strung up over the fireplace and cinnamon scented candles flickered on the mantlepiece next to the wooden scene of the nativity that I have known all my life. I poured myself a glass of wine just as my phone pinged and I checked it straight away. Was it a text from Ethan?

I'd been hoping to hear from him all day. Willing him to get in touch.

To my surprise, the text was from Gloria Goldman.

Lori. I need to speak with you. Call me back in exactly half an hour.

I stared at the text and felt a deep concern over what this might be about.

If this had been a regular message to chat and reconnect then surely it would have contained the words 'Merry Christmas.' But it didn't. Just a few words that on my phone looked ominous and foreboding. Half an hour passing felt more like ten hours as I waited to call Gloria back.

When I did, she answered straight away, and her voice sounded hushed.

'Lori, I must warn you that Damion knows about the protection application.'

My newly subdued mood crashed to a new low with this bomb-shell.

'He knows already? How? The offices on Tortola are now closed for the holidays.'

I'd hoped that the holidays would have provided us with a buffer period.

'Well, we are on Tortola right now.' She confided to me in almost a whisper. 'As you might imagine, Damion knows someone in the government offices here.'

'Damn,' I said. A feeling of stone-cold dread washed over me as I wondered what Damion might do with this information. 'So, he's sure to have seen my name on the petition and also the name of my expert witness?'

'He doesn't remember your name, Lori, or know of your witness. I overheard him saying that he thinks it's a competitor trying to cause trouble. But I can tell you that he immediately put plans in place to fog the island with a pesticide and it will happen tomorrow.'

'A pesticide! How can he even do that? It will kill everything on the island!'

'I just know he's hired a licenced pesticide company to irradiate mosquitoes and other insects on the island ahead of excavating for the new waterpark at the waterfall. That's all I can tell you. If I find out any more, I'll text you.'

A sob escaped my throat. Tom and I had re-established all our Green Morpho at the waterfall because that's where we'd found the Butterfly Pea plant. Fogging the island would kill them all. And it was all completely legal. So, basically, there was no way to stop him.

No way to prevent him from wiping out all insect life on the island.

And, with the government offices closed for another

week, there was no way to file a petition or a conscientious objection. No doubt, by the time the board had reconvened to consider the application for a protection order – and they send out their independent assessor – all the Green Morphos will have been wiped out once more. I sat still considering this while becoming more and more angry. My plan was failing right at that moment and I was totally helpless to stop it.

Ethan was right. Damion is ruthless. He'll stop at nothing to get what he wants.

I felt totally deflated. All of mine and Tom's efforts have come to nothing.

And I've lost the island. Ethan has lost the island once again even though he didn't know it.

Oh poor Tom too! He's also going to be so upset when he finds out.

But I really didn't have the heart to tell him about this yet. Why spoil his Christmas?

Especially as he's getting married tomorrow in Cancun Mexico.

I was grateful to Gloria for risking the wrath of her husband in contacting me.

If she hadn't, I'd certainly be none the wiser. And, I suppose ignorance is not always bliss.

Chapter 17

I got through Christmas as best I could. I developed a stress headache over feeling miserable about Waterfall Cay and also because I'd still not heard from Ethan. No news is good news he always says about being out of touch. But that didn't stop me worrying about him. On Christmas Day, although I could have just stayed in bed wallowing in misery, I'd decided I'd go with Mum to work in the kitchen at the shelter and help feed the homeless. I'm glad I did because it buoyed my mood. It was hard not to be swept up by the wonderful Christmas cheer and with the carol singers and all the joy being shared over a hot Christmas meal by those who appreciated it so much. In the end, it was like I'd had a day of respite from thinking about my own worldly problems.

But, despite all the evidence to the contrary, annoyingly, my mind was still convinced that there must be a way to save this situation. For some unknown reason, I simply could not let this go. My head was achingly full of seemingly relentless 'what if' scenarios and situations and my poor brain was in overdrive. I couldn't sleep. I couldn't concentrate. Was it because I was still holding onto my belief in the tarot cards? Cards that had been read by a woman who had claimed to see my future. Who had seen the whole world as my ultimate prize?

On Boxing Day, I had another text from Gloria. It simply said: *I have an idea!*

I texted back immediately. Her reply was for me to call her at exactly 5p.m. my time.

'Where are you now?' I asked her, when at exactly five pm she picked up my call.

'We're still in the BVIs. Staying with friends on Necker until New Year.'

'Can you see Waterfall Cay from there? Did it get fogged?'

'Yes, and yes. I'm so sorry Lori. Damion has been beyond furious. He's determined to stop a protection order halting his plans. But I do have an idea. It's a long shot. But I've been mulling this over since we talked. Ethan inherited a property in Scotland from his parents. It used to be the family home. I believe it's somewhere just outside Edinburgh. I really think it could be the one thing that's been keeping them divided over all these years.'

'So, you're saying, if Ethan still has it then he should offer it Damion in exchange?'

'I'm not saying it will work. He's pretty angry right now. I'm just saying it might.'

'Okay. I'll speak with Ethan. Although, I haven't heard

from him and I won't see him for a few more days. He's supposed to be coming to London for New Year.'

'We'll be in Edinburgh.' Gloria told me. 'We have tickets to the Hogmanay street party.'

'Okay. Then let's stay in touch!'

On the 28th December, I was in despair through boredom and monotony and disgruntlement because I still hadn't heard anything from Ethan. I'd called The Goldman Foundation headquarters and this time I'd actually reached a person who was manning the office at 'Twixmas' – which is what I call that strange time between Christmas and New Year.

I was told that Ethan's expedition team was currently in the air and on route to Argentina, from where they were flying on to the USA. I was hoping that Ethan would call me the moment he landed in the States. In anticipation, I've been holding onto my phone all day, checking that it's fully charged and that the volume is up high, and that I've always got a full signal.

When it finally rang, I jumped out of my skin and juggled with it for a few moments.

Then I saw it was HIM on the caller display. 'Ethan!'

'Lori! Hi sweetheart. How are you?'

'Oh my goodness – I'm fine. It's so good to hear your voice again.'

'Aye, it's been a while. I'm sorry I just haven't had a chance to call you.'

'Did the expedition go okay?'

'No. Not really. Plagued with problems but all sorted now. I'll tell you all about it soon.'

'So where are you now?'

'New York. I'm on my way back to you and boarding soon.'

'Text me your flight details. Are you flying into Gatwick?'

'Aye. Gatwick. Can't wait to see you, sweetheart.'

My heart was fluttering and I was bursting with excitement. My life might have been turned upside down lately but seeing Ethan again and being in his arms was what I needed right now.

Gloria and Damion Goldman and Waterfall Cay were all pushed from my thoughts as I drove to the airport to collect Ethan. My mum was super-excited to hear he was coming to stay with us. She had even cancelled her bingo session to stay in and polish her ornaments for when he arrived. I was beyond excited. Christmas had been a non-starter for me, but I was ready to make up for it now. I was keen to hear about Ethan's adventures in Antarctica – but perhaps while we were all cosy and sitting by the fire with a mulled wine – as the thought of all that ice and snow made me shiver like crazy. At least here in London today it was cold but dry and there was a blue sky and that made all the difference in the world too.

In the arrivals hall I watched the monitors. His flight had arrived and was disembarking.

I watched people coming through the doors from immigration and baggage claim.

I bobbed about searching among them all for sight of the man I loved.

The man I was going to marry if he'd still have me.

Then suddenly I saw him. He had his padded jacket slung over one arm and a small backpack in the other. He looked handsome and rugged all at the same time. Exactly how you'd imagine a hero might look on returning from an Antarctica expedition. I surged forward through the masses and when he saw me his face lit up and he rushed up to me and dropped everything onto the floor to swing me off my feet into his arms.

We held onto each other tightly, muttering words of endearment, until we broke off to look at each other at arm's length and to grin and laugh and even weep a little.

'Oh, Lori, how I'm missed you!' he told me with so much enthusiasm that my heart sang.

'You too. It's seemed like forever. I'm so happy to see you Ethan!'

We locked arms and moved through the terminal together towards the car park.

In the car, while I negotiated the car park and the traffic, we kept to small talk.

'How is your mum?' Ethan asked me.

'She is absolutely fine. Better than fine actually. She cannot wait to meet you.'

'And your boys?'

'You'll see Lucas later. He's coming over to meet you. But we won't see Josh or his fiancé Zoey until after New Year. They're in Cornwall. There's been so much snow down there that they've decided not to travel back just yet. But they're looking forward to meeting you too.'

'Ah, New Year. I wanted to ask you if you fancied going up to Edinburgh?'

I almost ran a red light on hearing his words and had to break hard to stop in time.

'Sorry. You said Edinburgh? For Hogmanay?'

'Yes. I have two tickets for the street party. A Christmas present from my team. I haven't been up to Edinburgh in years. What do you think? It might be fun.'

'Sure.' I shrugged. 'That sounds great.'

But my head was reeling in shock. Gloria had told me that she and Damion would be in Edinburgh at the street party too. But then, of course, so would ten thousand others, so what were the chances of bumping into them? Right now, the thought of seeing Damion Goldman filled me with fury. But if I could talk to Ethan about the property he has there, and introduce the idea of a swap as Gloria had suggested, then maybe this was an omen?

Back at the house, my mum gave Ethan a warm welcome and offered him a cup of tea using her best china tea set. I don't think I've ever seen her so flustered. You'd think the Queen herself might come calling. It was kind of amusing as she certainly hadn't reacted this way when I'd first brought my ex-husband Charles home to meet her.

'Now, do sit down and make yourself comfortable, Sir Ethan.'

'Oh, please. Just call me Ethan, Mrs Dobbs.' He said to her, obviously embarrassed.

'Well, all right. But only if you'll call me Margaret!' My mum gushed.

She handed him a cup and saucer so delicate that he had to wrap his hand around the cup.

'Fig roll, Ethan?'

After chatting for a while about everything and nothing, Lucas arrived.

I jumped up to do the introductions. 'Lucas, this is Ethan Goldman. Ethan, this is my son Lucas.' Lucas smiled warmly and they shook hands. I was so relieved.

'It's nice to meet you at last, Ethan. Mum's told us lots about you and about the important work you both do together. It's all sounds very brave and adventurous I must say.' Lucas said.

'You should be very proud of your mum. She's a remarkable woman.' Ethan said.

I blushed in the dizzy heights of delight at how well this was all going.

Very soon, the two men had wandered off into the kitchen.

'He's very handsome, Lorraine? I don't think you mentioned that about him, did you?'

While I chatted with mum, I kept one ear listening out for what Ethan and Lucas might be talking about.

The house is only small. The sitting room connects to the kitchen through a short hallway. So I could easily overhear Ethan chatting with Lucas.

Ethan was asking Lucas about his work. Lucas has an important job in the city. He told me recently that he'd been given a big promotion. I'm so proud of him.

'I'm not really very happy with my job to be honest.' I suddenly heard him say to Ethan.

I was so shocked to hear this because I thought Lucas really enjoyed his job. And, I know he has been a bit moody and introspective these past few weeks, but I'd presumed that was all entirely down to him being unhappy about the situation between me and his father.

'Listening to mum telling us about what you've been doing all over the world, saving turtles, marine conservation, standing up against illegal whale hunting, it's all so—well, important.'

I was completely taken aback by this sudden revelation and I held my breath to listen.

I zoned out of my mum's innate chatter about Ethan and zoned in on eavesdropping on Lucas and Ethan's conversation instead. I really had no idea that Lucas actually *approved* of what we'd been doing – what I'd been doing – because he always seemed so critical.

'Well, yes. It is important. Saving the planet is the most important job in the world right now' Ethan replied. 'And, I hope you are as proud of your mum as she is proud of you, Lucas.'

'I am. She's an amazing mum. I miss her but I want her to do what makes her happy. I'll be honest with you, at first, I thought she was doing wacky radical and wildly dangerous stuff on her own. But now I see she's part of something much bigger and more organised: the GGF.'

Lucas was being far more candid right now than I would have ever expected.

'You know about the GGF?' Ethan answered.

'Yes. I looked it up. I looked you up too. You are actually a very cool guy, Ethan.'

I heard Ethan laugh. He sounded delighted with the compliment.

'Let's get back to why you aren't very happy at work, Lucas? Why is that?'

Lucas sighed. 'I was recently given a promotion, but it's not turned out how I thought.'

'That's a shame. In what way exactly?' I heard Ethan respond.

'I moved from consumables to high end luxury goods and, to be honest. I've found dealing with my VIP clients all rather soul destroying. And, let's face it, working in sales and marketing isn't really saving the world is it? Nothing like the kind of thing you and mum are doing now.'

'So what would you rather be doing, Lucas?' I heard Ethan ask him.

I might have broken the world record on holding my breath as I waited for his answer.

'I'd like to do something more worthwhile. Something

to do with helping the environment. I'd like to travel and make a difference in the world. Just like you and my mum are doing.'

'Well, with your skills in marketing and communication and sales, Lucas, I know you would be highly capable of securing a position as an Organisational Operations Manager.'

'Really? You think? And what kind of job is that, exactly?' I heard Lucas ask.

'All environmental organisations need dedicated individuals to run the business aspects of the company. It's behind the scenes work but it's also a crucial role in saving the environment.'

'Wow. Yes. I can see how that might be the kind of thing to suit me better.'

'Then, if you like, I'll put you in touch with our London office of the GGF. We just happen to be looking for an OOP right now. Interviews are being held during the first week in January.'

They both came back into the sitting room with a can of beer each, still chatting.

'The biggest problem in Antarctica is the melting ice-sheets and rising sea levels.' Ethan was now saying.

'And what were your responsibilities out there, Ethan?' Lucas enquired; his expression rapt with interest.

'I was there to provide a study on how a loss of habitat will affect the Elephant Seals and the Emperor Penguins. And, to collect enough depressing data to help fuel the new GGF campaign, to make the waters off Antarctica into the world's largest wildlife sanctuary.'

'Wow. That sounds—really impressive.' Lucas told him.

Ethan laughed. 'Only if we succeed.'

'While you've been away, Lorraine's been busy too.' My mum boasted to Ethan.

I immediately shot her a warning glance. Perhaps it was more of an irate glare.

'Yeah, Mum's been campaigning against one use plastics outside the supermarket, haven't you Mum?' Lucas divulged.

Ethan smiled at me and looked incredibly proud.

'And she's been setting up a wild life sanctuary too.' My mum spurted.

My glare should have evaporated her on the very spot where she was primly sitting.

But she was still there and ready to spill my news before I could explain it all to Ethan.

'Sounds like you've been busy.' Ethan remarked, raising his eyebrows at me and grinning.

'I need to talk to you. Can we go to the pub? It's only a two-minute walk.' I urged.

We grabbed our coats and walked down the street towards the local, our breath becoming clouds of steam in the freezing air. Inside, the pub was warm and welcoming and noisy with chatter. We were lucky to grab a table for two in the corner, just as another couple were leaving.

Ethan then went to the bar and ordered a pint of draught beer and I had a glass of wine.

I tried to relax. It felt good to have him all to myself even if we were in a crowded pub.

I watched and smiled as he returned to sit and sup through the creamy head of his pint.

'Oh, that's so good. It's years since I had a proper pint of English beer.'

'Isn't it just the same as Scottish beer? I asked, attempting to steer the conversation.

'Scottish beer is even better.' He remarked adamantly.

'Then perhaps we should stay for two nights in Edinburgh?' I suggested.

He looked pleased at this idea. 'Sounds great. I'll arrange it.'

'Good. I'm glad. Because you'll know Edinburgh better than me. I've only been there once and it was a long time ago.'

'Well, Edinburgh isn't a place that ever changes much.'

'I remember you saying that you were born in Edinburgh.'

'Aye. Well, just outside the city.'

'Do you still have a family home there?'

'I do. It might be a good idea to pay it a visit while we're there to sort out a few problems.'

'What kind of problems?'

'Maintenance. Glencorrie, that's the name of the house, has been rented out for years. It was being used as a care home facility. But for the past two years it's been empty and, from what I'm told, the old pile sounds like it might actually fall down this winter if I don't do something about it.'

'And have you ever thought of living there yourself?'

Ethan looked at me curiously as he supped on his beer again then he shook his head.

'Nah, I prefer a palm thatched hut over a drafty old place in Scotland.'

'So, do you think you might want to sell it?' I asked him.

'Oh no. Never. I'll never sell it. Not at any price. It's been in the family a long time.'

I took a deep breath and steeled myself to get this over with now I'd broached the subject.

'I have something I need to ask you and I want you to promise me you'll stay calm.'

He looked at me intently and wore an expression of concern. 'Okay. Ask away.'

'Would you consider not selling but swapping your family home in Edinburgh for Waterfall Cay?'

Ethan stuck out his lower lip as he considered his answer carefully.

'Is this one of those truth and dare games like we used to play on Koh Phi Tao?' he asked.

'No. It's actually something that could be an option. If you wanted to pursue it?'

He looked completely surprised as soon as my words hit home.

'What have you done Lori? What have you been up to while I've been away?'

'I've been trying to get the island back for us. I've been in the Bahamas. I've been in the Caribbean. I've been back to the BVIs. I've tried – and believe me I have tried very hard indeed to take back the island from Damion – but all my plans and my efforts have failed. You were right about him. He is ruthless. But I'm in touch with Gloria and we've become friends.'

'Gloria!' He repeated her name and slopped half his beer onto the table.

'Yes. She's become an unexpected ally. Unbeknown to your brother, she's come up with an idea to help us get the island back and I said that I'd talk to you about it.'

He narrowed his eyes in confusion. 'And Damion doesn't know anything about this?'

'No. Not yet. But you must promise me that whatever happens you won't implement Gloria. The information she's given to us is in the upmost confidence. You have to understand; she's not doing this to go against Damion. She loves him. Like me, she just wants you both to get what you most want in life. And, Gloria and I would like to see you both reunited as brothers.'

He laughed. 'I'm sure that's the last thing Damion wants!'

'Gloria has told me that the one thing that Damion really wants – what he's always wanted in fact – is the Goldman family home. The one left to you when your parents passed on.'

'And what else did Gloria tell you?'

'She told me you were once together. Long before she

met your brother. And, what a shock it was to everyone, when she introduced you to each other unknowingly.'

Ethan sighed as he recalled it. 'Yes. It was a bit awkward to say the least.'

'Well, what you might not know, is that it almost ended their marriage.'

'Oh, no I didn't know. I'm sorry to hear it.'

'It was apparently during their marriage counselling sessions that they got to talk things through and she found out about how Damion felt about you and your ongoing sibling rivalry.'

Ethan frowned. 'Damion was always one to take things personally. As the eldest son, he always thought that he should have been left Glencorrie.'

'And did your parents have a reason for excluding him from any inheritance?' I asked tentatively.

'Yes. It's a piece of history and he doesn't appreciate anything until it's value can be measured in money. And, I have to correct you here, but they didn't exclude him. He got an equal share of their Estate. He got exactly the same as I did except for the house. My parents considered themselves guardians of Glencorrie. They knew if they left the family pile to both Damion and I jointly, then we'd have been forever fighting over it. I'm sure they thought he'd sell it. Whereas I never would!'

'Well, maybe they were wrong about Damion? He seems emotionally attached after all.'

Ethan gaffed. 'Damion? Emotionally attached? Never. Not in a million years.'

'Well, I trust Gloria on this. I think you should trust her too.'

He looked rather blown away by all of this and his eyes were wide and incredulous.

'Really? Damion wants Glencorrie House?'

I nodded my head slowly and sat quietly while he processed this information.

'Wow. Lori, you certainly have been busy while I've been away.'

I wasn't sure it was meant as a compliment.

I considered for a moment if I was being naive in recommending that Ethan trust his brother?

After all, he hadn't thought twice about murdering all the small creatures on Waterfall Cay.

He didn't care a jot about the pristine reef or pouring concrete into the sand either.

'Erm, perhaps just to be on the safe side, might it be possible to transfer ownership to him on the proviso that it can never be sold?' I suggested as tactfully as I could muster.

To my relief, he nodded his head and shrugged. 'Yes. It's possible.'

'Then perhaps we should arrange to meet up with Damion and Gloria in Edinburgh.'

Chapter 18

We drove up to Edinburgh on 30th December in a hire car. While Ethan was at the wheel, concentrating on joining the motorway on the long journey north in the cold and icy weather, I was on my phone talking to Josh and Zoey in snowy Cornwall. They told me they'd been invited to a New Year's Eve party with Zoey's extended family and they looked forward to meeting Ethan when they got back. Lucas had already told them he was impressed with Ethan and really liked him a lot. When I spoke to Lucas, he said he was including his Gran in his end of year celebrations, by taking her into the city to watch the fireworks at midnight.

I relaxed after being told all this. My kids and my mum were fine and this only reaffirmed my belief that everything and everyone in my family, as long as they were in possession of their health and happiness, didn't need me tending and fretting about them after all.

The drive was a pleasure because we were riding high in a top Range Rover with big comfortable heated leather seats that felt soft and wonderful on my derriere. Ethan said we'd need a four-wheel drive vehicle to be able to get up to Glencorrie House. I was really looking forward to the next few days. Although, I would also admit to feeling nervous about meeting with Damion and Gloria again. If Ethan was nervous, he certainly didn't show it.

We headed up the motorway chatting. I wanted to know how his Antarctica trip had gone.

He obliged me with a few details but then continued to press me to tell him more about my own adventures while he'd been away. I told him about how I'd gone from the Bahamas to St Lucia after meeting with Gloria and about meeting up with Tom at the butterfly exhibition and how we'd both gone together to Luminaire to collect the Green Morpho and how he'd helped me with the butterfly repatriation. It was quite an adventurous story after all.

Despite me relating it all as lightly as I could, Ethan drove with a tense expression on his handsome face and he drove with what looked to be an overly firm grip on the steering wheel.

Then with an element of hesitation, in case it muddied up our next move to negotiate with Damion over Glencorrie, I regaled him with the news that Damion had fumigated the island.

After I'd told him this, he didn't speak for such a long time, that it felt like forever.

'I don't know if to be flattered or furious with you, Lori. This is an awful lot to take in.'

I nodded and decided to be quiet until he decided on which one he would conclude.

I braced myself for the worst as we approached the motorway service station turn off.

I expected he might pull over and then do a U-turn to take me back to my mother's house.

And indeed, he did indicate for the turn and pull into the service lane.

I felt my heart beating in sync with the rhythm of the indicator and the windscreen wipers.

When he swung into the service station car park and turned off the engine, to turn his body in the seat and give me the benefit of his full attention, I felt physically sick.

'What on earth made you think of doing this? I mean, what on earth possessed you?'

'You did!' I interrupted him. 'You did, Ethan. First of all, you instilled in me a belief that one person really can make a difference in this world. Then you showed me how it is possible, should it be necessary, to travel great distances across the world in order to pursue what is right and decent. And, you convinced me that dreams do matter. I really want you to have that island. Your dream has become my dream!' My tears were rolling down my face as I spoke. My words became shuddering sobs. 'You also told me that you loved me and you showed me a special place, a paradise, where you wanted to build our dreams together and where you wanted to build our very own home. And, you asked me to marry you and—'

'And, will you? Will you marry me, Lori?'

His voice was softer now but still urgent and his eyes were full of emotion.

'Yes. My answer is yes. I love you. I want to marry you, Ethan.'

And before I even finished saying his name, he swept me up into his arms and held onto me, squeezing and hugging me so tightly for a moment, before he released me enough to tenderly kiss my wet eyelids and then my trembling lips.

'Lori, what you've done over these past weeks is extreme to say the least, I can hardly contemplate it.' His voice was deep and unsteady. His face was also wet with tears.

Then he started to laugh but I'm guessing it's more from incredulity than humour.

'And, I'll admit that it's hard for me to remain angry with you, when I'm so incredibly flattered by all of this. What you've just told me about the island and Damion and Gloria, it's well—it's incredible. It's beyond astonishing. It's crazy. It's also the bravest and the most foolish and yet the most romantic thing I've ever heard in my life. So, I've decided to be grateful to you, Lori. Thank you so much, my darling, for all your efforts and for your love.'

As we drove on through the Scottish Borders and into open rolling countryside, the weather worsened and the sideways icy sleet turned into heavy snow. Ethan was leaning forward and peering intently through the windscreen into the blizzard.

'Is Glencorrie House in a remote place?' I asked him. I was a nervous passenger. I might have sailed on a ship through a storm, but I was still worried about driving in blinding snow.

'Aye, the house stands in its own grounds. I was going to say gardens, but then I wouldn't want to disappoint you.'

I was now imagining a cold grey ruin of a house at the end of a long barren driveway on a Scottish moorland, like the one in *Skyfall.* Probably because the road we were travelling on now resembled the one James Bond and M had taken in the Bond movie of the same name.

'We're not too far from Edinburgh. I'm thinking, because of this weather, we should go straight to our hotel and leave Glencorrie until the morning. Besides, I believe we have other, far more urgent business to attend to involving soft lights, chilled champagne and a large comfortable bed.'

He gave me a sideways smirk and I got instantly lustful butterflies in my stomach.

We'd shared a bed in my mum's house, but we'd only spooned and snuggled.

The walls between bedrooms were far too thin to allow for our unfettered intimacy.

'I agree. And I suspect our urgent business could take all night long.'

I'm now wondering where he'd managed to book for us to stay in the city.

I'm guessing it's not easy to get a last-minute room over Hogmanay.

We'd been originally booked at The Balmoral. Always his first choice, Ethan told me, when he stayed in Edinburgh. But then, when I'd let Gloria know of our plans and confirmed our arrangements to meet up with her and Damion by 'pure coincidence' in a restaurant the following evening, she'd informed me they were staying at The Balmoral too.

So Ethan had hastily arranged for us to stay elsewhere instead.

'Ah, it's a secret. I think you'll love it. Spookily, I managed to get in after a cancellation.'

I could tell he was making a game of it. Ethan particularly liked guessing games.

The clues were always in his emphasised words and I so guessed it was 'spooky'.

I was intrigued. As we drove into the old city I imagined there were plenty of spooky places.

I knew from my days as a travel agent that Edinburgh had a ghost tour and secret vaults beneath the city and a dungeon beneath the castle itself. 'Are we staying in the castle?' I asked.

He gave me the sideways smirk again and I fizzled with excitement.

Well, excitement, but also nervousness. This isn't just an exciting and romantic New Year's Eve getaway. It's our chance to negotiate over Waterfall Cay and Glencorrie with Damion and Gloria. There's so much at stake here. I'm sure Ethan must be feeling the same way, but he also has the added pressure of facing his brother again. The last time they met they almost came to blows. There's no real way of knowing exactly how things will go and how this might resolve. Except of course, I do have my utmost faith in Ethan.

And I know Gloria will do her best to steer Damion around on the issue of Waterfall Cay.

'From what you've told me, I think Glencorrie House also sounds a bit spooky.' I said.

'There is a resident ghost, actually. It's a woman who was murdered in the music room sometime in the sixteenth Century. It's said that she appears at night as a misty apparition.'

I looked at Ethan in horror and saw he was enjoying himself.

'And have you actually seen this ghost yourself?' I ask him in disbelief.

He laughed at my question, but he didn't answer it.

'I'm really looking forward to seeing were you spent your childhood.' I told him, not imagining *Skyfall* this time but perhaps *The House on Haunted Hill.*

After negotiating a maze of one-way streets, we eventually drove up the Royal Mile. The tyres on our car thudded heavily against the steely grey wet sheen on the old cobbles, as Ethan drove slowly towards the famous castle. I could see it ahead of us, shrouded in an icy mist.

The dark shadows of a December twilight fell all around us, but I could see from the warm glowing lights in small pane windows, that all the restaurants and bars around here were busy.

A bagpiper busking outside St Giles' Cathedral was dressed in the full highland tartan garb as he played 'Flower of Scotland' on his pipes, as tourists and locals and early revellers bustled by and threw him their spare change into his collection box.

Hearing the pipes and seeing the piper felt to me like a proper welcome to Scotland.

When we reached the gates of the castle itself, Ethan pulled the car over to the kerbside and we were approached by a uniformed valet, who would park the car for us and then a porter came forward to carry our luggage. I climbed down from the Range Rover to see we were outside a small hotel called The Alchemist that appeared to be built into the very walls of Edinburgh castle itself.

I was enchanted as we were ushered through the single entrance door into a tiny and ancient looking reception area and greeted by an exceptionally friendly and melodic sounding receptionist.

'Och, Mr and Mrs Goldman, welcome to The Alchemist. I'm Ailish. Now, let me get you checked-in straight away as we have our most spacious suite all ready and waiting for you.'

I was blushing at being presumed Mrs Goldman.

Ethan eyed me naughtily while surreptitiously pinching my bottom.

Ailish escorted us through a narrow bare stone corridor that she called 'the close'. It had lots of ancient weaponry and tapestries on display on the walls and a stone floor worn smooth by centuries of people coming and going. The air was chilly and felt unnaturally heavy in this narrow space. I could see my own breath hovering in front of me like a small ghostly spectre as we were shown towards a door that looked like it could have been the castle dungeon.

Then when Ailish turned an enormous key and flung open the door to our rooms, my breath was literally taken away by the sumptuous sight in front of me. The suite was stunning. It was all oak panelling and hanging tapestries and historic portraits. It looked more like a debauched inner sanctum than a hotel suite. It was also decadently warm inside after the bitter cold outside and felt all-embracing with so much red and gilt and heavy brocade and velvet.

The bedroom too was a sight to behold with a high off the floor four-poster bed draped with blood-red drapes. I spotted an ice bucket on a stand with a bottle of very good champagne sitting in it and I licked my lips in anticipation. It all looks so wonderfully eerily dramatic and gothic and romantic. And, did I mention, spooky and haunted?

I decided it was a good thing that I didn't intend on sleeping tonight anyway.

As soon as we were alone in the room, Ethan and I fell into each other's arms.

We hung onto each other as if we were back in the first

moment he'd come back to me from the Antarctic and when I'd accepted his proposal all rolled into one. His lips crashed onto mine and his fingers moved lovingly through my hair while his other hand moved down to caress the parts of my body where my ardour was desperately aching with desire for him.

He then scooped me up into his arms and carried me over to the four-poster bed without taking his mouth off mine for a moment. Then he lay gently on top of me, slowly removing my clothes, as I desperately tugged and pulled at his so that we could be together again at last.

In the morning, my head was fuggy from last night's champagne and late dinner and even later lovemaking, when I was woken by a determined knocking sound at the heavy door of our suite.

Two knocks, actually, then nothing more. I looked to Ethan, who was still sleeping soundly.

Then I slipped out of bed and slipped on a gown to investigate. 'Who's there?' I queried.

When there was no answer at all, I opened the door and peered outside into the passageway.

There was no one to be seen but when I looked down, I saw a large wicker picnic basket.

I thought this rather strange, but also quite delightful, so I picked it up and took it inside.

Inside the hamper, I found a flask of hot coffee and also one of breakfast tea. There was a pile of warm toast wrapped in a large linen napkin, portions of butter and a selection of fresh fruit, and small glass pots filled with yogurt and muesli. I delved deeper into this trove and found sweet pastries and an assortment of preserves. This was a veritable breakfast feast.

But, I also saw it also came with a formal invitation, to eat a full hot breakfast in the restaurant as well, if we so wished. I imagined that we would because Ethan always enjoyed a hearty breakfast and had said that he was excited for me to try a traditional Scottish one.

Apparently, it consists of square sausage and haggis and white pudding.

I was rather intrigued. Although, the sound of the ingredients involved sounded odd.

However, it was still early yet, so plenty of time to work up an appetite between breakfasts.

After our mid-morning second breakfast, during which Ethan entertained me with tall tales about wild haggis and haggis-shoots and how these cunningly woolly creatures had adapted to life in the Scottish glens by growing three legs, so that they could apparently run straight on the hills, we headed in a northerly direction out of Edinburgh crossing the bridge over the Firth of Forth, towards the snowy Kingdom of Fife.

Fife, Ethan told me, was the ancestral home of Scottish monarchs as well as his own linage.

'Fife might be famous for its golf courses,' he boasted

to me, 'but it's also home to Scotland's oldest university and to countless castles and palaces and, of course, whisky distilleries.' His eyes twinkled. I do know that Ethan appreciates a good single malt.

His words reminded me of a night on an island turtle sanctuary in Thailand where we'd first met. It was the night before we were leaving the island, when he'd offered me a 'wee dram' of Scottish whisky as a nightcap before we said our goodbyes.

Knowing now how all of that had all worked out, I sighed happily.

I gazed out of my side window at the white Scottish countryside. I enjoyed looking out for all the sights and places of interest that Ethan had mentioned to me as we drove through historic looking small towns and quaint villages. Today, in stark contrast to yesterday's white out conditions, the sky was the bluest of blue and completely cloudless.

High in the sky ahead of us, two airplane trails had crossed, and Ethan took great delight in pointing this out to me. 'Look, Lori, there's a Saltire in the sky. That's just how King Angus saw it in the first Century. No airplanes back then, of course, but he saw it as a white cloud formation against a blue sky and a sign from St Andrew of sure success in the forthcoming battle with the English.'

'And did he succeed?' I asked, hoping this sign in the sky was an omen for us too.

'Indeed. He did. And the Saltire became the official flag of Scotland.'

Chapter 19

From here on, the subdued northern mid-winter sunshine shone down on the seemingly endless white patchwork of fields containing lots of fluffy white sheep until, not long after driving through the town of Glenrothes, towards the gently rolling Lomond Hills, we took an unnamed road flanked by dry stone walls into what looked to me like the middle of absolutely nowhere.

In the middle of nowhere, there was another, even narrower road, a one lane track. It was only passable by one vehicle at a time and this road went on for many undulating miles. So, when I saw another vehicle coming along the same road and heading our way, I wondered how we'd both pass without resorting to one of us pulling off into a snowy field.

But Ethan had spotted what he called 'a passing place' in the road.

As we pulled over to let the old land rover pass, I noticed the person in the other vehicle raise his hand, so I waved back. As he came level with us, he stopped and brought down his window. The man gave us both a delighted and craggy looking smile.

Ethan had brought his side window down too and it became immediately apparent that these two men, in the middle of nowhere, happened to know each other.

'Well, I'll be damned, if it isn't the Laird himself!' the man said in a tone of astonishment.

I can tell you that I was pretty astonished myself when he'd addressed Ethan as a 'laird'.

Was this yet another title bestowed upon the esteemed Sir Ethan?

'Good to see you again, Mac!' Ethan enthused. 'How are you, old friend?'

'Oh, I'm still going strong. Getting' auld but not as auld as these hills.'

'We're just going up to check on the hoose.' Ethan told him, pointing ahead into the snowy vista and with his Scottish accent sounding a little stronger now he was on his own turf. 'It's been a while. Is the old pile still standing?'

'Aye, only you might need to buy a new roof after this winter?' Mac laughed.

Ethan introduced me to his friend and a few more pleasantries were exchanged.

Then Mac insisted on offering us a brace of pheasant. He grabbed two shot dead birds, tied together by the neck and in full flock and feather, from the back seat of his land rover and handed them over to us as a gift. Thankfully, Ethan managed to decline politely and without offending him.

'So, who is Mac. Is he a friend or family?' I asked, once we were on our way again.

'The gamekeeper. He lives in a cottage here on the estate.' Ethan told me.

'He called you Laird. Does that mean you are a Scottish Lord, or something?

'Nah, not a Lord. In Scotland, Laird is just the name of the landowner, that's all.'

Then, all at once, a tall grey stone turreted tower came into view and my eyes practically popped out of my head with shock and amazement. This historic structure had obviously been built up and fortified over many centuries and by many generations. The more I looked, the more turrets I saw with actual arrow slits for windows and cute cone-shaped snow-capped roofs. Below the towers and turrets were rows of battlements and below these where so many rows of rectangular sash windows that I couldn't possibly even count them all.

This wasn't a house as Ethan had claimed. Glencorrie is an actual castle.

'Oh, my goodness, Ethan. It's like something from a fairy-tale. It's—beautiful!'

'You're not telling me you'd rather live here than on a tropical island? He suggested.

I was so enchanted that I didn't quite know how to reply to that question in that moment.

From a distance, Glencorrie looked like a considerable monument to Scottish history.

But then, as we drew closer, I realised that Ethan had been right about the place being run down. The evidence of this ancient building's demise and decay over the past few winters was now glaringly apparent. As we parked up, I could see that the huge oak front door was off its hinges and the lintels supporting the once grand entrance had collapsed. We went around to the side, where Ethan said it was safer to enter, into the vast kitchen area and through into the Great Hall. Inside, ivy had invaded the room through gaping cracks in the walls, but I could see there were still dusty family treasures on display. I was amazed that the place hadn't been ransacked for its treasures, but if there were still people living on the estate and in the cottages around the area, then maybe they were keeping a watchful eye on the place.

Ethan took my hand and led me up the sweeping staircase in the main hallway and beneath the central tower. All along the walls of this upper landing where historic portraits of illustrious looking people in various poses. Some holding guns aloft while dead partridge and grouse lay at their feet. I saw Ethan hesitate at a large painting of a glamourous and good-looking couple.

'Your parents?' I asked him. He nodded and then we took the final flight of stairs together.

All the rooms on this level showed evidence of when the place had been rented out as a care home. There were still care beds in place but now with smelly damp and mouldy looking mattresses on them and the odd zimmer frame in the corner and old wires hanging around of what would have been a call system. The place was now bone-chillingly cold and filthy dirty and full of dusty spider webs.

On seeing all of this decay, my enchantment had crumbled too.

'How have you let this amazing castle get into this terrible state, Ethan? I don't understand.'

'Because renovating an old property is costly and time consuming. I've always felt my money and my time were better spent elsewhere. But I agree that the time has come to tidy the place up a bit. I'm quite happy to hand that considerable task over to Damion and Gloria.'

'Well, I'm sure they'll have this place spruced up in no time at all.' I said, looking around me and feeling aghast at the sheer amount of work and expense that would certainly be required. We walked around for a while longer and Ethan assessed what needed to be addressed. 'We'll also have to get Historic Scotland and Scottish Heritage on board of course.'

'Come on, it's freezing. Let's get back to Edinburgh.' I said, wrapping my arms around him to both benefit from his body heat and also to comfort him as he gazed around nostalgically.

'Aye. Let's get back. We also need to go shopping. You'll need some warmer clothes if we're going to a street party tomorrow night. And, if we're collaborating with my nemesis in a swanky restaurant tonight, you'll be needing a new dress. It'll be very interesting to find out if my brother and I can actually agree on something, for a change.'

The restaurant that we'd agreed on for our chance meeting was in Edinburgh's sophisticated New Town area, a short distance over the New Street bridge and across from Princes Street gardens, in an area known for its sophisticated champagne bars and casual bistro scene.

We entered the restaurant at exactly 7.30p.m. It was very busy and noisy inside.

I was a little disappointed with our choice of establishment on account of how rowdy and boisterous it was in here. It was hardly an atmosphere conducive to holding an important discussion. But then again, if things turned nasty or heated, then it might actually be helpful.

I'd previously arranged with Gloria that they should arrive first, at 7p.m.

Then when we spotted each other we would feign complete surprise.

I was feeling quite weak-kneed and flustered with nerves as Ethan and I stood waiting to be shown to our reserved table. My eyes flitted over towards those seated at the bar and at those sitting at the tables lining the long narrow room. I was looking to see if I could spot where Gloria and Damion were sitting. I must have glanced quickly around two or three times, but to my dismay and escalating panic, I couldn't see them anywhere.

I was suddenly worried that Damion hadn't liked the

look of the place either and insisted they go elsewhere. If so, then our plan would be foxed. But then, I saw that half of the room was set out with tables and chairs while on the other side it was all booths, making it hard to see half the diners in the room. I searched amongst all the women I could see for Gloria's striking red hair. 'I can't see them.' I hissed to Ethan.

If he was nervous, he didn't look it. He told the waitress his name and that he had a reservation. I saw how she smiled at him but then also looked a little confused. 'Goldman?' She questioned. 'Are you dining with the other Goldman's who are already here?'

My relief was palpable. I sensed that Ethan was about to decline when I interrupted.

'No, we're not. But perhaps you could take us over to them, so we can say a quick hello?'

A moment later, we were being escorted right towards the back of the room.

In a high-backed booth, Gloria and Damion were sitting perusing the menu and sipping wine. When they looked up and saw us, I could immediately see that Gloria was relieved as well as nervous. Although, it was also clear that we'd caught Damion by complete surprise.

He flustered for a moment and then he stood up.

'Well, Ethan. We do meet in the most unlikely places these days, don't we?'

The waitress left us to it, saying she'd be back in a moment or two to seat us at our table.

'Oh no, please, do join us. We have plenty of room here in this booth. Isn't that right, darling?' Gloria gushed, grabbing Damion's arm as if trying to seize control of his response.

'Erm, yes, of course. Please do join us. We haven't ordered yet. Perhaps I should warn you that service is a little slow tonight.' Damion was frowning as he ushered us into the seats opposite him and Gloria. The waiter rushed over with menus and fussed over setting our places at the table with glassware and crockery and pouring wine, which thankfully, allowed us all a moment of repose before we needed to re-engage in conversation.

'How lovely to see you both again—' Gloria began, now smiling diplomatically.

'Yes, it's lovely to see you, too. What a coincidence, again. Are you going to the street party tomorrow night?' I asked, ever so innocently, although I was guilty of knowing the answer.

'Yes. We are. And we're looking forward to it very much, aren't we, darling?'

Gloria nudged her husband to respond favourably, clearly worried that he wouldn't.

Damion grunted, now clearly convinced that this meeting was as staged as it seemed.

Ethan, who didn't ever stand for any nonsense, suddenly stood up and spoke to his brother.

'Damion. A word, if you don't mind. Let me buy you a drink at the bar. Whisky?'

Gloria and I looked at each other in concern.

A waiter came over thinking we might be ready to order but we sent him away.

Then, each cradling our large glasses of wine, we sat and watched our two men as they stood at the bar together, hunched over glasses of single malt, in a seemingly animated and intense rapid-fire conversation. At one point, Damion glanced over to me with his eyes as dark as the devils. The room was so busy and full of background noise that it was impossible to hear what was being said. But soon, I saw it was Ethan who was doing all the talking and Damion appeared to be listening. Was Ethan telling him that it was me who'd tried to take back Waterfall Cay?

Then it was Damion's turn to do the talking while Ethan listened in careful consideration.

Gloria and I sipped tentatively on our wine and waited for the eventual outcome.

We saw another two drinks served to the men and their stances becoming less hunched.

'Do you think they might be having a conversation now or another argument?' Gloria asked.

I thought it was hard to tell. Over half an hour had passed before the two men returned.

When they approached us, Ethan's smile told me everything that I needed to know.

'It seems we have you two ladies to thank for this clever exchange tonight.' Damion said.

Gloria reached for my hand under the table in a tight collaborative squeeze.

Then seeing the four us all seated at the table again, a waiter rushed over to ask if we were finally ready to order, and Ethan immediately ordered up a bottle of their finest champagne.

A bottle was produced. The cork was popped. Our foaming flutes were raised in the air.

We all paused for a moment as Ethan stood to propose the toast.

'Here's to islands and highlands,' he said, looking to his brother.

A smile appeared on Damion's face as he too raised his glass.

After our meal, during which our conversation was carefully confined to casual chat about how beautiful Edinburgh looked in the snow and of course the Hogmanay celebrations, we all took a 'wee stroll' along Rose Street. A narrow and cobbled alley behind Princes Street, in a search for a pub that served Ethan's favourite type of Scottish beer. Once we'd found it and consumed it, we made our way back onto Princes Street, to catch sight of the torchlight parade that was due to kick off the traditional Hogmanay celebrations tonight.

It was amazing and exciting to see so many people marching with torches from the historic old town to the sound of so many bagpipes. Everyone was dressed up warmly and many were dressed in tartan with sashes for the women and full highland garb for the men. It was an experience that had the hair on the back of my neck standing on end. I could only imagine what it actually might be like to be part of the Hogmanay party tomorrow night. And, to see with my own eyes, the spectacular firework display over the castle at midnight to bring in the New Year.

From Princes Street, in the gardens beneath the castle, we could see the stage being prepared for the next evening's concert in the gardens. Although I was wrapped up warmly in my new cashmere woollen coat and scarf, bought this afternoon at Jenners department store, I was shivering with anticipation and excitement in knowing that we now had so much to celebrate.

Once we were able to do so, we escaped the crowds and walked back towards The Balmoral.

Gloria and I walked together, linking our arms as we walked along the icy and busy street behind our men, who walked side by side in conversation as if all the years and animosity between them had never existed. Gloria and I agreed it was like a miracle.

Ethan and I said goodnight to Gloria and Damion and then we carried on, arm in arm, over the bridge and onto the Royal Mile and back to our own fabulous room beneath the castle.

I couldn't wait to get back and to get Ethan on his own to find out exactly what had been said tonight. Back in our room at The Alchemist, a real log fire had been lit in the gothic fireplace. The room was warm and luxurious and glowing with flickering firelight. I pulled off my outdoor clothes, slipped out of my heels, and sat on the cosy rug in front of the fire, warming my hands. Ethan soon joined me. He handed me a cut-glass tumbler. 'Care for a nightcap?'

I took it from him and patted the space next to me on the rug.

'Come here. Sit down. I need to know what happened tonight. What was said and how on earth you managed to negotiate with your brother so easily and so quickly? Gloria and I were amazed – and of course absolutely thrilled – how all of this has worked out so well!'

Ethan was grinning from ear to ear. 'Funnily enough, Damion said he'd been intending to get in touch because he needs my help. Can you believe it? It seems he's in big trouble. His businesses all over the world are struggling. He's losing investors left right and centre and he's being held to account because he hasn't been sensitive enough about environmental and conservation issues. To put it bluntly, he's in the shit.'

He laughed and took a slug from his glass.

'So, what has he asked you to do for him?'

'He wants me to consult with him on his projects. I agreed. I like the idea of consulting.'

'But then, after that, you talked about the island and Glencorrie?'

'Yes. You and Gloria were right. All this time, he's been bitter about our parents leaving the house to me. I told him that I honestly didn't know that he'd wanted it. I had to remind him how he'd managed to sell off every asset our parents had ever given him and every family heirloom that he'd managed to sneak out of the house to the auctions. He tried to justify it all by saying it was how he'd kickstarted his stocks and shares portfolio, which of course, is now famously volatile but worth an absolute fortune. Then we did a deal. Glencorrie for Waterfall Cay.'

'A straight swap?'

'Not quite. He's had to agree to the no-sell clause and to pay for the damage on the island together with all Glencorrie's renovations. It's likely cost him ten million.'

'Gosh. And you said Damion was ruthless!'

'I also told him we were getting married and asked him if he'd be my best man.'

I held my breath in anticipation at how well this was going. 'And what did he say?'

'He said he'd be delighted!'

'Well, let's drink to that. Cheers!'

We chinked our glasses together and as we sat in front of the warm fire, bathed in flickering firelight, I revelled in the joy and happiness that I saw reflected in Ethan's eyes as he realised that his dream island was finally his to enjoy and that he had his brother back in his life at last.

'Lori' he said, turning his attention to look deeply and lovingly into my eyes.

'Yes, my love?'

'Hypothetically speaking, if I was to retire – not entirely of course – as I do like the idea of being a consultant on conservational and environmental issues, would you have any objection to me getting Lucas onboard to oversee my interests at the GGF?'

The following evening, on Hogmanay, we invited Damion and Gloria over to our much smaller hotel to dine with us in the intimately proportioned Alchemist's restaurant. The restaurant itself seemed to be a room carved out of the rock beneath the castle. The setting was sumptuous and unusual and incredibly impressive. Indeed, the four of us were seated at a table right next to an A-list Hollywood action star – who will remain nameless – but who also happened to be Scottish and incredibly handsome. I was totally star-struck.

Gloria was beside herself with excitement, until Ethan rose to his feet and intervened to introduce us to the star – as he apparently knew this person – and probably because he was keen for the sake of all involved to re-establish an atmosphere of nonchalance in the restaurant.

Damion, cool as a cucumber, merely nodded his head when he was introduced.

I'm sure my face was as red as the lobster being served to me when the star winked at me.

As we finished our meal and enjoyed coffee, we could hear the first whizzes and pops and booms of the first of the countdown firework displays over the castle to rally the crowds.

At 10p.m., we wrapped up warm in our coats and hats and scarfs and made our way over to Princes Street, to join the throng of revellers in the shadow of the castle on its hill. It was standing room only in the street and the atmosphere was electric. Music was blasting out from the massive speakers either side of the main stage and everyone around us was caught up in the beat, dancing and singing and whooping with revelry in the street.

Gloria and I joined in with it all in wild abandon. We bought glow sticks to wave in the air as we sang our hearts out along with Franz Ferdinand and the incredible crowds what was surely the best New Year's Eve party in the world.

At midnight, we stood in awe and excitement with hundreds of thousands of other people and with our eyes in the sky over the castle as the countdown to the midnight bells began and the fireworks exploded in an incredible choreographed display.

It was so big. So noisy. So incredible. So amazing.

Then we locked arms, the four of us with everyone around us, to sing *Auld Lang's Syne*.

Of course, Damion and Ethan knew all the words and sang them loud and proud.

Gloria and I leapt about laughing and joined in with the chorus.

For auld lang syne, my dear, For auld lang syne

We'll take a cup of kindness yet, For auld lang syne!

My phone was suddenly vibrating in my pocket. I check it to see it was my boys.

But it was impossible to hear them. No doubt they could only hear the roar of the crowd.

But we shouted out Happy New Year to each other anyway before we hung up.

I held onto Ethan's strong arm and my eyes were filled with tears of joy.

I looked at his handsome face and my heart was bursting full of love and happiness.

I was sure that this new year was going to be the stuff that dreams were made of.

Indeed, this was the year we were getting married!

I stood on my tip-toes and reached to kiss Ethan on the lips with all the passion I could muster. He responded in kind and when our lips parted, he smiled at me slowly, his eyes shining like beacons in the darkness and without dropping eye contact with me for even a nano-second, he took my left hand up to his warmed lips to kiss my icy fingertips and to slide onto my finger an enormous diamond ring.

Chapter 20

Six Months Later

Waterfall Cay: British Virgin Islands.

Lori and Ethan cordially request the pleasure of your company at their wedding tomorrow. No shoes required.

This morning, in bright sunshine and on calm waters, we're sailing towards Road Town, Tortola. I gaze out from my viewpoint on the forward deck at what must certainly be one of the most beautiful sights in the world; a chain of tropical islands laid out like an emerald necklace. I'm sitting back, relaxing, with my sunshades on, enjoying the warm breeze and the clear vista ahead of us as Ethan stands proudly at the helm of our boat *Butterfly*.

He says it's his dream boat. I'm certain, given half a chance, he'd spend all day and every day driving it up and down these straights and around the BVIs if he could.

He's enthusiastically wearing the new shirt I bought him. As an avid collector of colourful shirts, I knew at once he'd love it as it has large butterflies printed on it. He's left the buttons open, so it's flapping in the wind and the butterflies look like they are flying along with us, as we sail through the Sir Frances Drake Channel.

We did this trip yesterday, too. As we're ferrying our wedding guests back to our island as they arrive at the airport on Tortola, from various corners of the world. Yesterday, we were excited to welcome Ethan's brother Damion and his wife Gloria, who flew in from Edinburgh, where they are planning to spend the most part of this summer supervising the renovations of their new Scottish home, Glencorrie House.

I'm beyond thrilled that my fabulous friend and travelling companion through Thailand, Summer, is able to join us with her fiancé, Nate. And George and David, whom Ethan and I had worked with on Koh Phi Tao at the turtle sanctuary, and wonderful Tom, my butterfly man, together with his new husband, also named Ethan.

This morning, we're meeting our final special guests: my family, my mum and two sons and their girlfriends. My mum is giving me away on my wedding day. Josh and Lucas are to be our ushers. Zoey, who is to be my daughter-in-law later this year, and Lucas's girlfriend Lucy, are to be my bridesmaids. Gloria, who is now my very best girlfriend as well as my sister-in law to be, has agreed to be my Maid of Honour.

I'm prone to bursting into tears at random moments because this all means so much.

We are all going to be together as one big happy family.

We've managed to achieve so much in these few incredibly busy months, although we've had teams of designers and architects and builders on site to help us this whole time.

During the time in which the beach house and guest bungalows and caretaker's cottage were being constructed, I've been preoccupied with my own keen conservational interest here on the island. We have established a new turtle sanctuary. We discovered very soon after moving here, that on the far side of the island, we have a nesting beach for leatherback turtles. These are the largest and most vulnerable of the sea turtles. To me, it seems entirely fitting that as we didn't manage to establish a sanctuary for the largest butterfly in the world on our island, then we could at least provide an important sanctuary for the world's largest turtle.

Another preoccupation of course has been our wedding arrangements.

My darling groom has been busy supervising the reef reconstruction here at Waterfall Cay, which has been worked on meticulously by a whole team of marine biologists from his foundation. We're told the results look encouraging and, although the coral is slow growing, it's expected to recover well. Damion has been generous in footing the bill for this reconstruction and making good any other damages incurred here on the island. I know that Ethan really appreciates both the contribution and the apologetic sentiment behind it.

'So, what do you think?' I said to my family as we sailed towards Waterfall Cay.

I watched their faces as they caught their first sight of our island and the beautiful new house at the top of the beach above the lagoon. The response was as expected and one of awe and open-mouthed silence. We were met at our new dock by an enthusiastic and happy reception committee of our friends who were already ashore, who greeted us, welcomed us home, and then helped everybody to lug their bags from the boat up to the house.

'Go and get freshened up.' I yelled up the staircase to my flight weary family as they followed Ethan and David and George and their luggage up to their rooms. 'Then come down and join us on the terrace for some lunch!'

I checked outside and saw Tom and his Ethan stoking up the barbeque.

What is it with men and fire?

Summer was stretched out on the beach, sunbathing on a lounger, reading a magazine.

I sighed with happiness. My world felt complete.

I loved how everyone looked so relaxed and happy.

Right now, it literally and figuratively, feels like my life has come full circle.

And, I'm so very very thankful.

'This place is perfect.' Gloria exclaimed to me, as I invited her into my bedroom for a sneak-peek at my wedding dress. It had arrived this morning and I couldn't wait to show it to her. Especially as she had been the one to suggest the designer to me when I said I wanted something in keeping with the theme of our wedding – casual but elegant – and suitable for a tropical beach setting.

'Look!' I said, proudly uncovering the dress. 'I went for a slightly boho look, with a v-neck and an antique lace bodice in white-ivory. It's simple and drapes beautifully. I love it.'

'It's stunning. I love all your ideas for your wedding theme and for the house. It's bright and breezy and elegant. But where are you getting married tomorrow – here in the house – or out on the beach?'

'Oh, we're getting married on the beach.' I confirmed. 'No shoes required!'

'Oh, how dreamy. And, you will be the most beautiful bride!' She enthused, hugging me.

'We're having the ceremony out on the edge of the lagoon.' I explained. 'Ethan's built a beautiful driftwood arched pergola and, by tomorrow, we'll have it all decorated with frangipani flowers from the garden and little seashells and drapes of dreamy white voile, to provide us some shade from the heat of the afternoon sun.'

Gloria went from admiring my dress to appreciating the open views from the bedroom.

'Damion and I had a small wedding with just a few close friends in attendance. His lawyer was his best man.' She laughed but then looked sad. 'Being here and being part of your wedding makes me wish we could do it all over again. Now that we're all a family.'

Suddenly, I felt a rush of love and inspiration from her words and from her wish.

'Then why don't you and Damion renew your vows tomorrow after our wedding? After all, we have a Minister coming over from Tortola. What do you think? You'll already be dressed up for the occasion?'

Gloria hesitated. 'Really? Should we? Oh, no, Lori. Tomorrow is yours and Ethan's day!'

'Tomorrow belongs to all of us. Why don't you speak to Damion? I think it would be wonderful. It would be our honour and privilege. Damion might even want Ethan to return the favour and to be his best man?'

Gloria looked quite ecstatic, but I said no more. The decision was between her and her husband. But I did hope they would want to renew their vows tomorrow and make the whole day even more special. But, between now and then of course, there was so much to do.

In keeping with the casual theme, Ethan and I weren't having separate pre-wedding parties with 'hens' and 'stags'. After lunch today, we were simply planning on having an afternoon of relaxation, followed by some fun and games in the lagoon and then a big get together tonight for everyone to enjoy sing songs around a bonfire on the beach and dance under the stars.

'Okay, what can I do?' My mum demanded to know as soon as she'd appeared from her unpacking. She wasn't a woman who knew how to be idle, but I thought it was time she learned.

'Nothing. I've already delegated everything.' I told her. 'Ethan's in charge of everything to do with food. Our wedding meal will be a seafood extravaganza, cooked on the barbecue tomorrow evening by all the men, so there'll be plenty of hands to help. Tomorrow, after lunch, tables will be taken down to the lagoon and all the ladies will help to decorate them with flowers. I have floating candles and sea glass lanterns and our 'message in a bottle' wedding favours (I'd handwritten personal thank you messages with a scoop of the fine white sand from our beach for all our guests as a keep-sake). Champagne has already been procured by the case load and is in the chiller. A three-tier wedding cake, decorated with edible pearls and faux corals and shells made in icing, by a very talented wedding cake specialist from Virgin Gorda arrives tomorrow morning. So mum, please, go, sit down, and relax!'

A short time later, I was ecstatic to see that my mum had actually done as she'd been told.

I spotted her sitting on the swing seat bench in the shade of the front porch, gazing out onto our tropical garden and to the white sand beach beyond it, just as I'd always hoped she would.

I also saw my sons having an introductory lesson in scuba diving with Ethan on the reef.

*

All of our closest friends and family are now on the island. So, after lunch and drinks and during the late-afternoon heat, while some are relaxing in the shade or taking a siesta, Ethan and I have decided to sneak away and be alone at a private spot at the top of the island.

Hand in hand, it was good to walk off our lunch and follow the central rainforest path to our special place, at the emerald pool beneath the waterfall. It's our secret grotto. Heavenly and private. Here in our own natural spa, we can skinny dip in the cool silky waters and make love to the rhythm of the rainforest and then lay back in the cool water, to relax and gaze up at the emerald coloured walls and lush foliage and watch tiny green butterflies fluttering in the air through the misty spray. The place is so beautiful and such a draw, that we selfishly hadn't included it in our guest's tour of the island, so we could keep it all to ourselves.

'It's half a year tomorrow since you proposed to me,' I told Ethan, as I sighed happily.

'And since you tortured me while I awaited your answer,' he reminded me.

'I needed to be sure.' I told him.

'You haven't changed your mind? You will still marry me tomorrow, won't you?'

'I haven't changed my mind. I won't change my mind. Besides, I had to help you get the island back and your brother too, or you wouldn't have had a best man for your wedding!'

'And for that I will be forever grateful to you, my darling.'

'Well, family is everything.' I reminded him, kissing him as we faced each other in the pool.

'Talking of family. Am I to assume you'll take my family name? Only we haven't yet discussed it. You don't want to do the double-barrelled name thing do you?'

'No. Tomorrow I will be Lori Goldman.' I told him proudly. 'I want you to know, my darling, that I'm so happy right now. You and I are together and all the people that mean the most to me in the whole world are here on our island.'

'It's wonderful.' Ethan agreed. 'But when they're gone, we can begin our honeymoon.'

'Oh, Ethan. I didn't expect to go on a honeymoon. Not when we have Waterfall Cay?

'So, if I told you our honeymoon was right here, then you wouldn't be disappointed?'

I threw my head back and laughed in relief. 'No. I'm happy to stay right here!'

'Well, that's good because I ordered extra champagne just for the two of us.'

And as our lips met again, this time for a softer and even more delicious kiss and our warm bodies pressed together, skin to skin, heart to heart, in an embrace that would undoubtably lead to us lingering here for even longer in late afternoon passions, the shimmering refracting sunlight around us closed in and a sudden darkness was cast over us.

A shadow that caused us both to stop kissing not in alarm but in curiosity.

At first, I thought it might be a fruit bat. They often come down from their roosts in the tree canopy here, to scoop a drink from the pool. But this time, the fluttering shape was a butterfly.

Only, its wingspan was huge, more than six inches across.

Its colour was iridescent and reflecting both the green walls and the emerald pool.

I held out my hand aloft as it played just above us in the misty orbs that streamed in from the forest canopy above. I watched it hover over us with its dark glimmering underside and I held my breath as it settled lightly on my hand.

Its wings moved as if they were flying in slow motion. I gasped in wonder.

This was magical. This was a miracle. This—was a Green Morpho.

'And finally, I see you here, where you belong.'

The End

Acknowledgements

Writing the second book in The Backpacking Housewife series really has been the next adventure for me as a writer, as well as for Lori, the heroine of my stories. Once again, it has been a pleasure and a privilege to work with my publisher HarperImpulse - the romance imprint of HarperCollins. I want to thank Charlotte Ledger and her team at HarperImpulse for their expertise and for their enthusiasm in supporting me as an author and in getting behind this series of backpacking romantic adventure novels.

You might have noticed that one of the main themes of this book is about the importance of family. Wherever we or they happen to be in the world, I want to thank my lovely family, to whom I've dedicated this book, for being so loving and supportive during the past six years that the backpacking husband and I have been nomadically travelling. We may be apart for long periods of time, but we are never out of touch or ever out of heart and mind, and we are so grateful for the strong and close family bond that we all share.

Over this past winter, while I've been working on The Next Adventure, my backpacking husband and I have been 'housesitting' for homeowners who want to travel. This arrangement allows us some downtime from our own travels and is also conducive to me meeting my writing deadlines. We've been living in the South of France, caring for an old 'bastille' farmhouse with a menagerie of animals: a horse, two donkeys, a herd of sheep, a flock of geese, a whole selection of poultry, four cats and a dog. It was a fantastic experience during which time I did get to write and finish The Next Adventure. So huge thanks go to our homeowners Philippa and Ashley.

In the Spring, we moved from the South of France to wine country in South West France, to stay in the same beautiful 500-year-old chateau where last year I wrote The Backpacking Housewife. Thank you so much to our lovely homeowner Frances, for inviting us back to care for her home and very fine cat, Mr Smudge, and for facilitating the writing of the third book in the Backpacking Housewife series over this coming summer.

Between writing The Backpacking Housewife in 2018 and The Next Adventure in 2019 I took some time out to travel. I've been fortunate to explore some amazing places in the world and to have had some fantastic travel experiences. Like Lori, I have circumnavigated the whole world - moving from France to the UK, then onto Singapore, Malaysia, Cambodia, China, South Korea, across the Pacific Ocean to the USA, and then onto the Caribbean – where I spent five months researching and writing as well as working on my website thebackpackinghousewife.com before returning to the UK and then back to France once more.

So, as you might imagine, many of Lori's adventures are my adventures too, as I use my own travel experiences to provide insight and inspiration for my stories. I hope you find my books inspiring. If you do, and you'd like to get in touch, then I'd love to hear from you via my website or my social media channels. I promise to reply from wherever I am in the world as soon as I get an internet connection.

Lastly, a special thank you to everyone who entered the recent 'Name A Character In My Next Book' competition draw via my website at thebackpackinghousewife.com which was won by Jules Knight. Congratulations Jules - who chose the name 'Taryn' for one of Lori's friends in The Next Adventure.

Happy reading and backpacking!

Love, Janice xx

